THE GLORIOUS FIRST

THE GLORIOUS FIRST

BY

M. HOWARD MORGAN

www.Penmoprepress.com

The Glorious First

M. Howard Morgan

Copyright © 2023 M. Howard Morgan

This is a work of historical fiction. While based upon historical events, any similarity to any person, circumstance or event is purely coincidental and related to the efforts of the author to portray the characters in historically accurate representations.

ISBN-978-1-957851-22-8(Paperback)
ISBN 978-1-957851-21-1(e-book)

BISAC Subject Headings:
FIC014000FICTION / Historical
FIC032000FICTION / War & Military
FIC047000FICTION / Sea Stories
Editors: Lauren McElroy, Chris Wozney
Cover Design and Painting by:
Acknowledgements to Oliver Hurst, illustrator and artist for permissions
Covers: Emilija Rakić PRB.Emilia'sWorld of Design
All correspondence to:

Penmore Press,

920 N Javelina Pl,

Tucson, AZ 85737

First published in 2014

The Glorious First of June, 1794, was a protracted and fragmented action. It is widely regarded by historians as one of the bloodiest battles of the Revolutionary War with France. It was the first major fleet action of that period, and it tested the British Royal Navy, which had not seen a major action since the conclusion of the American War of Independence in 1783.

The British fleet was significantly undermanned, but not completely lacking in training or commitment, even though many experienced officers had retired. The French fleet, too, was undermanned, partly as a result of Revolutionary fervour, partly by the intervention of such persons as the deputy of the National Convention, Jon-Bon Saint André, who must have been a major irritation to the French admiral.

Study of the logs and journals is revealing; some myths are severely dented, such as that of French ships always firing into the rigging and sails of British ships. Villaret Joyeuse, commanding the French fleet, demonstrated, for me certainly, sound tactical and strategic management of his force. Villaret Joyeuse managed to avoid battle when he had to, almost certainly controlled the battlefield as well as Earl Howe, but most importantly, from the French perspective, he ensured the safe arrival of the enormous grain convoy into Brest.

The French lower deck men had recently mutinied and paid the price. Hundreds of officers and men were executed, incarcerated in prison or banished from the Republic. Junior officers were promoted to positions of seniority; merchant captains and even enthusiastic civilians were given command of warships.

Earl Howe was undoubtedly a fine, outstanding officer and deserving of the praise that came his way. He was an inspiring, innovative leader and an example to many officers who came after him, including a young rising star of the Royal Navy, one Horatio Nelson. Howe declined any further honours from King George, which may be a measure of the man.

Readers who wish to know more can do no better than to read the excellent work of Sam Willis, *The Glorious First of June*. Dr Willis is, to my mind, the outstanding historian of the Great Age of Sail. He follows in the footsteps of Professor N A M Rodger, surely the leading maritime historian of the present time.

This tale is fiction and is the second I have written to feature Lieutenant Jack Vizzard of the Corps of Marines. Charles Hamilton Smith did exist. He was a talented artist, artilleryman and spy. His work included experiments with camouflage, nearly a hundred years before the British recognised the need. Lieutenant Lapenotière also existed and acquired fame as the Captain of *Pickle*, the sloop that brought the news of Trafalgar to England in 1805. I borrowed both characters, and who knows, they may have been involved in such circumstances as I have invented. A third book about Jack Vizzard is in preparation for subsequent publication.

ACKNOWLEDGEMENTS

My thanks must go to my wonderful wife, Tracy, for allowing me to the time to indulge my 'hobby,' to the friends who generously or unwittingly assist and support me, be they known personally or through the medium of the interweb. A great debt of gratitude is owed to ('Sir') Keith Penny, my editor-in-chief and instructor in matters of swordsmanship. His help has been invaluable.

I am also indebted to Oliver Hurst, illustrator and artist, for permission to use his work on the cover of this title. I stumbled upon his painting very late in my research and knew instantly that it was the one to adorn this book. Do please visit his gallery at: http://oliverhurst.com

Finally, but not least, a special thank you to a special young lady, Ashleigh Yates, a talented graphic designer who designed the cover.

I

The sense of foreboding he felt this morning really did not agree with Lieutenant Jack Vizzard. He could usually be found fully awake and busy, preparing breakfast shortly after dawn had cast its watery light over Portsmouth Town, but this morning his head ached, and his mouth was as dry as a ship's biscuit. He felt morose, which was unlike him and, something more; he was inexplicably fearful. Too much port wine, he decided; it was a weakness of his. And he was at risk of being late for his appointment.

He lit the candle and splashed ice-cold water on his face, shaking off the spectre of dread, blowing through his hands as the kettle sang over the blackened kitchen stove, shared with another family. The rooms in the small, terraced house at 17 Great Southsea Street were furnished but sparingly by their landlord. Jack and Mary had slowly added to the home, but he did, occasionally, wish for the comforts of his father's home, Lampern House, in Gloucestershire.

Pouring half the contents of the kettle into the bowl, he quickly lathered some soap with the tarnished silver brush and scraped the stubble from his chin with a practiced hand. The blade was quite keen and in good condition, for which he was grateful. Taking a pause he stared at his face in the highly polished silver mirror. He could never do so without thinking of the night, so long ago, when he had killed a man. The face of a murderer. He silently spoke those words to himself every morning. One evil man and how it had changed his life. He should have shot the judge, too, but then he would have hanged. He was grateful for the goddess Fortuna's indulgence for his escape from a scaffold.

Jack Vizzard was thought a handsome man by many, not least his wife. Six feet and one inch tall—well above-average height. The dark hair, curling upwards at the collar, so much like his mother's, was like the face—strong, but with a soft glow, always coloured by the sun. A modest nose, neither aquiline nor concave, it served to inform others of his imposing, confident personality. Full, wide lips graced a strong jawline and the eyes, a hybrid green and bright blue, were this morning slightly blood-shot, evidence of the excessive consumption of the previous night.

Taking a cloth from the side-cupboard, he dried his face, then reached for the teapot, placing two spoons of the rich, aromatic tea that Mary so enjoyed in the pot—part of a set gifted to them by the parish of Woodchester on their return to Gloucestershire after the tiring voyage from New Holland. He followed with the remainder of the boiled water, stirring the leaves thoroughly, as Mary insisted he do. The aroma of the tea floated into his nostrils, aiding his recovery.

Reaching for two of the decorated cups from the sideboard, he almost forgot the saucers; placing them with care on a tray, he stepped quickly along the still-darkened hallway to the pair of rooms that had been a drain on his pay. Now however, the new lodging allowance of six shillings a week covered the expense, but rents were again rising. A stark contrast from the rough log-hut overlooking Cockle Bay in Sydney Town and, in contrast, it was luxurious accommodation.

The Glorious First

As he entered the bedroom, Mary raised herself onto her right elbow, rubbing sleep from her eyes, and smiled. 'I do so miss you when you are late home. At what time did you return last night?' She accepted the tea with her left hand, carefully edging herself upright, so as to drink it. She plumped and pushed a pillow against the headboard for support.

'Did I disturb you, my dearest?' Jack sat on the edge of the bed, placing his own cup on the floor as he searched for his boots. 'As best I could tell, it must have been approaching four bells of the middle watch. The coach was late—delayed at West Meon with a lame horse. I had to walk across the common—not the easiest of tasks with last night's fog. Yes, it was probably nearly two of the clock before I opened the door.'

He found the boots, one under the bed, its partner beneath the worn spoon-back chair, and pulled them on with ease, the leather supple and thoroughly polished.

'You were snoring, and I had no wish to disturb you,' said Jack, 'although I did wish for a peg to stop the infernal noise you were making!'

Mary gave him the look she reserved for the times when she was mildly annoyed at his language, raising her right eyebrow with obvious disdain. Her hair hung about her face, with natural waves, a soft copper shroud, framing a small face, with high and obvious cheekbones. Her smooth skin, unmarked by any blemish, glowed with health in the soft candlelight. Above those cheeks, large and bright eyes of hazel, with minute flecks of the palest green, looked on the world with interest and intelligence. Her mouth, wide and with full lips, opened, revealing straight, clean teeth. 'I do not believe a word of it, Jack Vizzard; I do not snore, unlike the man to whom I am married!' She drank fully from the small cup, placing the empty vessel carefully onto the saucer. 'However, I do feel I may be contracting some ailment. Yesterday I felt as though all my bones were aching, and my throat does feel exceedingly tender this morning. Thank you for the tea.' She sipped from the cup, a sigh of pleasure coming from her throat.

'I have the unenviable task of reporting to the dockyard this morning.' Jack reached for his uniform coat. 'The commandant believes I may be required to embark for duty aboard one of the fleets 74s. Howe has requested more marines than we are able to muster. He has already demanded men from the infantry, and it seems I may have an appointment to one of the Channel fleet; the *Brunswick,* it is thought.' He buckled his sword belt. 'Am I presentable d'you think, my dear?'

Mary Vizzard fixed a smile on her face, distressed at this news; turning away from him in order to hide her emotions, she slipped from under the heavy blankets covering the bed, and embraced her husband. The Channel Fleet; it could be worse, she thought. The service could send her dear man anywhere, leaving her alone for years. Detached to Richard, Earl Howe's fleet, he would not be on the far side of the world. He would surely be in a position to return to Portsmouth once in a while.

'As ever, you appear the model marine, my love.' A street cloak, protection against the early morning cold, draped over her shoulders, she made her way to the kitchen and said, 'Have you eaten, Jack? I can readily have something for you to eat.'

'I have so little time, dear. I am due at the Navy Office at eight o' clock, and it is now well after seven. I must be on my way.' He followed her from the bedroom.

'Oh, well then, be sure to find something for luncheon, please. You have yet to fully recover your strength. I know your duty in

New South Wales took a greater toll on you than ever you care to admit.'

Making small talk disguised her feelings, concealed the fear in the attic of her mind. Idle conversation was not one of her strengths, preferring directness and honest open talk to mere chat for its own sake. Of late, she had been reflecting on their life and the inner desire he failed to disguise; eager again for something more than the routine of garrison life. She was not, should not be, surprised at the enthusiasm barely concealed in his eyes.

Vizzard smiled again, his mind recalling those desperate days. He had lost a good measure of his muscular frame, and though his appetite was always healthy, he had yet to return to his former physique. His frame appeared wiry, muscular, but lacking the full strength of earlier years and the thick, dark hair of his Oxford days had thinned and lost something of its gloss. Barrack duty had made a poor restorative and his regular pleas for active duty were declined by his superiors so frequently he had convinced himself his conduct in New South Wales had not been seen as 'exemplary' as Governor Phillip had reported to the Colonial Office and to the Commandant of the Corps.

'Do not fear m'lady, I dined well enough yesterday, and may well do so again today. What plans do you have for the day, Mary?'

Mary had reached the kitchen and found a solitary egg and the remains of a leg of ham in the small larder. She added some coals to the sleeping stove with a pair of tongs and placed a heavy, iron pan onto the top.

'I intend to take coffee with Helena Squires. It was last week when she sent the invitation, do you not recall, dearest?'

Placing the meat onto a hot pan, she added some bread and a knob of butter, and poured milk from a pitcher into a pewter cup.

Jack wore a puzzled expression

'She wishes to meet more of the wives of the battalion officers, and gives me to understand there may be several ladies attending this morning. Be gone, Lieutenant, before I ruin this. I wish to prepare and I have much to do.'

Jack looked deep into her eyes, in wonder and pride. Her natural beauty had captured his heart near on eight years ago, but how much she had changed since! It was a lifetime ago. Mary, the coy, simple country girl, whose one ambition had been, was still, to become better educated, to improve her station in life. His heart swelled. 'Give Annie a kiss for me when she awakes, my dear.'

Jack and Mary Vizzard had adopted a girl, Annie, the daughter of a convict friend of Mary's. The child had never known her mother, Lizzie Parker, who had died in Sydney Town shortly after arriving in the new colony, some five years past. A sweet-natured child, Jack adored her, but privately longed for a son of his own. He had not discussed this desire with his wife, believing time would bring his wish to fruition. They had lost a baby in New South Wales, a pain both still felt, but never discussed.

Mary kissed him lightly on the left cheek, and he left, pondering absently on why the major's wife should be arranging such social occasions. Major George Squires had recently taken command of the right wing parade company, following a prolonged lack of a field officer for the duty. He impressed Jack at once with his zeal and energy, and forward thinking. Squires was the man with whom Jack had an appointment, at the naval dockyard.

* * *

It was a good twenty-minute walk to the Victory Gate, and he set off at a brisk pace, his mind working on the prospect of a sea-going appointment, after the tedious barrack duty. The cold, bright January air lanced his lungs, sending small clouds of vapour from his mouth as he strode across the common; after ten minutes he was sweating, the linen shirt glued to his back. The belief of many officers who had served with the Corps that the three years in New Holland would lead to widespread promotion, had proved misplaced. Jack still wore the epaulette of a second lieutenant, but the chance of employment on a ship of the line did promise elevation to lieutenant. Why else had he received the summons to attend on Major Squires at the office of the Navy Board? As the appointed hour approached he felt a growing excitement.

A guard at the gate proffered a too-casual salute as he passed by the Porter's House. He was of a mind to reprimand the man for his disrespect, but decided against it. He merely glared at the man, who froze, understanding his mistake.

He made his way to the Navy Board office, and was gratified to see he was on time. Major Squires was intolerant of unpunctuality in his officers. He introduced himself to the clerk and was ushered along a short windowless corridor to the Port Admiral's office.

Major George Squires was a stocky man, a little less than six feet tall, with an untidy mop of black, wiry hair, greying at the temples, and inclined to stoop. A smile, not evident in his grey eyes, flicked across his face as he rose to his feet when Jack entered the large, airy, sunlit room, the sudden brightness causing him to blink.

'There you are, Vizzard. Punctual, as I expected.' He extended a hand in welcome, which Jack, unsettled for a moment at the familiarity, grasped firmly. 'Captain Powlett, I present Second Lieutenant Vizzard, one of my officers, and lately returned from New Holland.'

The Naval officer seated at the large mahogany desk waved a hand in welcome, but did not rise from his chair.

'Please, do take a seat Mister Vizzard. I am delighted to make your acquaintance.' Jack removed his hat, placing it under his left arm before sitting opposite the naval officer, who glanced at a paper he had evidently been studying before Jack's arrival.

'Snuff, gentlemen? This is a fine Spanish Prize,' said Powlett, offering up a tortoiseshell case, declined by both marine officers, he continued. 'New Holland, heh? Must have been a damned hard commission. I have read reports and accounts, of course, but would be interested in your opinion of the place.' The back of his hand to his nose, Powlett coughed and sneezed several times, his chest wheezing. 'But another time perhaps. I have to place a number of appointments, and Major Squires believes you may have the qualities I am seeking er... for a particular assignment.' He looked toward the major, indicating consent. The major turned to Jack.

'I received certain information and orders only yesterday, Vizzard, which cause us to advance certain plans recently discussed in London.' Major Squires looked keenly at Jack, who returned a level gaze at his senior officer. 'You will no doubt see it in the broadsheets later, but now the damned French have gone too far. Vizzard, they have executed their king!'

Jack jerked back at the news as though struck in the face. All of England had watched nervously as France's revolution had become more strident, more demanding, ever more violent. The food riots had attracted little publicity, but the massacres in Paris last September had caused great anxiety and concern in government quarters. The French war against Austria demonstrated the First Republic's expansionist plans, as had the occupation of Belgium only last November. Jack was aghast, realising the French seemed set on a policy of aggression against all Europe. 'This is terrible news, sir,' he replied. 'How are we to respond to it?'

His mind raced. Why was he here? He knew Pitt's policy of neutrality reflected the feelings that France was set on a path of destruction, for itself and other nations of Europe and that he could no longer remain aloof from the events across the English Channel. It would surely mean expansion of the Corps, and could only lead to promotion and more adventurous service than the routine of barrack life. He felt invigorated, as though his body had instantly received an influx of purpose.

'If the Colonel Commandant is correct, Vizzard, then England must surely prepare for war with France. Pitt cannot ignore this. The damned Frogs are stirring up rebellion in Holland, which will affect our trade there, and this news can only cause agitation in the country.'

Squires pulled some papers from his bag. 'The Commandant received orders yesterday to add to our division—we are depleted, as you will know—but there is also word some important intelligence is to come from Paris, *'of the utmost importance to the King of England.'* It seems the government have an informant anxious to be in England without delay.' He looked meaningfully at Jack. 'I have instructions declaring that an attempt must be mounted by the Portsmouth Division to locate this informant, and return him safely to London.'

Jack Vizzard now had an inkling of why he was present. The Major's next words confirmed his fears.

'Colonel Souter has the view you are a suitable officer to lead such an expedition, to locate this man and escort him, alive, and with whatever documents or information he seems so anxious to bring us.' He cleared his throat. 'I did suggest this was a dangerous activity; it will need a landing on the coast of France, and the risks are great.' He pulled another document. 'Whether you like it or not, Vizzard, this is the colonel's written order... oh, and confirmation of your promotion to first lieutenant. Congratulations.' Squires's face was impassive.

For the second time during the morning, Jack was startled. Of course; the Corps could not have a lowly second lieutenant landing on the coast of France on a clandestine mission for the government.

'I would have preferred to have shared this honour—I must be candid about this—however, I am assured none of the senior officers available to me have the necessary, ah... attributes to undertake this duty,' Squires added.

'Ahem.' Captain Powlett had sat silently during the major's discourse, and now felt bound to contribute. 'I have any number of junior officers suitable for such a task, Major Squires. However, I understand my orders are limited to providing a suitable vessel and crew for the... how shall I put it... the expedition.'

Powlett appeared irritated, the rivalry between the two crown services evident in his manner, but was also mindful of his own orders for more ships to be commissioned and officers and crews found for them. 'We have a fast cutter available; at least she will be in a day or two. I have a suitable man in command of her. How many men will you be taking, Mister Vizzard?'

Jack hesitated, and looked to Major Squires.

'The Colonel and I thought a platoon, Vizzard?'

Jack half inclined his head, as though signifying agreement. 'Where am I to find this informant, sir? Will the arrangements require me to travel inland any distance?'

'Colonel Souter expects further information tomorrow, or the day following, but at present, the intention is that you should meet this gentleman near Cherbourg, but then use your discretion as to whether to return to Portsmouth or another port.'

'Then, I would prefer to keep the force small, sir; a dozen at most. I will also want Sergeant Packer,' Jack added.

Squires smiled. 'The Colonel expected you to ask for him. You served together in New Holland, I understand?'

'Yes sir. He is a first class soldier and is familiar with my methods.' Jack's mind went back in a flash to the business in Capetown during the voyage to New Holland and the lessons he had learned there. It was his first action and he had lost a man, for which he had blamed his lack of forethought, planning and execution. 'He has the necessary experience and ability, sir.' He added for emphasis.

'I doubt there is any officer in the Corps with the requisite experience for such a task, but I take your meaning, Vizzard.'

They talked for another half an hour, on the details of the supplies and equipment needed, the expected duration of the landing and the limited information of the destination. Jack requested a chart of the area for study.

'Then if you lobsters have completed your business, I would be obliged if you would allow me to complete mine. I have plans to prepare for your excursion!'

A chair scraped on the wooden floor as Major Squires rose and Jack followed, with a nod to the naval officer, and left the room behind Squires.

At the steps, Squires halted and turned toward Jack. 'This may be a bloody business, Vizzard. The message we have states our man is on the run, and the revolutionaries may now know his intentions. It could be damned bloody if you are caught.'

'I recognise the problem, sir, but have no intention of meeting the French at close quarters!' He grinned boyishly, his breath clouding in front of his mouth.

Major Squires's grey eyes drilled into Jack's as though exploring, seeking an uncertain reception. His voice lowered. 'The Colonel told me a tale of a certain duel he seems to think took place in New South Wales. It is one of several rumours which have come to his attention.'

Squires looked enquiringly at Jack, who merely fixed him with a benign smile. 'Really, sir? It is little or no surprise to me. Sydney Town was awash with the wildest speculation when I departed for England.'

'You should be aware, Vizzard, Colonel Souter holds you in high regard. I hope his successor will share his view.'

Jack's eyes widened. 'His successor, sir?'

'Of course, you would not know. Harry Innes assumes command next week. Fine man is Harry. A fighting man, Vizzard. Just the man we need for the difficult times I fear lie ahead. He will attend the colonel's retirement dinner on Friday. You will probably miss it, which is a pity. I will get word to you as soon as I can, but for now, I believe you have preparations to make.'

Major Squires donned his hat, Jack doing the same. 'I will see you in barracks later and will have your promotion posted in Divisional Orders. Well done, Vizzard.'

He strode off in the direction of the guardhouse, leaving Jack to wonder at his good fortune—he now had another shilling a month— and to contemplate the onerous task ahead. He walked to the barracks with a slower, measured pace and in a more sombre mood.

CHAPTER 2

He arrived in the barracks nearly thirty minutes later, and found several officers in animated conversation. 'Vizzard, there you are. Have you heard the news? Pray, come join us.'

The loud voice belonged to Captain-Lieutenant Matthew Varlo, the officer commanding Jack's company. An ineffectual officer, he was old for his rank. He beckoned to Jack to take a seat, pouring Madeira wine into a glass. A broadsheet paper was on the table in front of Varlo.

'There, the damned French have done it. They have executed Louis and such barbarity must surely send the cat amongst the pigeons, don't you think?'

Jack gazed around at the others. 'I believe it will, sir, and I will give you my opinion, if I may. The country will be outraged and Pitt's government obliged, I would suggest, to better prepare our forces. The Navy is prepared; however our own Corps must be augmented, in my submission. We will need a larger force if war is on the horizon. I for one feel France has shown its new colours and is bent on acquiring territory.' Jack had followed the reports in the London papers of the events on the continent. He was alarmed at the violence perpetrated in the name of reform.

Around the table several nodding heads indicated agreement. 'Is it your opinion then, that war is likely, even inevitable?' asked another officer: First Lieutenant Dick Adamson, seated opposite Jack. A smart, intelligent officer with a patrician manner, he looked for promotion and trained hard to improve his martial skills. He frequently sought out Jack as a partner for sword practice, readily acknowledging Jack's superiority in combat.

Jack looked at him, tugging on his right ear, as was his habit. 'I believe it does, Dick, and I tell you why. The first duty of a government is to protect its people - its national security if you will. England will wish to protect the Netherlands and the trade in the Scheldt. Prussia will be self-serving, Austria would like either the Netherlands or Bavaria; it minds not which. I believe Pitt will have to seek some alliances because the Army is in no fit state to fight a campaign on the continent; it would be hard pressed to defend our own shores. The major task will fall to the Navy... and to us.'

Varlo stared at him. 'You seem to have a good understanding of the situation, Vizzard.' He stretched back in his chair, so it balanced on only the two rear legs. 'How do you see the Corps in all this mischief?'

'I do hope we can lunch soon, I grow hungry!' Jack paused while a ripple of laughs rolled around the table. 'The Navy will have the brunt of it, and it can but mean more employment for the Corps, be it on ship or on shore. I fancy we will see a deployment to the West Indies, to protect our own interests there; and to see if one or two might be taken from the French!'

'Hear hear, Vizzard. I for one agree with you. A drink then, to the Corps and damnation to the French!' Varlo raised a glass, imitated by the others, as Jack rose.

'Now perhaps we can eat. All this talk of war does nothing to ease my appetite!'

* * *

In Castle Street, across the road from the grammar school, Helena Squires was entertaining half a dozen ladies, all wives of serving officers, with the exception of Margaret D'Aubant and her mother. She was particularly pleased with the house; she and the major were the first occupants, the building work only completed before Christmas last. The rooms still carried the odour of new paint, which Helena tried hard to disguise with bowls of *potpourri*, and vases of lavender.

Heavy velvet curtains aided in keeping the cold January air at bay, the ill-fitting windows in need of some adjustment if the draughts were to be removed. The walls were covered in a pleasing flock patterned wallpaper with a tasselled border in a deep burgundy which complimented the curtains. A large, rather plain open fireplace crackled with unseasoned logs the Major had diverted from the barracks; wisps of smoke slipping from beneath the mantle rose to the ceiling in a silent wave. An unlit ornate silver candelabrum reflected the dancing flames.

Helena Squires was no beauty, having a plain complexion and a neck which was overly large and extended for her rather small head. Cheeks unfashionably rosy were veined on close inspection, and her hair, a chestnut brown, was inclined to grey and hung a little untidily about her face. What she lacked in facial attractiveness however, found compensation in her eyes, which radiated a good and contented nature. She enjoyed entertaining, and was fortunate to enjoy a wide circle of friends.

'Mary my dear girl, welcome, welcome,' she enthused as a young marine orderly announced Mary's arrival. 'Please do come and sit with me. Is this your daughter? She is quite lovely, my dear. May I suggest you sit by the window, child,' she directed Annie, who looked displeased.

'I am so happy you were able to join us. Allow me to present my special friends; Catherine Spencer, wife of Lieutenant Charles Spencer; on the right by the fire is Margaret D'Aubant—her husband is a merchant in the town.' The ladies named inclined their heads, without speaking. 'And here we have Maude Prater—her husband is a most important official at the Navy Board, my dear.'

'I am delighted to have made your acquaintance.' Maude Prater spoke softly, and with genuine warmth.

'Finally, but by no means least, I am pleased to introduce Rachel Varlo, wife of Captain-Lieutenant Matthew Varlo, who commands your own husband, I believe.'

Rachel Varlo smiled. 'I am so pleased to meet you at last, Mistress Vizzard. I have heard something of you. Lieutenant Vizzard is always so anxious to return home to you, so my dear husband relates.'

'Thank you. I am similarly pleased to have been invited.' Mary responded to the various introductions and took a seat next to her hostess.

As though summoned by some silent signal, the door to the spacious room opened, the same sour-faced orderly standing aside for an elderly maid to enter, pushing before her a trolley, bearing on it a selection of small cakes and sweetmeats, tidily arranged on Wedgwood Jasperware platters. Two large teapots from the same manufactory promised refreshment, and the maid poured tea into small cups.

Watching the maid carefully, Helena spoke to all present. 'I have wanted to meet so many of you for some time. I do believe the Corps is akin to an extended family, and it seemed appropriate that, while the men are busy playing their games of soldiers, we should become better known to each other.'

Rachel Varlo agreed. 'I am certain it is an excellent idea, Helena. There are all manner of reasons for us to meet socially. We must support our menfolk. It is expected of us.'

Margaret D'Aubant felt less certain, but chose not to air her thoughts at once. Her husband was profiting from the expansion of the king's forces, and she enjoyed a good life as a result; however, she also believed that associating with the wives of mere soldiers was beneath her station. She expected her husband to receive some honour from the king. He had paid handsomely for the Admiralty contracts, and had been encouraged to believe some noteworthy honour would be bestowed on him soon.

'I er, I mean to say your idea is an excellent one, Helena.' Mary offered, a little shyly 'My husband spends most of his time in the barracks, and would spend more I am sure, if I permitted him.' She carefully raised the cup to her lips, hoping she would not spill any of the contents.

'Take comfort in the knowledge Jack Vizzard is extremely well spoken of, my dear girl,' said Rachel Varlo. 'My husband cannot speak too highly of him, and tells me he is viewed as an ascendant star in the regiment.'

'I thank you for the compliment, Rachel,' replied Mary with genuine gratitude. 'I know he has worked hard to master his duties.'

'He conducted himself most honourably in New South Wales I am told, Mary.' Helena smiled. 'Governor Phillip's despatches to Lord Sydney mention him more than a few times.' She reached for an almond cake before continuing. 'I am cousin to Lady Sydney, a Powys before becoming a Squires—and was at a dinner at Frognal last year,' she explained, nibbling delicately at the confection before returning it to the side-plate

'Poor Governor Phillip, he had such weak officers to assist him—the boor, Ross for one. I think Major Ross's presence made him the more grateful for supportive officers such as Mister Vizzard.' She hesitated, then added, 'There was talk of Major Ross being defeated in a duel?'

At this, Mary coloured with acute embarrassment. She felt uncertain of her company and how much was now known of the episode—of Jack's defeat of a bully. How much could she relate, when clearly Helena Squires already knew a good deal? It was a matter Jack, for one, preferred not to discuss at all. She had learned of it herself only from Lieutenant Dawes, and then because he, mistakenly, believed her to know of it already. 'I am aware there was bad blood between Jack and Major Ross. My husband felt it his duty to support the governor's aims for New South Wales, whereas the major did not.' She sipped at her tea, choosing her words with care. 'As to a duel, I know only the common knowledge that there was some altercation between the two.' Her words lacked conviction and she knew it.

Helena Squires wished to probe a little deeper 'Come now, Mary, why so coy? I am confident we would all of us be flattered to see our men fight for our honour.' She laughed almost girlishly. 'My information is your husband handsomely defeated the boorish Major in swordplay —expertly done by a master, my dear Helena, according to one who was present—so my cousin related.' She raised an eye, inviting a reply.

Mary was at a loss. When she accepted the invitation to morning tea, there was no expectation her private life, or Jack's, would be subject to such interrogation, however well intentioned. Their time in New South Wales had been most cruelly endured. She, a falsely convicted criminal; Jack, her dear beloved husband, had unknowingly become her salvation. Destined for penal servitude, for a crime of which she was wholly innocent, she and Jack Vizzard were reunited miraculously only on arrival in the newest colony of the English Crown. Yet, she had come to know an inner comfort, born of strength, of a resilience she never knew she possessed. She had matured quickly in the harsh environment of New Holland, losing her former innocence and finding an assertiveness she never possessed before.

'He contemplated murder—Major Ross, I mean of course. It was not proven, could never have been and Jack will not thank me for discussing these matters, however true they may be. Ross became insane—I am convinced of it. Indeed, I believe he was unbalanced before ever the fleet left England. My husband is highly trained and eminently skilled in swordsmanship, it is true; I have observed him at practice in the salon. He did defeat Ross in a duel, for which gallantry I am so proud of him.' She spoke defiantly, challenging her hostess.

'My dear, I know the heartache such a business must have caused you. We shall speak no more of it, but allow me to say how much I—and others—admire your courage, and fortitude. Mister Vizzard is an example for all in the Corps to follow, or so believes my own husband.' Again, Helena smiled, a warm smile of friendship, and Mary felt more at ease.

'You are too kind.' Mary answered, with the feeling she had found a new friend.

'Do forgive my curiosity, Mary, but it has been a matter of some speculation—you were—how may I say this...? Well, let me speak plain... a convict?' Rachel Varlo had heard it spoken in discreet circles. 'How did you come to be so? I also hear you received a Royal Pardon—is such truly the case?' She found Mary a subject of the greatest interest, having learned of her through whispering amongst some of the officers, so she had felt emboldened to ask directly.

'Indeed it is true. I was falsely accused of a calumny, of theft, by a wicked, evil man who gave Irish evidence at my trial; but my father-in-law, Sir Henry Vizzard,' she spoke proudly, 'after tremendous endeavours on my behalf, was able to establish my innocence and secure my freedom.' Mary steeled herself, conscious of the interest Rachel's questions had aroused amongst the ladies present.

She spoke defensively; long convinced she would carry the stain and the stigma of felony for the rest of her days. She spoke of Sir Henry Vizzard's prolonged correspondence and personal visits; his preparation of an appeal from the judgment of the trial judge, and how, after some years, had been able to secure a Royal Pardon from the king. Others listened, wide-eyed, as she recounted some of her experiences on the voyage to New South Wales. She told of the women on the transports, and of the poor conduct of several of the officers, and most of the men.

The conversation moved to other topics of more general, more local interest, although Mary sensed, that a pair of eyes was studying her, quietly and surreptitiously. As she looked around the room, she could see nothing but innocent, interested faces, but still kept a sense of being observed.

She found it greatly unnerving.

CHAPTER 3

As Jack Vizzard rose from the lunch table, an orderly approached and spoke softly to his right ear. 'Mister Vizzard, sir. Major Squires's compliments, sir, and he requests your attendance in the adjutant's office as soon as may be convenient, please sir.'

'Very well, Hicks. I shall report immediately. Thank you.'

He walked briskly around the drill-ground, mildly curious as to the reason for the summons, suspicious some mundane chore might be assigned to him, running over in his mind the tasks recently completed before knocking on the adjutant's door and entering smartly at the major's command.

'Ah, Vizzard. Do please take a seat. There has been a development since we spoke this morning.'

He sat in a small leather chair, positioned directly in front of the large table serving as the duty officer's desk. Behind it, Major Squires sat with Captain the Honourable Alexander Wemyss, the divisional field adjutant. The captain was a confident officer, who, unlike Squires, had seen no sea-service, nor indeed any action, but was nonetheless regarded as efficient and conscientious. His pale features contrasted with the dark hair, worn short. A slim-built man, he appeared to Jack to be some thirty years of age. He had recently transferred to the Portsmouth Division from Chatham.

'The adjutant received an urgent despatch during luncheon. As it concerns your forthcoming expedition, I thought you should be aware of it. The Admiralty received a messenger last evening, from Paris. The agent they require us to assist has information *"of the gravest import to England."* Our man is in Normandy, making for the port of Fecamp. He will likely reach there tomorrow evening or the following day.'

Jack let out a low whistle. 'Then we have to go, and go quickly.'

'Indeed, Vizzard I must order you to prepare at once. I do not know what this important information is, but it is our clear duty to see to it this man... and whatever he knows, is delivered to their lordships as quickly as we can manage it.'

Captain Wemyss spoke for the first time. 'My wager, Vizzard, is this man has knowledge of plans by the French to raise insurrection in the United Provinces. The damned Frenchies want the trade and the wealth of the region and the Dutchmen will have no stomach to resist them. The Dutch will look to England for help for once.'

Wemyss slapped his hand onto the table. 'Vizzard, personally, I hold the opinion—not shared by all—they will not stop there! They are already in Belgium, and where next, eh? The government must act soon, but for now, we hold our neutrality; so go to France, find this man, and bring him back.' Wemyss stood up, the chair scraping on the worn timber floor.

'Report to me at, shall we agree, five o' clock?' I am away now to see Powlett about your transport. I suggest you select your men and equipment. We shall have written orders for you later in the day, and we can talk more later of plans.'

Jack stood, returned his hat to his head, gave a formal salute, which neither of the others acknowledged, and left the room. Standing outside, he looked at a squad of marines under training on the drill-ground. They were recruits from Worcester and Gloucester, brought in by Lieutenant Tom Archibold. They had been examined by a surgeon, attested before a magistrate and now were receiving their first taste of drill and manoeuvres. He smiled and made for the sergeants' mess, where he expected to find his troop sergeant, Joseph Packer. He found him in an adjacent office, discussing with a corporal the content of the morning's Divisional Orders. Packer straightened at Jack's entrance and offered a salute.

'Many congratulations, Mister Vizzard, sir.' Packer was beaming, a broad grin across his face. At Jack's puzzled expression he went on. 'Orders, sir, just posted. Your promotion has been announced.'

'Ah,' Jack grunted. 'I thought the order might be displayed tomorrow. Thank you, Sergeant.' The corporal attempted a smile, but his reserve in the presence of an officer caused it to appear as a smirk.

'Joe, a word with you please.' Jack glared at the corporal, who slowly registered understanding, and left the room.

He closed the door behind the man, and sat on the corner of the desk.

Sergeant Packer pulled a chair and sat astride it, the seatback between his legs.

'This looks inauspicious, if you ask me. Your face gives you away, sir.' Packer had been with Lieutenant Vizzard since the day Jack first walked through the archway into the barracks seven years before. A seasoned marine, Joe Packer had experienced much in his twenty years' service with the corps. Ramrod straight, head shaved to a close crop and skin stained from years in India. Broad shoulders and as strong as a bull, Packer had little time for officers until Mister Vizzard had entered his life and earned both his trust and respect. Vizzard led men; he never asked a man to do something he would not do himself. He fought without apparent fear and he was the best shot in the division.

'Perhaps we know each other too well, Joe; but you are correct. We have an excursion to make, and, it is one with some hazard, for we are to sail... to France.'

Joe Packer grunted 'No wonder you look so bloody serious. Who thought this one up, sir?'

'We are to assist a government agent, return him safely to London and make damned sure he is in one piece. It is of the "utmost importance, the gravest importance to England," I am told, Joe; and we leave tomorrow, assuming a fair wind.'

'Which is just Jack-a-dandy, sir. An outing to France with the whole bloody country in uproar, revolutionaries running all over the place, butchering and chopping folks' heads off, and you and me wandering around like toy soldiers. Should be an easy jaunt!'

Jack laughed. His sergeant always had a joke or two ready in bad times. They had fought together, and—against orders—had drunk together. Jack had tremendous respect for his sergeant, a man who had endured much in the service of His Majesty, and who had taught Jack a number of skills.

'How many men do you want to take, sir? It's only one man to catch, so no more than a dozen, I'm thinking.'

'I thought so too, Joe. I will know more later but you may wish to take a corporal, and shall we say ten men.'

'If this man is as important as you say, perhaps it would be better to have near platoon strength, say twenty men. It's not as though we want a battle there, but a few extra hands might come in useful.'

Packer understood men could become lost or injured, even killed, when they were most needed. If he was going to wander around France, he wanted some good men and plenty of them.

'Then you had better start selecting them, Joe. I want this kept quiet. Nobody is to talk about this, right? We will probably sail tomorrow, but I will tell more, when I know more. Make certain they are all reliable, steady men, with some experience. This is not a job for those new recruits standing outside!'

Joe Packer thought for a moment. 'I know about a dozen straight and true men when they be sober, and will think on it for the others.'

Jack stood and looked through the window at the recruits, still seeking mastery of a simple march in step with each other. At this rate of progress Jack thought, it would be another week before they learn to wheel in line. 'I must see the Q.M. and assess our stores and equipment. I favour short muskets ashore, but I am uncertain we have enough.'

Sergeant Packer nodded assent, his mind already turning to the task of selecting suitable men for the task. They need to be calm, experienced men, able to think independently. Not enough of them, he reckoned.

'Joe, I have another idea which I must ask you to think on. If we are to be ashore in France, perhaps we should dispense with our red coats and white cross-belts. We would stand out like the cross of St George in the enemy's country. Some dark overcoat or jacket perhaps. A disguise, if you like, in the event of meeting with French patrols. Think on it will you? I know the Corps would not approve, so I shall not seek the colonel's consent.'

Packer shook his head. 'Vizzard is a rum bird,' he thought. 'Always doing something different. The bugger looks excited about this—found garrison duty heavy going he has, and no mistake.'

'Can't see any of the field officers thanking you for ideas of such ilk, sir,' he spoke aloud. 'Mind you, I can see 'ow it might be an 'elp though.'

'Go and find the best men for me, Joe. I will see you in the adjutant's office later.' Vizzard left the sergeant wondering.

* * *

The quartermaster, an elderly lieutenant by the name of John Bartleman, was a lugubrious, portly man of perhaps fifty years. An untidy mass of curls framed the weary, veined, florid face; evidence, not of years spent at sea but of too many hours spent in taverns and dining rooms, was dominated by a grog-blossom nose. Fortunately though, he was able to satisfy Jack's needs for the shorter land-musket, and, amidst much puffing and panting, arranged for the weapons to be put aside. He reserved for Jack a sufficient supply of powder and ball, but he looked askance at Jack's request for dark-coloured overcoats or jackets. 'Why on earth would you ask for such, Mister Vizzard? I have no clothing of such ilk in my stores.'

'Perhaps some canvas jackets or coats, such as the Navy use at sea?' He asked hopefully.

'If you wish non-uniform clothing, Mister Vizzard, you will have to seek it elsewhere, for I cannot supply it.'

Jack Vizzard pleaded with him, begged him to find some suitable covering, enough for some two dozen men. He cajoled him to the point where Bartleman agreed to try, with 'no assurances, of course,' but he would endeavour to meet Vizzard's needs.

Satisfied he could do no more, he next left his sword with the armourer, in the adjacent building, requiring a fresh keen edge be honed on the blade. He spent an hour in the adjutant's office, poring over an Admiralty chart of the Cherbourg Peninsular and Normandy, making notes of coastal villages, and such features as rivers. The clock on the wall chimed five o' clock and within three minutes, Major Squires walked in.

'You now have a vessel to take you across the Channel, Vizzard. She is the *Nimble,* a cutter of fourteen guns, I am told. Captain Powlett has detailed a Lieutenant Lapenotière to accompany you. Know nothing of the man; Powlett believes him fit for the command —he has some experience of small boats and of the coasts of Brittany and Normandy.' Squires halted his discourse, and sat at the table. 'Sounds too much like a damned Frenchie to me!' He exhaled a sigh.

'That is not all, Vizzard. Powlett has instructions from the Admiralty to provide all possible assistance to our mission. However, the First Lord was awoken during the night, received a visitor it seems. Our man has a most gallant servant, a Frenchie but a Royalist who sought refuge in England some months past. He has just arrived having ridden all night and all day. I have just arranged for him to eat and sleep, for he was most desperately tired.' Noting Jack's expression of surprise, he continued, 'Yes, the man is here and reports his master is proceeding, not to Fecamp, as we first thought. His mission, I mean his attempt to return to England, has been discovered, he believes, and he travels now to Dieppe. Evidently he is most anxious to leave France.'

Jack looked at the chart he had studied, and pushed it away. 'Dieppe. Hell and damnation! I have just spent an hour or more poring over the chart of Cherbourg.'

Squires gave him a wry smile. 'Sorry, Vizzard it's to be Dieppe, and tomorrow night. If our man fails to show, Lapenotière has orders to lay offshore, and return the following night. You of course, will be ashore. A suggestion has been made for a rendezvous at a church in the centre of town. You are to watch for a young man, shabbily dressed. He will wear a white lily in his hat!' Squires laughed, and Jack looked wide-eyed.

'All rather strange to me, Vizzard, I don't mind telling you. Cloaks and daggers and a white lily!'

'I am expected to sail to France, make my way to the centre of Dieppe, and watch for a young man wearing a lily? More than a little strange I would say, sir. Bloody dangerous would be more appropriate. I hope the information he has is worth it.'

Jack thought over the prospect for a moment. He had learned a little of the French language when at King's School, but not enough. He was right to think of covering his marine uniform, though we cannot simply march into a French port, dressed as toy soldiers. We will have to masquerade as civilians, he decided.

'This French manservant,' Squires intruded on his thoughts, 'he has volunteered to go with you, to act as a guide. Seems he is anxious to ensure his master reaches England safely. I have agreed to his request, and trust such is acceptable to you. Actually, their lordships request it, Vizzard.'

'Today has been one of many surprises, sir. It may be useful to have a guide, certainly one with command of the language. With your leave, I should like to return to my wife, unless you have further need of me this evening?' It was already dark outside and Jack was anxious to be home.

'No, Vizzard. I will be returning to my home also, but first I have to speak to the colonel. I need his advice on certain matters relating to this business. I will see you in the morning.'

CHAPTER 4

'It was a most curious sensation, my dear. I truly felt as though I was being observed, in a secretive fashion.' Mary had recounted her visit to the home of Helena Squires earlier in the day. 'Yet, I am certain none of the ladies present were doing so. It truly made me feel most uncomfortable.'

Jack ate his evening meal without enthusiasm. He had not spoken much since returning home, preoccupied as he was with his own thoughts and contemplating how best to tell Mary his news. He swallowed another mouthful of the baked fish pie Mary had made, and raised a pot of water to his mouth, pausing as he searched for the words.

'I am sure there is nothing to it, my love. Do not fret over a simple feeling. I, too, have had an eventful day.' He drank to refresh his mouth. 'I had a meeting with Major Squires this morning at the dockyard, as you know. The major was kind enough to confirm I am promoted to first lieutenant.' He thought it preferable to impart some welcome news first.

'Oh Jack, what wonderful news,' said Mary, a broad smile lighting her face. 'Not before it is due, in my opinion. I felt you should have received your due shortly after our return from New

South Wales. Oh excellent, Jack; your father will be so pleased—proud too, of course. I shall write to him this very evening.' She cleared away his plate, taking it to the pail used for washing their crockery. 'There is another matter, my love. Something less than wonderful I regret to say.' He looked at her with affection, not wishing to cause her upset.

Mary stopped, alerted by the tone of his voice, and gazed back at him, her hazel eyes full of anticipation.

'I am to travel to France, on urgent government business. I cannot tell you what I am to do there, and it does... it *may* hold some small degree of hazard.' He paused, his throat tightening a little. 'I will have some good men with me, and I am sure it will turn into an adventure. Joe Packer will be with me, and I will be back in Portsmouth within a few days.' He smiled, hoping she would be encouraged, knowing she would worry. 'The colonel has entrusted me with a most honourable employment and instructs me much depends on my "diligence and skill". He was kind enough to say he doubted not success would be assured in my hands.'

Mary sat on a chair, taken aback at the news. She had not expected this. France was in such turmoil at present, as all knew, because the broadsheets carried stories of horrors committed in Paris and elsewhere. Now they have murdered their own king surely they would not hesitate to kill an English soldier, if he were caught. She stared at him with wide, glistening eyes.

'Oh no, Jack. I will not cry. I know you must go and you will be brave, as I will be.' She went over to him, and embraced him firmly. 'Just come back to me. I could not bear to lose you.'

He caught hold of her, marvelling at her strength, her courage and her love for him.

The following day was her birthday. France declared war on

England the day following that. The news reached England a week later.

* * *

Colonel William Souter knew the French declaration of war had found Britain militarily weak and ill prepared for another armed conflict. Her allies, Prussia and Austria, had already deployed her armies following the declaration against Austria in April; and had they only been placed under a united command with a clear direction, they could well have destroyed the French Revolutionary Army within a week, he thought. The French National Convention needed a distraction to divert the people's attention from the failing economy and the failure of the previous year's harvest. Cynically, the convention had reasoned that a war would unite the people behind the revolution. In preparation for that, Souter knew, an accelerated plan of enforced conscription had been ordered in France.

Britain had a weak, small, and ill-managed army. Pitt, the king's minister, had resolved that Britain's role could only be financial and naval. By contrast, the Navy was well supplied with ships, dockyards, munitions, supplies of victuals and a trained and a disciplined force of men. Indeed, manpower was the one resource lacking for the wartime Navy—men to crew the ships, and men to fight on them.

The Corps of Marines would need expanding. The force was half-trained and under strength, but the heart of the Corps was sound. Tired as he was, Souter felt proud. Proud of the Corps and filled with a sense of purpose, he was conscious of the conflict he realised was coming.

Colonel William Souter displayed the evidence of a sleepless night, as indeed had been the case: these thoughts, and more, running through his mind. He had been in conference with two of his majors until midnight, and then he had called for the French servant, who had been sleeping in barracks under guard. He had questioned him carefully and shrewdly for two hours. Then he had written a long despatch to the Admiralty, sending it in the care of a junior lieutenant before dawn.

He felt his chin, and noted the rough, grey stubble which covered his face. His eyes were red and sore and his bones ached. The little hair he had left was thin, lank and in parts quite white, and now was dishevelled. He stood and stretched his aching limbs and called for his servant, who slept in a bunk in the adjacent office.

'Wilkins, where are you man? Wilkins, I have dire need of some coffee,' he growled. 'Please arrange it before I expire.'

The unfortunate marine, a veteran of nearly twenty years' service, swung his legs over the side of the bunk, rubbed his eyes and shivered with the cold. 'Not my fault you bin up all night,' he muttered under his breath, 'some of us 'ave been tryin' to sleep.' He slouched away to roast and grind some beans to make the brew the colonel always demanded in the morning.

Colonel Souter splashed some cold water from a bowl onto his face, starting at the sudden shock. He quickly honed his razor on a leather strop, and painfully scraped the stubble from his face, wincing as the edge pulled at the bristles. His wife always left a bottle of lavender water in his private room and he dabbed some on his cheeks and chin.

He felt better, but desperately wanted coffee. At least now he had a good idea of the demands to be made of young Vizzard and his men. God in heaven, we are at war again. He would see the men away, but then he would have to complete the packing and arrange for the transport of his effects to Chatham. He should have been there yesterday, he thought. No use worrying about it now. This order from the Admiralty, no less a person than the first lord himself, had to take precedence. He had a glimmer of understanding of the importance of the task. We know now some move is afoot, but where, when and by whom, and in what strength? Only their Lordship's agent in France knew the answers to some of those questions. Vizzard must get the government's man back to England, and damned fast.

Wilkins shuffled in with a pot of steaming coffee. To assist Colonel Souter reach a good humour, he had buttered some toast and added on the strong Scottish orange jam his superior so favoured. Bitter stuff, thought Wilkins.

'At last, man. Thank you.' Souter's humour returned with the aroma in his nostrils. He took the pot and poured the steaming contents into a dented and tarnished pewter mug which was of great personal value. Adding a generous measure of cold milk, he drank the contents without pause. 'Pour me another will you please, Wilkins,' he requested, biting into the toast, savouring the bittersweet taste of the conserve, liberally spread on the bread.

He read again the clerk's copy of the despatch sent two hours ago. With luck, it will be with the first lord by supper. Light crept into the office as the weak, wintry sun rose over Spithead, slowly bringing some degree of warmth to the cold room.

Jack Vizzard knocked and entered the room, hesitating just long enough for Colonel Souter to call out, giving consent. 'Mister Vizzard, good morning to you. I trust you slept well?'

Jack had not. His mind had been too full of thoughts of the forthcoming day; and of the passionate farewell Mary and he had made during the night. He had lain still beside her as she slowly subsided into troubled sleep, to face her own nightmares. He had dressed quietly and quickly, and left Great Southsea Street before dawn, walking slowly through the dark deserted streets.

'Thank you, sir. Well enough I believe, in the circumstances. Is Major Squires to join us, sir?' He pulled the cloak from his shoulders, hanging it on a stand by the door.

'Help yourself to some coffee, Vizzard. I know you enjoy it. No, he is not expected here today—said he had to attend to some matter in Winchester. I spent much of last evening conferring with him. I asked him for some time with you alone, as I wish to brief you personally.'

Colonel Souter motioned Jack to a seat, and proffered the copy despatch for him to read. As he read, his eyes slowly widened.

'I see you comprehend our difficulty, then.' Colonel Souter smiled wryly. 'It is thus vital to our cause this agent of their lordships be found and brought to London. No price is too high to pay to ensure his safety.' He paused to allow the full effect of his words to be appreciated. 'No price, Vizzard; I speak plain. Is all clear to you?'

'Sir, yes, I understand.' His brain absorbed the implication. He understood all too clearly and suppressed the sensation of ice along his spine.

Souter sighed. 'I am glad you do. We have learned the French will be on the move soon, but desperately need to know where and when they intend to strike, and in what numbers. The information, if we can get it, will be of enormous value to our country and our allies.'

He pulled a rolled chart from a rack and spread it out, weighting the edges with a brass paperweight, and a heavy book; Vizzard couldn't determine the title. 'It has been decided the Navy will land you here.' He pointed to a place on the chart, a short distance from the port mouth of Dieppe. 'From there you will move along the *Rue de Chastes* to St Jacques Church. He will make himself known to you, but you should be looking for a young man, likely to be in uniform. He will be wearing a lily, but I understand you know this.'

Souter smiled benignly. He lit his first pipe of the day, a marbled clay pipe inherited from his father, filling the room with clouds of aromatic smoke, and coughing briefly as the tobacco caught his lungs. 'Now, Vizzard, this man's servant, a rather sour-faced man, perceptibly loyal to his master, tells me his master's identity and possibly his intent, has been discovered by The Committee for Public Safety, which is what passes for the ruling body in France these days—little more than thugs and murderers, in my book.' He sucked on the pipe, savouring the flavour. 'The man is on the run, and hunted. We have to find him first. We have a fast cutter to take you to Dieppe, and by all I hear, a good man to command her. Once you are ashore, the Navy will retire to a safe place and return exactly at mid-night. You must signal seaward, with three, long green flashes. Two lanterns will be with your party.' Souter sneezed, as smoke entered his nostrils. 'The Navy will reply with five white flashes, at which point, Vizzard, you will be on the beach, with our man, ready to embark. Is all clear?'

Jack nodded and opened his mouth to speak. Souter continued without waiting for a reply 'The Navy will not wait if you do not appear, but they will return the following night, again at precisely twelve of the clock. Same signals to be applied. If you are not on the beach, they have orders to assume you have either been captured or worse, and to return immediately to Portsmouth.'

He poured another coffee, and rested his elbows on the table. 'Now, some good news for you. The fellow's servant knows Dieppe well. Grew up there it seems. He will take you to the rendezvous, and back to the beach. Be wary, Vizzard. Who knows with a Frenchie, eh? Fellow seems *bona fide*, but... well, just be careful and keep your wits sharp!'

Lieutenant Varlo entered, florid of face, as though he had run a dozen miles in as many minutes. 'Good morning, sir. I have a message from a Captain Powlett. The wind is westerly and a good, steady breeze. He would like your party to be at the sally port by eleven o' clock at the latest. He does not wish to lose this breeze, so I have sent a runner to confirm our lads will be there. Do you... er... have any orders for me, sir? I would be honoured to have the command of the...'

'No, not this time, Varlo, this is a matter for Lieutenant Vizzard only. The fewer who know of the detail of this enterprise the happier I will be. My orders are very explicit; only the officer commanding, that is to say I, and the officer leading the patrol, are to know of its nature and purpose. None of the company commanders are privy to the details. Is all ready, Mister Vizzard?

'I arranged matters with Sergeant Packer last evening. With your leave Colonel, I will go and collect him and the men.' He stood.

The Colonel extended his hand. 'Good luck, Vizzard. Remember my words. God speed to you.' Souter strode through to another room calling for his servant.

'I will come with you, Vizzard. See you off, if you like,' said Varlo, clapping him on the shoulder. 'Have to say though, I would rather be commanding this expedition in your place.'

'I am curious as to the decision to give me the task, Matthew; but Major Squires and the colonel have been adamant, the honour is mine. It also means that the responsibility, should I fail, is mine too. Junior lieutenants are expendable, you know.'

They left the Colonel's office and found Sergeant Packer

inspecting a line of men on the parade ground. Joe Packer turned to face them and threw a smart salute, directed more to Captain Varlo than to Jack.

'Good mornin' sirs. The men are ready, sir. I've spoken with the QM and our equipment has been loaded onto yonder cart, sir. All as you directed, Mister Vizzard.'

As he spoke, the corporal of the guard, accompanied by a private, marched from the barracks, a tall, gangling, miserable looking man walking between them. He was dressed in black breeches, tucked into black calf-length boots, with a dark brown coat over a faded, crumpled white shirt. His head was covered with a simple, dusty stack hat in which a white lily wilted.

'This will be your guide, Vizzard.' Varlo stepped forward to dismiss the guard, and welcomed the Frenchman with a cold stare. 'Good morning to you, Monsieur Bontecou. I trust you have rested. I have the honour to present Lieutenant Vizzard, the officer commanding this expedition, and charged with escorting your master. Do you understand me?'

The Frenchman turned his head a fraction to look at Jack. 'I 'ope he is a good soldier, *Monsieur* Capitain.'

His voice and his words carried a meaning, and Jack felt a moment of concern. He spoke English, which Jack was pleased to learn, because he had never fully mastered French.

'*Oui m'sieur. Oui. Monsieur Vizzard est l'un de nos meilleurs officiers,*' replied Captain Varlo.

'*Je suis ravi d l'entendre, commandant. Il peut être necessaire. La France est une endroit dangereuxmaintnant.*'

The narrowed eyes of M Bontecou looked across at Jack. His manner was not patently unfriendly, simply naturally suspicious. Jack understood the man was trying to take the measure of him.

Joseph Packer stood next to Jack, his face inscrutable. 'Beg pardon, Mister Vizzard, but what are they talkin' about?' he growled softly from the side of his mouth.

Jack replied, without taking his eyes off Bontecou. 'As best I can understand, Joe, he hopes we are up to the job of rescuing his master.'

'Cheeky bastard,' Joe Packer grunted.

'*Monsieur* Bontecou.' Jack addressed him directly. 'Your knowledge of our English language plainly is very good. How did you come to learn our language, sir?'

'Ah, Lieutenant, I spent some years here, in London, when I taught at Westminster. I am a teacher, by profession. Now I serve a good man—also I think a teacher. He has been hunted by our enemies.' Bontecou extended his hand. Hesitatingly, Jack took it, and gave the Frenchman a firm handshake. 'You will find my master a good and honourable man, Lieutenant. I trust you to find him protect him and return us both safely to Britain, yes.'

'I will do my duty, *monsieur*,' Jack snapped. 'I trust you to do yours, sir.'

Jack Vizzard strode across the parade ground to examine the contents of the cart, which Sergeant Packer had prepared with the assistance of the Quartermaster. Casting his eyes over the neatly arranged stores, he was gratified to see a quantity of dark canvas coats had been included, after all. There were food rations for three days for the men; sacks of bread and biscuit, a barrel of beef, one of water and an ample supply of musket balls and powder.

'Sergeant Packer, I wish to examine the men. Who have we got for this outing?'

'The best I could scrounge from the garrison sir, but don't you go tellin' 'em now.' Packer grinned. Most of 'em you will know, but some are from Major Walters's company. The colonel's orders sir,' he explained, at Jack's puzzled expression. 'He wanted you to have trusted men, sir.'

Jack walked slowly along the line of assembled men, Sergeant Packer with him. 'Tom! What in God's name are you doing here?'

His question was directed at young Tom Clutterbuck, his servant and fellow conspirator in the death of the Reverend Barnwell, all those years ago. The youth, now an experienced man of twenty-three, returned his officer's gaze equably and spoke with acquired confidence, 'Sir, Sergeant Packer sought to discourage me, but if you are off looking for a fight, well, I have a duty to be with you and watch your back, sir.'

'A fight is the last thing I am seeking, Tom, but so be it. I am content you are with us.'

He spoke briefly to other men from his own company, pausing when he came upon an unfamiliar face. 'Davies, Paul; Private, sir.' The man slapped his musket to the present position.

'Welcome, then, Davies. How came you to the Corps?'

The man stood straight and still and recounted how he had been in the 55th regiment of Foot, but had transferred in December, hoping for a more active role.

Jack progressed along the line, speaking similarly to several men he did not know, trying to measure their worth, but wanting also to know who they were. It was of importance to him, to know his men. They too, found it of value, if a little unusual. Had Jack been aware of it, one of the men selected was Major Squires's orderly. He had volunteered—indeed the major had pleaded with the colonel for his selection.

Having completed his inspection, Lieutenant Vizzard concluded that he and his men were ready to proceed. He saluted Captain

Varlo, and ordered Sergeant Packer to start the men on the short march to the dockyard. 'Good luck, Vizzard. Wish I was coming with you. God speed your safe return, my lad.' Varlo turned and walked back to the adjutant's office.

Jack Vizzard watched him for a moment, noting his limp and wondered how Varlo had been injured. Making a mental note to ask him one day, small clouds of breath marking their march, he led his men on a steady path to the sally port, where a young midshipman awaited with a ship's launch to transfer them to the *Nimble,* anchored in Portsmouth Harbour.

'Good morning, sir. Mister Vizzard, I believe?' The young officer addressed Jack as he approached. 'My name is Bird, Richard Bird, sir, but I am known as Dickie.'

The midshipman grinned. He was of short stature, with broad shoulders, and an untidy tangle of hair, of quite the reddest hue Jack had seen. His face, browned from exposure to the sun, was peppered with a myriad of freckles. Bright green eyes sparkled with enthusiasm.

'Good morning, Mister Bird. I am delighted to meet you.' Gesturing to Joe Packer, he said, 'This is Sergeant Joseph Packer, my right hand. You do have room for us all in your boat, I trust?'

'I was told to collect two-dozen lobsters... beg your pardon sir, marines. Yes, I can take you all in one trip, have no fear. He addressed Joe Packer. 'If you could bring 'em down the steps, Sergeant, I will have my crew assist with your stores.' He detailed two large sailors to lend a hand as Sergeant Packer ordered two of his men to start unloading the cart.

'The captain is anxious to weigh, sir. The wind favours us, but it may not last.' Dickie Bird offered a hand as Jack stepped on board the jolly boat. 'The crossing may be lumpy at this time of year—

mind your head, sir—the tides are inconstant in the Channel.'

The lateen sail unfurled and Bird ordered the lines cast off, pushing the tiller over, as the wind plucked at the sail, cracking as it filled, and the small craft gathered momentum. 'Lively with that sheet, Roberts, you lubberly bugger.' Bird looked over his shoulder, picking his course to the sloop, which came into view as they rounded a frigate. 'There she is, sir. Pretty as a picture, is she not? Just to larboard of the seventy-four, the topsail schooner, gaff-rigged.'

The description was lost on Jack but he followed the middie's outstretched arm, picking out a small ship, some seventy feet in length, two masts and a solitary row of closed gun-ports. Jack counted them—only four.

As if reading his thoughts, the midshipman spoke, 'Fourteen 12-pounders, sir. Ideal for the inshore work we have to do, Mister Vizzard. We have a crew of just thirty, so with your marines we shall feel a might crowded during the crossing.'

Bird's eyes narrowed as he approached, adjusting the tiller to bring the launch onto the starboard quarter of the little ship. 'Clew up there,' he called out, 'smartly now.' The two forward-most sailors hauled quickly. They each grabbed a boathook, preparatory to catching the boarding ladder. As they caught on, Bird shouted again, 'Hook on smartly now, Roberts. Here we are then, sir. Have your men get aboard first, if you please. Steady now.'

Vizzard's men clambered uncertainly up the short rope ladder hanging from the cutter's starboard quarter. Following Sergeant Packer he quickly reached the top, to be greeted by a good-looking man in the uniform of a naval lieutenant.

'Welcome aboard, Mister Vizzard. John Lapenotière is my name. I am delighted to meet you.'

The tall officer returned Jack's salute and extended his hand in welcome, and Jack had time to observe a dark complexioned man of about his own age, ruddy of face with a dimpled chin, wearing a faded uniform coat, with a single, slightly tarnished, epaulette.

'Dickie Bird will show you where to go, just as soon as your stores are aboard. I am most anxious to get underway, as naturally, you will understand. I have the luxury of a small cabin, which please do me the honour by sharing. I will join you presently.'

He strode forrard to supervise the loading of Jack's stores, shouting at the chattering seamen labouring with barrels and cases and sacks.

Jack and Joseph Packer stood at the stern, close to the wheel, looking about in helpless attitude. The seamen, obviously working to prior orders and from skill born of experience, hauled on halliards, raising the jib; another group heaved on the sheets to raise the fore-stays'l. A third gang worked the capstan, raising the bow-anchor.

Lieutenant Lapenotière walked back to the stern, watching his crew at work. 'Bring her out, Mister Holt,' he called to the master's mate standing at the wheel.

The little vessel picked up a wind and heeled to larboard. Lapenotière moved to the windward side, peering alternately along her side and at the bowsprit. 'Another half-point to larboard, then we should be flying,' he shouted to the helmsman. The vessel responded, her sails filling, the mainsail whipped and cracked as it too, was hauled up, driving her bows forward, a surge of foaming grey water sliding swiftly along her flanks, as the rising mizzen cracked and filled, pushing the swift vessel even faster. Vizzard grinned at Packer, infecting his sergeant with good humour.

Dickie Bird returned from an errand below, and called out,

'Come with me, if you please, sir. Sergeant Packer, I will show you where to lay up.' He darted back below and Jack followed, Sergeant Packer close behind.

Vizzard remembered, fortunately in time, to duck his tall frame to avoid a beam. Sergeant Packer, not so familiar with small ships, forgot, and struck his head in the gloom below. 'Bugger this.' He cursed again, rubbing his forehead.

Jack laughed. 'Never mind your bloody head, Joe. I hope you have not dented Mister Lapenotière's little ship. He seems to be in love with her!'

I can see 'ow he feels about his vessel; she do sail smartly. Mind you, sir, seems we must rely on yet another ruddy Frenchie, sir. This one seems a mite more English, though.'

The midshipman's eyes flared in the low light. 'Mister Lapenotière is unquestionably an English gentleman, Sergeant Packer, I assure you, and a finer inshore sailor you will not find in the service.' His glaring eyes levelled at Joe Packer, challenging.

'I intended no slur on your cap'n, Mister Bird, grunted Packer, staring directly at the midshipman. 'My apology for any offence.'

Bird relaxed. 'His great-grandfather fought with Marlborough, Sergeant, and his own father was a post captain. They are Huguenots, Mister Vizzard, his family have been settled in Devon for a hundred years or more.'

'Regretfully I do not know of the family, Mister Bird, but I look forward to his company on our little expedition.'

'I have had a hammock slung for you next to the gunner, Sergeant Packer, just along here.' He stopped at a small curtained area, timbers creaking as the vessel rose under their feet. 'Mister Vizzard is to share the captain's berth, though in truth, it is no stateroom.'

Stooping low, he entered Lapenotière's private quarters, dropping his pack and musket behind the door of the small rear cabin. Unbuckling his sword belt, he sat on a chair, and helped himself to a glass of water from a jug in a rack. He had time to study the cabin, rudimentary as it was. A cot, probably too short for Lapenotière, was slung on the starboard side. A small round table and four spoon-back chairs were the substance of the furniture. A rack with half a dozen or so books hung on the larboard side; an eclectic mix of The Nautical Almanac, a Bible and what might be novels or books of poetry; Jack could not tell, as the spines were damaged by salt or mould. Three small windows in the stern allowed light into the cabin. A narrow bench, covered in worn and sun-faded canvas, was set into the timbers below, with a pair of small cupboards for storage of personal items. Jack could see some shoes and a pair of boots, one of which prevented the cabin door from closing.

Overhead the sound of running feet interrupted his inspection. The door to the cabin opened with a sudden flourish, and John Lapenotière stood crouching in the doorway. 'Ah now, there you are. I trust you are comfortable. We are well away now, and I can spare a few minutes. Joshua Holt is a reliable man—keeps a good watch. Belay that water, Mister Vizzard. Have a real drink!' He opened a cupboard, and pulled a bottle of brandy from its depths. Plucking a pair of pewter mugs from the rack, he poured generous measures into each.

'Good French liquor, man. You should enjoy it! Health to you, and damn the French, I say.'

Jack raised the mug taking a large mouthful.

'Health and fortune to you, Mister Lapenotière, although I confess I am curious as to the reason for your enmity to the country which is now our enemy.'

'Please, dear fellow, do call me John; I insist. Dickie Bird has mentioned my family, I see. No matter. I hold no allegiance to France; be in no doubt of my loyalty, dear fellow. My great-grandfather had to flee for his life, all for the sake of his faith. Wars, Jack, have their roots in religion, but perhaps the current revolution is an exception. Now sir, I have a briefing from old Powlett, and your Major Squires assailed my ears yesterday on the subject of this expedition of yours. Pull the chart down would you, there's a good chap,' he said, indicating a roll on the shelf behind Jack.

He did so and Lapenotière stretched the chart over the table, completely obscuring it from view.

'Here, I have marked our landing point. I know the coast quite well—it differs little from Dover, but without the cliffs. There is a small beach between Dieppe and Varengeville—there, close to Pourville. Be best to drop you there—you have a guide I believe?' At Jack's nod, he continued. 'Then it should be a steady march into the town itself.' He drained his glass and poured another.

To his mute enquiry, Jack declined. 'The entry to the town is not my chief concern, John. It is finding this man and getting him back that troubles me. The town is likely to be patrolled, so I am told. I have only a small and lightly armed force.'

'Yes, it will be, but they have no real troops in Dieppe that I am aware of. My bosun was there last week—how d'ye think we have such fine brandy? He reports no troops in the town and not even any armed men of any real quality. I can have him accompany you if you so desire, however, he has little of the French language of any value to you.'

'I hope his information is reliable then,' Jack replied. 'You are clear on the signals to be employed for our collection, I trust?'

Lieutenant Lapenotière looked sharply at him. 'You need have no concern about it. I am familiar with this coast and will not fail you. Count on it.'

Vizzard however, was not prepared to accept this officer's assurances and insisted on repeating them and the arrangements to be complied with, should he not return to the landing place at the appointed time.

Finally, satisfied Lieutenant Lapenotière understood his own orders, as well as Jack's interpretation of them, he rose slowly and announced his intention of checking on his men. Leaving the small cabin, Jack was followed by Lapenotière, who rapidly took in the condition of his command, with a swift glance aloft, and a more searching study of the seamen on deck. He stood by the helmsman, hands clasped behind his back, the fresh breeze lifting his dark hair forward over his head. His mouth formed a satisfied grin, showing clear, white teeth.

Jack moved toward the stem of the vessel, seeing Joe Packer arranging supplies and equipment with two privates. He staggered briefly, as a large wave raised the vessel, rolling her to larboard. He grabbed at the shrouds to steady himself.

'Sergeant Packer. Are we ready for this task, or shall I ask Mister Lapenotière to return us to Portsmouth?'

Packer smiled, knowing his officer's sarcastic ways, and understanding his anxiety over this business. He feigned a scowl, deceiving neither of them. 'Now then sir, none of your usual banter, if you please, it might upset the lads. They don't know you ain't serious.' He turned to one of the privates, speaking in the peculiar, gruff London voice the men knew so well, 'Make sure those water bottles are filled, Mortimer, and with water, not pusser's rum. I'll check 'em later.'

Turning back to Jack, he spoke more quietly. 'You think this excursion will be all right, sir? Only, some of the boys are a bit skittish about it all. Landing on a French beach at night, marching into a strange town; it ain't what they were expecting, you see.' Packer rubbed his chin, realising he had not shaved properly this morning.

Jack gazed back at the experienced, level-headed sergeant who had come to be more of a friend than he cared to admit, the bonds of friendship having been formed in the despair of Sydney Town, when nearly all but Packer and Vizzard had forsaken discipline and the spirit of the Corps. He smiled at the memory of those days as he answered.

'I have this suspicion, Joe,' he said, 'the coasts of France may become more familiar to us. This is a most important task, perhaps the first of several, and I have been left in no doubt as to its value to our masters.' He moved Joe away from the working party, seeking more privacy.

'Our man is obviously a spy, and he must be returned to England, whatever the cost, Joe. I confess I am anxious about this matter, rather the more so because our guide is one whom I instinctively dislike. There is something odd in his manner. Watch *monsieur* Bontecou carefully, Joe—most carefully.'

'I wouldn't trust the bastard, sir. I'll keep a close eye on the bugger.'

The subject of their conversation appeared by the mast, in conversation with the bosun, who seemed not to be listening to the Frenchman with any great attention. Vizzard took the opportunity to climb the foremast, as the pair walked aft, evidently seeking Lieutenant Lapenotière. From his vantage point, straddling the yard beneath the lookout, he watched as the Frenchman engaged

Lapenotière in conversation. The sea was darker now, and he realised that the sun, mostly only glimpsed during the day, had begun to vanish completely behind a curtain of dark clouds moving slowly up-channel, so it was all but obscured. The salt-filled air was becoming chill and soon the sea to the west was blackening, topped out with bubbling crests of dirty white.

Jack pondered on the mission that had brought him aboard this small cutter and inevitably he found himself thinking of the country in front of him, which within a few hours would be beneath his feet. An alien country, where his small group of marines were to be cast ashore, and destined for what? He desperately wished to avoid any contact with local people. Would it be possible? Would he find the man the Admiralty officials were so anxious to talk with? He speculated, with futility he understood, just what information he possessed that could be of such value. 'At any cost' he had been ordered. He understood exactly what was meant by the order. Was he prepared to sacrifice himself for Lord-knows-what man, for information he would never be a party to? Was death to be his duty? His fate? Could he sacrifice his life for some secret information he might never know... would never know? He doubted it and felt an inner cold seep into his bones.

A call from the deck brought him back from his thoughts to the present. He had been called to the deck by Lapenotière, and standing and stretching, he then quickly descended the shrouds, making his way back to where Lieutenant Lapenotière paced across the deck, from windward to leeward and back again, a puzzled frown on his face.

'Join me for a bite to eat, Jack, if you please. I need to discuss a matter with you.' Lapenotière moved towards the door leading to the small cabin in the stern, not waiting for a response.

The table had been laid with a piece of surplus sail-cloth in lieu of a table cloth, and on it Lapenotière's servant had placed two large wooden fiddles and some fresh baked bread, the aroma of which immediately made Jack aware of an appetite that had been dormant all day. Now he felt famished.

John Lapenotière poured some small beer from a stone bottle, pulled from his seemingly bottomless chest, into a pair of pewter mugs. Jack waited for him to speak, sensing the man now had some trouble to share and was struggling to form the words.

The servant clattered noisily through the door, kicking it ajar with no regard for courtesy to the ship's commander, and placing a laden tray heavily on the table. A dish of large, charred beefsteaks covered in browned onions brought saliva to Jack's mouth. He saw a bowl of steaming potatoes, still in their skins, dripping with fresh butter. He could be patient no longer. As the servant left the cabin, as noisily as he had entered, he glanced at Lapenotière. 'Come, sit and let us eat man. God, I am famished. This sea air gives one an appetite, is it not the truth?' He took a pull at the tankard of beer, and helped himself to the topmost piece of meat, adding a generous spoonful of onions and a large, over-boiled potato.

John Lapenotière spoke softer than was his habit. 'This Frenchman, Jack; he makes me damned uncomfortable.' Lapenotière stared at the food in front of him. 'He spoke with me—you may have observed—and now asks me to change plans and land you and your party further along the coast, to the west. I confess I am rather put out. He believes it would be safer for all, but I am troubled, and don't mind telling you. He could give me no explanation for his request, which he has not discussed with you—he confirmed it so. I sent him below with a sharp word or two, I can tell you.'

With considerable enthusiasm, John Lapenotière pulled a piece of beef onto his platter, taking and dropping one of the greasy potatoes, which rolled onto the table. 'Hell and damnation,' he said, stabbing the errant vegetable with his fork, placing it back on his platter. 'The bastard knows more than he has told, I have little doubt.' He sawed at the meat, thrusting a large piece into his mouth, a stray length of onion left hanging from the corner of his mouth.

Jack paused, considering this new development, which discomforted him also. Why should the French servant make such a request, with no consultation or word before approaching Lapenotière?

An impulse came to Jack's mouth.

'Go along with his suggestion, John. I too am curious, indeed concerned, but some instinct tells me to go along with this. How far along the coast does he suggest we now land?'

'Oh, only a mile or so from the original point, which is what is so odd. Why should he feel our chosen place is 'unsafe'—his word, Jack, his word.' Lapenotière hacked at the potato, and hesitated. 'He clearly knows the area well. Muttered something about the beach shelving steeply and access to the coast road at the point presenting a hazard. It will mean a longer walk for your chaps, I reckon.'

The point had not been lost on Jack. He had no desire to add to the physical burden of the approach to Dieppe, but his insatiable curiosity had taken over. Greater caution would be necessary, and he would need to be even more vigilant.

The Frenchman was playing out some plan, and he had to discover what it was. At any cost.

CHAPTER 5

He had left the portmanteau in the villa in Paris, and regretted it. There had been a dozen or so quite lovely drawings contained within it, which, probably, he would never see again.

The journey from Paris to Normandy had wearied him. The documents from the Legislative Assembly had helped him this far, but they were no more than clever forgeries, and the confusion throughout the country had assisted him enormously. Twice now he had met with a challenge *en route* from the capital. He sensed the tiredness in the horse; she had carried him from Evreux; twelve days he had ridden, resting when he could, always with an ear, and an eye, for trouble. And trouble there had been in plenty. Every town had witnessed one or more horrors. He had watched, frightened, saddened and at times disgusted with what he had witnessed. The Terror had spread from Paris to town after town and to even small villages, where communities now sought out any who were less than fervent supporters. Each town found a self-appointed leader of growing brutality.

Charles Hamilton Smith looked older than his years. His face, pale from years of study in engineering and more recently, artillery, was that of a plain man. Dark hazel eyes set wide apart had proved to be an asset. He was a talented artist, with a sharp observant eye for detail. At nineteen he appeared an upright, confident young officer, and his uniform, of an ensign of the Savoy Hussars, was effective as a disguise; none outside Paris would know of it. The blue coat with silver epaulette and a plain shako, displaying a single red plume above a gilt eagle, was sufficiently nondescript to arouse no interest. Once recognised as from the new 84th *département,* with the French language at his command—albeit with a hint of Flemish accent—he had, for the greater part of his journey, been left unmolested.

He had left Paris almost too late, with one of Robespierre's lackeys close to confirming his identity, after ensuring that his friend, *Monsieur* Bontecou, had safely reached England with his message. He was confident he would find an escort waiting for him in Dieppe. The Admiralty would be anxious to see him back. The Admiralty had promised him an escort from Paris but had let him down. Their man had been intercepted, he'd learned from his associate, and had disappeared.

He patted the mare's neck, encouraging her to continue the last mile or so of his journey as the old town of Dieppe unfolded before him in the fading light. He paused on a rise in the road to admire the old city, dominated by the chateau. He had visited Dieppe two years before and had spent a month or more sketching some of the churches and old buildings scattered about the harbour and the fishing fleet: then as now, safely moored within the protection of the port.

He squeezed his booted legs into the horse and walked her on down the hill into the town. He planned to rest for an hour or two in a hôtel, before the rendezvous by the church of St Jacques. Would the Navy be there, as he had requested? It was a question he could not answer, but he prayed they would be. If not, he intended to bribe a fisherman to take him across the channel; a more risky venture he knew, but he also knew that smugglers, greedy to earn hard currency, were sometimes willing to risk the fast cutters of the British customs service.

He rode through the town and into the courtyard of a hôtel, the *Mortier d'Or,* and paid for a room for two nights, overlooking the Eglise St-Jacques, from which he could observe activity in the square below. He washed and shaved, changed his stained breeches and pulled a clean shirt from his valise. After a light supper of fried fish followed by cheese, he returned to his room with a bottle of poor red wine, and prepared to wait. If his message had arrived in London, a small party of British sailors should appear... he consulted his watch... in just over an hour. Picking up his valise, he touched the brass pins on each side, hearing a reassuring, confirming click, as the base lifted on hidden springs. Lifting the base, he pulled a flat canvas packet from the hidden compartment, and read again the despatch of Jean Dalbarade, France's Minister of the Navy. This was exactly the information he had agreed to obtain. It had not been easy. He had recruited a Scots lady, Grace Elliott, to assist. She had proved significantly successful, well known to the French and English aristocracy. Drinking a glass of wine, he re-packed his bag, blew out the lamp, then sat at the table by the window and waited.

* * *

Mary Vizzard laughed at the antics of the pup, a collie, as it chased the ball of wool around the floor. Mary had decided to call it Charlotte, after Jack's only sister, as a courtesy, really, because she was not overly fond of her sister-in-law. She considered her too strong-willed, and a rather opinionated person. Jack called her stubborn, but remained fond of his sister, visiting rarely since their return from New South Wales. The loose-limbed pup, mostly black, with a white face, white feet and a white-tipped tail, had all the energy and force of personality of Charlotte Vizzard, and the same inquisitive temperament.

Abandoning the now futile attempt at knitting the long, thick socks Jack had such a fondness for, she picked the puppy from the floor and placed it on her lap. 'I wonder if your new master will be displeased.' She spoke aloud to the animal, which stared back at her with deep brown, uncomprehending eyes full of devotion. She had taken the animal in from her neighbour, Joan Fitzpatrick, on an impulse, taking pity on the creature, the smallest of a recent litter. The addition of an animal to the household would provide company for her, she reasoned, during Jack's absences from home. And he liked dogs.

Her thoughts immediately turned to him. They so often did. He was away again, this time some secret assignment on the coast of France. She worried for him, always. Jack inevitably dismissed her concerns with his usual good-natured scorn. 'I shall be perfectly safe, beloved,' he had said dismissively. 'Whatever chaos the forlorn country is in, at least we are not at war—for the present.'

Then, this morning all had changed. Outside the Phoenix Tavern, the town crier had brought the morning shoppers to a standstill. People stood like statues as he loudly proclaimed the announcement that the revolutionaries of France had indeed declared war on England. Wherever Jack was, she prayed he would learn of this, and take great care.

Within minutes it seemed, a patrol of soldiers arrived under the command of a sergeant. 'Come my lads,' he shouted, 'come take the king's shilling, for you have heard the news this morn. We are at war with France again. Come join the South Hampshire's own regiment, the 67th Foot. Do your patriotic duty. Come lads, come one and all, and take a pot of ale with me!' There would always be men willing to join the colours, rather than the harsh life of the Navy, he had learned.

He stood at the steps of the Phoenix, jangling a heavy purse, expectant of a small crowd of young men, eager to take a tankard of ale and listen to his stories of the last war; pleased to take his money. The sergeant had need of more men. The regiment was under-strength, and the ones he had were country bumpkins in uniform, he thought, smiling broadly at the group of men hoping to find more profitable employment at the dockyard nearby. One approached him, a youth no more than sixteen years, dressed in dirty, worn trousers, and an old coat which was evidently not his own, for it was too large for his small frame. The remaining men pulled hats over their eyes, dug hands deeper into trouser pockets, and moved quickly away.

Mary shuddered, the cold air only contributing to her chilled senses, and walked into a butcher's shop, one she had come to use more frequently when Jack was at home, for he favoured the sausages and pork pies the man made.

'Ah a good morning to you, Mistress Vizzard. How may I treat you this cold but interesting day? You have heard the news I take it? Is your gallant husband at home this week?' He stood at a bench, on which lay a stained and well-used board, a large boning knife in his hand.

'Good morning to you, Mister Richards,' she answered, smiling weakly. 'My husband is expected home from London tomorrow, and will be expecting some of those fine sausages of yours he so admires.'

It was none of his business where Jack might be, and knowing her husband as she did, he would not welcome idle gossip of his comings and goings. 'Mary, it is for the regiment, you and me alone, to know where I am or what I am engaged upon.' He had made abundantly clear his instructions to her, many times before.

'My pleasure indeed, my dear lady, a real pleasure as always.' Richards looked at Mary in a friendly manner, again enjoying her regular visit to his small shop, for she was a beauty to behold—she brightened his day. He turned to a stone shelf behind him, on which lay a variety of meats; loins of pork, trays of offal, pies of varying size and fillings and strings of sausages of varying contents. He was proud of his work, hard though it was, and glad he had the custom of the Navy and the Corps of Marines, for most of the townsfolk could ill afford to pay his prices.

With a swift stroke of his knife, he severed a string of a dozen of his most popular variety of beef sausages, deftly wrapping them in a packet of paper and passing it across the bench to Mary.

'Your bill will be tuppence please, my dear, unless you have a fancy for anything else? One of my fine pies might tempt you perhaps? Some rich venison, or a spiced pork?'

He spoke hopefully, knowing Mary occasionally purchased several other items during her twice-weekly visits.

'Thank you, but no, Mister Richards, it is all I require this morning. I wish you a good day.' She smiled and turned, the butcher pausing to admire her retreating form as she exited his shop, thinking it could be another week before her smiling face graced his premises once more.

The people of Portsmouth had largely dispersed as she left the shop, with one or two small groups of old men, former soldiers and sailors probably, who stood talking in low voices. She walked briskly past, ignoring the leering glances, intent on returning to the comfort of her home. She thought absently, of the first home she and Jack had made in Sydney Town; the poor rough-log hut leaking with every fall of rain. She had come to love their home, glad though she had been to leave it when, at last, Jack was free to return to England.

It was with some surprise she turned the corner into Great Southsea Street and found herself viewing the form of her recent hostess, Helena Squires, clearly in an agitated condition. She hesitated, but the lady had noted Mary's approach with such obvious relief she could not avoid the contact—she wondered for a moment why she should want to.

'My dear Mary, how pleased I am to see you,' she announced, with something of a forced smile. 'May I impose on you and invite myself for some refreshment please. I fear I have had some quite disconcerting news, and would share it with you, if it is not an inconvenience?'

Pulling the key to the door from her purse, Mary glanced sideways at Helena. 'Naturally. It will be a pleasure, I am sure.'

The door open, she stepped inside the gloomy hallway, indicating her companion to follow with an outstretched hand. She pulled off her cloak, hanging it on a hook on the wall, and made her way to the small room at the front of the house, furnished modestly with two armchairs upholstered in green leather, now showing the first signs of age. Henry had donated them, together with other items of furniture, as a contribution to their new home. Mary gestured again, 'Please, do sit and make yourself comfortable. I am sorry for the cold, but I have yet to make up the fire.'

Helena's eyes appeared troubled and agitated, but confused, too.

'Would you care for some hot tea, Helena? It will take only a moment.' She thought to provide herself with an excuse to leave the room and ponder the reason for this unexpected visit. Receiving a nod of assent, she left and busied herself in the kitchen, boiling water and spooning leaves into a pot. Helena was plainly troubled, she thought. But why come to me? Does it concern Jack? Is it to do with his absence? She picked a jar from the pantry, in which she had stored some shortbread, thinking it humble fare for her guest, but anxious to offer more than simple Indian tea.

The porcelain was old; had belonged to Jack's mother, of course. The set was incomplete and quite fragile and delicately decorated with images of primroses. It was another of Henry's thoughtful kindnesses. As the fusion of leaves and boiled water reached a conclusion, she smiled to herself with a warm thought for her father-in-law and resolved to return to the Cotswolds to visit both Henry and her own family.

Helena was gazing through the window to the street, watching flakes of snow float earthwards, forming slush in the mud, as Mary carried a tray to the table. 'I wonder if it is snowing in France this morning.' Helena spoke quietly.

'Why do you think of France?' Mary asked, instantly alert.

'Your husband is there, at least, so I believe.' Helena spoke softly, her eyes still watching the snow.

Mary sensed trouble in those few words. She sat quickly in one of the armchairs, the colour draining from her face. 'You must know he is, Helena. Please, what is wrong?' She felt her hands trembling, but refused to look at them, fixing her eyes on Helena Squires, willing her to speak.

'Mary my dear, I believe he is in some danger.'

CHAPTER 6

The day had died quickly, the cold sun slipping silently into the western sea as Jack Vizzard and Lieutenant Lapenotière took station at either side of the helmsman, the sailor searching the grey rolling sea ahead of his swift little craft, the marine grasping a ratline to starboard, feeling the wind combing his hair forward, seeking out the nape of his neck. The wind was increasing and a squall was rolling down the Channel.

Jack climbed up to the gunwale, the better to view the coast when it appeared. He steadied his swaying body and wiped spray from his eyes, slowly adjusting to the gathering gloom. His head turned slowly through ninety degrees as he searched the sea and stopped. He understood with immediacy that they were in harm's way. 'Astern, John. Look.'

Lapenotière spun round, eyes narrowed as he, too, realised his beloved vessel was about to be urned to matchwood.

'Hard a' starboard, man!' he roared at the helmsman. The sailor, a sharp, alert man, didn't hesitate, repeating the order as he swung the craft around. 'All hands stand to,' his shout audible throughout his command, immediately answered by the sound of men running to their allotted stations.

'Damn the lubber of a lookout. I wager you, Jack, she is the *Duc d'Ayen*; a privateer out of Dunkirk. I have seen her before. Fast and well-armed, she has twice our guns and thrice our manpower. And she is too damned close.' He snatched up a glass, trained it on the vessel astern. 'Dammit, I'm right, too!

Dickie Bird appeared in front of his captain. 'Your orders, sir?' A ball passed between them, the hot wind brushing their faces, an instant before it decapitated the helmsman, and sent a crimson shower across the deck.

'Another man on the helm, now please.' The order superfluous as a mate grasped the wheel while the dead man's blood still pumped from his body. Still training his glass on the approaching ship, he commanded; 'Please have your lobsters ready, Vizzard. I will have work for them imminently.' Calm and controlled he braced against a sudden clap as a second gun opened up. 'Note the log, Dickie; then have your division ready for boarding.'

'You are attacking?' Unable to keep the surprise from his voice, Jack reflected on his orders. 'Can we not out-run her, John? I must be ashore without the French navy at my back.'

'I may be *Nimble,* Jack, but have not the speed, and I have no choice in the matter. She has the gage and the legs to close with us. No, sorry, my friend, we must fight her or be taken. And I, for one, have no desire to be taken a prisoner at the start of this war.'

He ran forward shouting orders, catching the boatswain and speaking quickly but not within Jack's hearing because the gunwale on which Jack had stood moments before exploded into a dozen splinters, piercing the deck in front of them.

'Sergeant Packer, he shouted, 'I want the men up and picking them off, their officers first. Smartly now.'

Packer rolled his eyes upward and ran off muttering, 'Bloody hell. That's all we bleedin' want.' He directed a party forrard to the bows and the main body of his force astern, collecting a boarding pike and a cutlass as he joined Vizzard astern.

Lapenotière had sent a man below for swords and pistols, calling more orders in a calm firm voice, watching the enemy's actions with a steadiness Jack found encouraging. He emulated the sea-officer, placing his hands behind his back.

'Have you a plan, John? He is drawing on us, I detect.'

'Indeed he is. I need him to do so for my scheme to work.' He lowered the glass and glanced at Jack, 'I must get alongside him and damned quickly, if we are to have a chance.' He watched the approaching ship through narrowed eyes. 'I will get alongside, spar to spar, fire our pea-shooters, and then sheer off. I shall repeat the manoeuvre and your men must fire rapidly, Jack. I will give them no more than a minute or two at each passing. Then, if all is well, I shall board her!'

They responded to an order her master had given a minute earlier, *Nimble* heeling over with such speed that Jack lost his footing, sliding into the base of the mizzen as another shot hit the larboard quarter. Scrambling to his feet, he saw the gap between the two was closing too rapidly, now less than a cable length.

'She's all-amiss, look. They cannot move. Bring me alongside, Nicholls, quickly now,' Lapenotière called to the helm. 'Dickie, ready with those grapples... ten more seconds.'

With unexpected silence, *Nimble* was alongside the frigate, as the wooden walls met. Then came the splintering of timber as the spars and rigging caught, knitted together, bringing the vessel close aboard, with the guns of the French ship still elevated as a ragged fire rippled along her side. The *Nimble's* small guns fired at full elevation, with one or two well-aimed balls striking the larger armament of the French ship above them.

'Now sergeant, fire!' shouted Jack, a concentrated volley sweeping death across the gap. 'Make ready and fire.' Marines worked hard and fast, teeth biting on cartridges, ramrods flashing, smoke snaking across the deck. A second, less concentrated volley spat into the packed ranks of French sailors, spinning bodies aside in a wind of destruction.

'Bear away, Nicholls. Look sharp!' *Nimble* pulled away, her yards ripping the enemy's halyards from the port side clews and leaches as a ragged broadside finally came from the larger vessel. A ball punched a hole high in the mizzen as Lapenotière issued another order, the yards swinging, bringing his craft with skill across the stern of his opponent. Then his four-pounders cracked out in sequence as he slid speedily onto the opposite tack, confusing the Frenchmen already rushing to the larboard side.

'Mister Nicholls, the sea anchor... now.' Then, 'Hard a' lee... now!' He directed the helmsman, who grunted as he worked the ship to his master's will, spinning her almost as a top with a laughing child behind it. The man spat, wishing he had tobacco.

As she turned, Jack ordered his men astern, watching as *Nimble* came ever closer, the sailors steady by their guns, waiting on the command. When it came, they remained disciplined, the gun-captains pulling the lanyards, orders unnecessary, smoke filling the deck, the trucks squealing, boys running with more bags to fuel the guns, men shouting their fear.

'Now, Dickie, let's get at 'em.' Lieutenant Lapenotière leapt across the gap between the two, hauling himself up the side as a dozen men followed him.

Jack Vizzard called to his sergeant, and followed, hand over hand along a line, swinging his legs onto the gunwale of the larger ship, pulling a pistol from his belt as he did so, seeking a target. He discharged it into the face of a French sailor, awed when the man's face disappeared under a sea of crimson, clubbing a second sailor in the face before throwing the weapon aside, kicking a third in the crutch and pulling his sword, slicing a pike-man across the neck as he charged forward.

Vaguely aware of Lapenotière to his left and Sergeant Packer to his right and a sea of blue in front, he was stopped in his headlong rush by a French officer. A tall, slender man, with an aristocratic, arrogant expression, the man lunged, but was too slow. Steel rang against steel as the men sought an advantage on the now-crowded deck. A sudden thrust—he sidestepped and Joe Packer's pistol exploded by his ear as he put a ball into the Frenchman's chest, throwing the officer backwards.

'No time for fancy swordplay, sir,' he shouted, mouth wide, teeth stained from years of tobacco. Packer swung his pike in a wide arc, forcing the French sailors back.

'Thank you, Joe.'

Then he was slashing and hacking again as more French took form in the sea of bodies, screaming as wild men, desperate to repel the invasion of their ship. Steel clashed against steel, smoke filled the arena as, like gladiators, each man sought a weakness in his opponent, slashing, stabbing, clubbing, kicking and gouging to bring victory. To survive.

A searing, excruciating pain in his side removed, for an instant of time, the red mist in his vision, and Jack fell to one knee. A burly French seaman was over him, the cutlass high above. Instinct made him thrust his right arm upwards, skewering the man in his groin. The scream burst in his ears as he withdrew, rolled away and struggled to his feet, the pain all but unbearable.

He heard shouting, saw the French captain by the mainmast, attempting to rally his men. Jack slashed at another man, opening a face, to find himself in front of the French captain, the point of his sword swiftly at the man's throat.

'Surrender, sir. I urge you to yield, before more blood is shed on your fine ship.' He hissed in French, caring not for his accuracy. '*La capitulation, monsieur. Je vous conseille de céder, avant que plus de sang est répandu sur votre beau navire.*'

'*Oui.* Yes,' the crestfallen, sullen captain answered with shame in his eyes.

Dickie Bird cut the French tricolour from the jack-staff with his dirk, bending on a flag of St George, the only one he found in the flag locker before boarding. *It will suffice,* he thought. 'She is your prize, sir!' he shouted to Lapenotière.

It was over. The unthinkable had been achieved. As swiftly as it had commenced, it ended; Frenchmen motionless and open-mouthed lowered weapons as Jack's men stood threatening, muskets levelled and bayonets bloodied.

Marines were herding French sailors away from their captain with Packer prodding with a bayonet in encouragement, ready to kill more if necessary. Cutlasses and pistols littered the deck, gathered greedily by a bloodied sailor and a pair of marines, one lacking his shako. Tom Clutterbuck, Jack mentally noted.

The French captain proffered his stained sword. Lowering his own, Jack accepted with an inclination of his head. Lapenotière slipped his sword quickly into its sheath, moved closer and growled, 'The honour is mine, I believe,' his hand outstretched for the Frenchman's sword.

'As you wish,' Jack gasped, his lungs heaving from exertion and pain. He limped away, calling on Packer to bring his men. He fell at the rail, weak and exhausted.

In an instant, Tom Clutterbuck was at his side, raising him to his feet. 'Come along, sir. You've done enough for today. Let's get your wound looked at,' he said, noting the bloodstain on Vizzard's breeches. A gangway had been lowered across the gap between the two vessels and Tom helped him cross it safely.

Down in the cabin, Lieutenant Lapenotière pushed open the door and grinned at Jack. 'She is a most handsome prize we captured today, Jack. Worth a small fortune, I shouldn't wonder. Now I must get her and her crew to England. I can spare my bosun and Mister Bird with a couple of hands, but will have need of some of your lads to provide guard.' He sat and picked up a flask of water, and near emptied it in one go. 'I have their crew battened down below deck with a couple of your lads, but will need at least two more to ensure a happy return to Portsmouth.'

Jack looked at Tom, pulling his shirt down over the wound, hastily stitched with a couple of turns of catgut, which was all it required. Tom returned the look, understanding reaching his eyes. 'Oh no, oh not me, sir. Please no. My place is with you, Mister Vizzard.'

'I cannot spare Sergeant Packer, Tom, and you must see that Lieutenant Lapenotière is correct. I will issue you with an order, appointing you as acting corporal. If you discharge your duty satisfactorily, as I am confident you will, it will be ratified in time. It is inadequate reward for your past and present loyalty.' Jack gave the young marine a knowing look. 'Pick three others to accompany you and make sure those Frenchies are handed over the moment you land at Portsmouth.'

Acting Corporal! The news was unexpected and brought a smile to the young man's face. 'Very well, sir. I am mightily grateful to you. I shall collect my kit and go across now.' He saluted and left the cabin.

'Thank you, Jack. That was well done. The lad will be fine with Joshua Holt in command.'

'He has been a good support to me over the years. It is small return for his past service,' he added enigmatically. His thoughts returned to the night at the Vicarage, when Tom Clutterbuck surprised him in the darkness, just after he had dispensed his own justice to Mary's nemesis.

* * *

The surf splashed noisily against the shingle beach masking the marines' muttering, as the cutter's boat slid with a rush onto French land. A half-moon danced between clouds which seemed to sway slowly across the black sky, as Joe Packer leaped onto the shells and pebbles of the foreshore. A sailor quickly followed, pulling hard on the painter, and Jack and his men vaulted over the sides in pairs, up to their knees in the icy Channel water. He stared ahead, willing his eyes to become used to the darkened landscape.

'Quietly now, lads. Move up to yonder ledge and make ready,' Jack whispered.

He trod slowly and warily on the wet sand towards a rocky ledge some twenty or thirty yards in from the water's edge. His ears stretching and eyes straining for any sign the landing had been observed. Once he had his breathing under control, he looked for the Frenchman.

'*Monsieur* Bontecou, if you please. Which way from here? I can see no path off this beach.' Jack studied the sullen looking face of his guide by the thin moonlight penetrating the wispy clouds moving slowly up the coast from the Atlantic.

'Over there to your left, Lieutenant. A narrow path will take us through the dunes to the coast road.'

Jack looked across to where his sergeant squatted with the platoon of marines, dressed in unfamiliar green canvas jackets and grey trousers. He crawled on hands towards him, keeping low. He grunted as he knelt beside his friend.

'Time to move off, Joe. Up to the left, there is a track—so our French friend tells me. Lead the lads off please, no less than three yards apart. Keep your eyes and ears sharp, Joe.'

Growling an order in a low and commanding voice, Joe Packer moved off into the darkness, followed by half of the men. Jack watched for a moment, then, waving to Bontecou, he gestured to the man to walk ahead. He followed; his eyes narrowed as he stared into the darkness, alert for any unusual sounds. The marines moved silently through the sand dunes collecting in groups at the road.

'Move to the sides of the road men, two files not less than six feet apart.' He whispered the order, his head twisting from side to side as he waited for a challenge which never came. 'Sergeant Packer, take the lead if you would. We have a long march ahead, so let us be gone.'

He slung the musket over his shoulder, wrapped his jacket tighter about his neck and tugged at the leather gloves, lacing his fingers together against the cold. He walked with care, listening to the sound of the sea away to his left as he followed.

'The port is an hour away, Lieutenant, but the town is not a fortress. It should be easy to meet my master. I think you are perhaps too cautious, yes, to bring so many men.' Bontecou stepped alongside Jack, his presence unwelcome, obviously so to the Frenchman.

'If that is so, *monsieur*, please be so good as to explain why you advised a different landing-site?'

'Ah yes, naturally. The coast here has many cliffs, and this bay I thought would be easy for landing. I do not say the area is entirely free of soldiers. However, certain beaches are guarded because of Royalists like me who seek the protection of England's court.' He looked intently at Jack. 'You should alert your sergeant, there are small patrols and it will be necessary for us to avoid them. The beach that had been selected is one such, which is monitored; this I know.'

A murmured curse slipped from Jack's lips, and he sent a private ahead to direct Joe Packer to halt the advance party. 'It would have been helpful to have known of this before, *monsieur*.'

But what the Frenchman said made some sense. If indeed, the other beaches were being watched, the caution was warranted. Why was this beach clear of troops, though? His mind worked at the riddle without answer. Not enough men under arms he speculated; or they are not prepared for war on France's own shoreline. He could not help the suspicion that remained in his head, but he would, he must, remain alert for any sign of falseness or treachery. He looked hard at the Frenchman's face, seeing no guile or artifice in his eyes. Bontecou raised his shoulders in the irritating manner so typical of Frenchmen.

'Very well. Proceed, *monsieur*.' He gestured with his open hand, inviting Bontecou forward. As the man slipped quietly ahead in the dark, Jack placed an arm in front of one of the marines. 'Stay to the rear, Jamie, and keep your eyes on our arse-end for me.' The stocky Scotsman, a man with a reputation for keen eyesight, merely nodded and wiped his nose on the sleeve of his oiled jacket, dropping silently behind.

He listened to the soft crump of feet moving steadily ahead of him, smiling at the memory of the whistles and oaths which had greeted his order for the men to place long woollen stockings over their boots. It had seemed a simple measure, designed to silence the nails of the boots on stone or gravel, and for a time, perhaps half an hour, it worked. Now however, the wool had worn through, as the sandy track gave way to coarse gravel and stones, and the strident crack of nails on stones could be heard. In a moment of irrational thought, he decided he would raise the problem with the regiment's cobbler on return to Portsmouth. '*If* I return,' he corrected himself.

Silhouettes took form ahead and he quickly sensed some difficulty, confirmed as the crouching shape of Joe Packer approached rapidly.

'Two guards up ahead, sir. Slouching around, chatterin' and drinkin'. Brandy, I reckon; I was close enough to smell it!' His teeth showed against the dark of his browned face, not lost since his return from New Holland. 'There's a derelict farm just off to the right of 'em. Had a sniff around there too, but couldn't see or hear any more Frenchies. Reckon they are all alone like.'

'*Monsieur*,' he whispered, beckoning Bontecou to him. 'Your opinion, if you please. Are only two guards to be expected, or should I anticipate they will have others nearby?'

The Frenchman looked preoccupied but answered quickly enough. 'I would doubt there is a patrol nearby. 'My thought is another two will be sent from the town to relieve them. There will be more watching the port, I say, seeking more émigrés.'

'Quite possibly, *monsieur*, but I think we take a flanking route and leave them alone for now. I may have to deal with them on our return.' He pulled the straps of his knapsack tighter. 'Joe, we shall head across the fields behind the farm. Take the men off, if you please.'

He watched Packer's retreating back, glanced behind to ensure Jamie the Scot was alert, and moved off behind Bontecou, his carbine held across his chest. To his left could be heard the surf rushing over the shingle beach. The chill air pinched at his hair and ears. He followed the line of silent figures into the gloom across frozen fields, which lay bare and barren. The farm could be seen with no lights showing, giving every indication of being deserted, neither human voices nor animals to be heard. The line closed up as men slowed to pass over a wall, the stones of which had fallen haphazardly about its base.

'Keep moving,' he hissed. 'What's keeping you?'

'Sorry, sir, a man in front has stopped. Think 'e's 'urt, sir.'

'Hell and damnation.' Jack cursed. 'Let me see.' Vaulting the low wall and ignoring the pain in his leg he found a man on the ground, with another leaning over him. Peering into the darkness he recognised Private Hannan, a man regarded by Joe Packer as 'a fine shot, and handy with a bayonet, but keep him off the ale.' He crouched beside the soldier. 'Hannan, is it not? What is it, man?'

The man's face was twisted in pain, and on leaning closer Jack could see the left foot at an unnatural angle.

'Sorry, sir. I stumbled on a rock coming over the wall. Busted me ankle, I reckon. Heard a crack and it fuckin' hurts. Beggin' your pardon, sir.'

'Can you get up... no, of course not. Look here, Hannan, I cannot leave a man with you, and plainly, you cannot continue.' He was irritated at the unwelcome complication, but refused to let it show. 'Make yourself as comfortable as you can; I will not leave you behind. Stay close to this wall and I shall have you collected on our return.' Jack pulled him up against the wall, checked his water bottle and slapped him on the shoulder. 'Keep quiet and keep alert.'

The line moved forward, leaving Jack now more anxious at the passing of time. He decided to increase the pace. He half ran to the head of the line, urgently commanding the men to speed up as he went by. Reaching Joe Packer, he said, 'We need to move a bit faster, Joe. Time is slipping by if we are to make our rendezvous with this agent.' He stood aside as the men moved on, the step just noticeably quicker. He took his place in the centre as the men walked briskly towards the town. It seemed colder, and he rubbed his ears, introducing a little warmth, as he strained for any unusual sounds, his eyes training from left to right, keeping his distance from the grey shadowy form of the man ahead. Freezing grass cracked under his boots, sounding like pistol shots to his sensitive ears, each footfall bringing an expectation of entrapment and capture. His mouth was dry and his head throbbed with tension.

After the months of mundane, banal routine of barrack duty, the days craving some adventurous duty, he was now experiencing it. He could sense the unease in the air, exuded by these men who had no comprehension of his task, their duty to follow his lead and obey his commands. *"For I am a man under authority, having soldiers under me: and I say to this man, Go, and he goeth; and to another, Come, and he cometh; and to my servant, Do this, and he doeth it."* The quote came unbidden to his mind. Where from? Of course, the Bible. One of the Gospels—but which, he could not recall. A distant memory of the words of a sermon by the vicar of Saint Giles, his parish church. Odd how such things came to mind, when his active brain ought to be directed to matters more serious.

The minutes ticked by; he pulled the watch from his pocket but could see nothing of the hands. He dare not stop to light a match. He stumbled into the man in front. 'My pardon,' he whispered to the tall marine, pushing forward to where Joe Packer was crouched behind a low wall.

'There's another patrol, sir; but half a dozen of 'em this time.' Packer nodded in the direction where a ragged group of men were slowly making their way up the winding road towards them.

Vizzard turned and gestured to the marines to lie flat, as he had trained them. Instantly the gloom and ground mist consumed the small force. He sat with his back to the wall, slowing his breathing as the low French voices approached, his heart thumping in his chest. He had, for a moment, considered attacking the French, setting an ambush. He had just as quickly dismissed the notion. He did not want to attract attention to his presence. It was a clandestine mission, after all. *'At any cost.'* He could not risk jeopardizing the expedition for the doubtful benefit of killing half a dozen Frenchmen. In two or three long minutes they were gone, and he slowly raised himself, judging it safe to continue.

'We must be close now, Joe. It's time to separate the men and send in the first of them.' In planning with the colonel, Jack had outlined his ideas to enter the town in small groups. Packer was skeptical, and had argued, with some passion, for the safer option of keeping together. He opened his mouth to repeat the advice, but Jack silenced him with a stern expression which left Packer in no doubt—Vizzard was not in the mood for further debate on the subject.

He nodded towards the forward group of men, who rose slowly and, in crouched positions, moved towards the wall. With a hand on the first man's arm Jack smiled, inserting a confidence into the act he did not feel, and watched as they slowly walked with exaggerated casualness towards the town. Once they were lost in the darkness he summoned the next group of four men, and then waved for Bontecou to approach.

'Now, *monsieur*, we go,' he said curtly. 'Joe, leave two squads behind, one either side of the road, to cover our return. Follow me as soon as they are in place. I will wait for you at the end of the road.' Beckoning to his French guide he crawled over the wall and set off, eyes flicking from side to side. Packer quickly detailed two squads, whispered an order and set off after his friend, his mouth set in a grim line.

CHAPTER 7

On a cold stone bench overlooking St James Park, William Pitt blew on his hands to warm them. He had been sitting alone with his thoughts for half an hour, after the warmth of the Long Room and the hot air generated by his officials and admirals. He needed to think and formulate his administration's policy for what must be a conflict which could envelope all of Europe. His advisers had been full of suggestions, ideas, fantastical schemes, words of caution; the usual mixture of bulls and doves. He rose and walked. A brisk walk always aided his thinking and he walked with a quick, firm step, his head erect, his appearance haughty.

It was inevitable now; the execution of Louis had settled any doubt. What could, what must England do? *Our army is weak; short of men, short of equipment, short of leadership. We must, then, buy time to rebuild and seek alliances within Europe. Alliances will involve money, a good deal of it, and everyone will be seeking to advance his own interests. Thank God the Navy was in good condition. Black Dick Howe and his Corps of Marines had ensured it. More must be done to get more men—we have the ships, just enough, but damnation, we need the men.*

Information! We need intelligence of France's intentions. Now at last, a useful man had become known. His name had been kept from him, but was evidently an educated engineer and artilleryman, one who had studied and lived on the continent. This afternoon he had learned this spy was on his way to London with much needed information. Courtesy of the Navy. *Good,* he thought, '*but when the blast of war blows in our ears....' The poet Shakespeare, naturally; he always had a ready word or a line to describe the moment. Well, we shall hear the blast soon enough, and this time we must be ready, and this time we must defeat them utterly and completely.*

To do so, we need information; sound, reliable, and regular. Information of all kinds; intelligence of the enemy's shipping, dispositions, intentions. More agents. More true Englishmen willing to serve our country and to take risks for information. Eccentric landings on the enemy coast; a favoured idea of his late father, the First Earl of Chatham, would serve well, if properly managed. Perhaps a campaign in the Mediterranean, or the Caribbean—there was so much to be done. *We could, no, we should, augment the army with mercenaries. Hanover and Hesse. I must speak to the king of this. And alliances or a coalition; Grenville must negotiate with some of the other powers on the continent: Austria, Prussia, Spain—perhaps Naples and Sardinia.*

He pulled a flask from his coat and drank deeply. He continued along the short path overlooking St James Park for another twenty minutes or so. On the third perambulation he stopped gazing into the snow, which fell from a dirty grey sky, realised he was chilled and pulled the flask, emptying the contents into his mouth, relishing the warmth of the liquid. An audible sigh escaped from his wide mouth; he turned quickly and strode into the warmth of Ripley House.

If William Pitt found good reason to congratulate himself for the defeat of Charles James Fox, he also had good reason to regret the circumstances that had made his victory more certain. He had struggled long and hard to prevent the French subjugation of the United Provinces. He recognised that the preparations to increase the strength of the king's forces had been in haste; much had been neglected and now must be put right.

The state of the army was lamentable. It was contemptibly small, with perhaps two-thirds of it dispersed among garrisons in India and the West Indies. He had less than 14,000 men in England, for the most part poorly trained and poorly led by country gentlemen with no experience of warfare or overseas service. He knew he could not send an army into Europe with any hope of success. Any alliance against France would primarily rest on the Navy. That service was well led by professional officers. For the army, Pitt needed to find senior officers capable of organising the king's forces, modernising its structure, developing a modern force which would acquit itself well in continental fields.

He slumped into a worn leather armchair, stared into the flames of the fire and ordered a servant to bring him a bottle of Madeira and a glass.

* * *

Helena Squires alighted from the carriage with worry lines etched on her chilled face. She had been married to George for nigh on three years and believed she knew her husband well. His service to the king, his devotion to the corps was beyond question; or so she had always thought. Theirs had been a fast-moving courtship; friends of her family, her parents too, had advised caution, but as the younger daughter of an indulgent father, she had forced her will and married George a mere five months after their first meeting.

Her husband had seemed so... well, dashing was the word that came to mind. He was a man of action and glamour, well-connected with friends in Parliament and at court. She had been impressed, perhaps too readily, she now reflected. Never before had she found reason to question his frequent absences, nor the seemingly unlimited funds to which he had access, even though his pay from the Corps could not possibly have supported his extravagances. Then there were all those unexplained absences. She had believed him without reservation. Recently she had become unsettled, sensing her husband's mood had altered, his absences were longer, with ever less plausible reasons given. His expression, too, usually cheerful and confident, had become solemn and grave. He had become distant, uncaring, cold and inattentive.

His orderly, the furtive man who declined to utter more than an obligatory grunt when she directed him in some task, had avoided her completely, holding urgent whispered conversations with the Major, breaking away sullenly if she should encounter them together. Naturally, she had grown suspicious, curious. Her inquisitive nature urged her to become ever more watchful, ever more secretive.

Then she had found the note. It had fallen from her husband's second tunic as she picked it from the chair where he had so casually cast it, simply to hang it, for the orderly's attention. As she glanced at the folded paper before returning it to the inner pocket, she noted it was written in faded brown ink. She assumed it was of some age, but then observed it consisted of clusters of numbers and jumbled letters. Instead of returning it to his jacket, she kept it hidden. It had left her confused for days. Several times she had considered discussing it with George, but something deep in her consciousness held her back. The more she wondered, the more concerned she became. For many hours she had tried to recall what she had seen, but nothing clear appeared in her mind. Simple groups of letters and numbers, but a pattern for sure. Each group had four characters. She decided to hide it behind the large wardrobe in her bedroom until she reached a decision as to what to do with it. The note occupied her thoughts for several weeks. George wore a constantly troubled expression and spent much time in London. When she returned to read it a third time, it had vanished.

It had been Rachel Varlo who had persuaded her to consult the colonel. She had met the new colonel commandant of the division—one of those balls the Corps seemed so determined to hold in the grand mess. He had tried to be reassuring, but she knew he was troubled by her information. The smile on his face had belied the concern in his eyes. She had returned home distressed and was now convinced her husband was at best a charlatan, at worst an imposter, a double-dealer. A spy.

Her life changed with the thought. Her husband, the man who had filled her life with meaning and purpose, was a traitor. She was betrayed, felt anger and shame. She felt helpless and insecure. Yes, she felt she was in danger. If he knew she had discovered his secret life, she was at risk. He was in London this week, or so he had said: 'I will be in town for some time; business with the Admiralty and so forth.' His words hollow now. So where had he gone?

Then she knew. With a flash like lightning she understood. How ignorant she was; how naïve she had been. Squires, she could not now think of him as George again, was in France, amongst the turbulence raging uncontrolled through the country. My God. Then she realised he was involved in some intrigue, some treachery and it must involve Lieutenant Vizzard. She had flown to see Mary, to take her into her confidence. This was how she found herself in the small rooms in Great Southsea Street, emptying her heart to this young woman of whom she knew so little, but who exuded such understanding and compassion. As she did so, she felt a symbiosis, a closeness she had never before shared with another person.

She had cried. Not one much given to tears she now sobbed deeply, her eyes red and her face becoming blotched and lined as the tears ran into the labial folds of her cheeks as Mary ran to her and embraced her with soothing sounds, as though comforting a baby.

'Hush now, Helena. We must think. If you are really in danger, and my dear Jack also, we must get away from here, to a place of safety, and I think I know exactly who we should see.'

Helena allowed Mary to take charge. Two valises appeared and a small, confused little girl was told to gather her favourite doll and a toy while essential clothes and toiletries were hurriedly packed. Within half an hour, the two women were hurrying through the cold evening air to the coach at *The George*, for the eight o'clock Royal Mail service to Bristol. From Bristol, another would take them to Gloucester, which could be met on the road near Stroud. No time for a note to Henry, thought Mary. We will have to make the best of it, she said to herself, her heart competing with her mind for attention. Thoughts and fears reeled through her head as she took in the impact of Helena's news. Jack in danger. She could not contemplate what he might be facing across the dark, freezing water of the Channel.

A coachman, wrapped in a deep scarlet cloak, his tricorn hat pulled down over his eyes and his neck swathed in a woollen warmer, was stamping his feet as the leading Cleveland bay snorted great gusts of vapour from flared nostrils, shaking its head as if anxious to be on the road away from Portsmouth. The two women looked at each other, concerned to see a solitary passenger, a young man, seated within the carriage.

'To Gloucester, you say,' the coachman answered Mary's question, 'yes there's room enough, if you have the price.' He looked on their worried faces. 'The fare's 28 shillings each; same for the girl.' He snorted, resembling the Cleveland whose bridle he now grasped, settling the animal. 'It will be eighteen hours to Bath, say twenty to Bristol, and I can have ye in Gloucester for this time tomorrow, easy as you like.'

It was more than Mary had expected. Her scant savings were no more than three guineas. She knew that, once in Woodchester, Henry would come to her aid, but now her wilful nature took over.

'Nonsense man. Why, I could buy a pair of your nags for the sum.'

'They're not my rates, miss. I can't take thee for less.'

'Look, your coach is all but empty and I don't see you taking any more passengers this evening. And it hardly seems fair to charge the full rate for my small daughter. Three more guineas will please your masters, surely?'

The man shuffled from one foot to another, conceding her argument. 'Oh, dammit, madam, pardon my language, but do not you speak a word of this, or I will not keep my job.' He returned her smile, with a show of carious teeth. 'You an officer's lady, mistress? Only such would speak to me thus.'

'Not that it's of your concern, but yes, we both are,' she said, 'which is why I would not pay your asking price.'

During this exchange Helena was fumbling in her valise for a purse, slightly relieved to learn that the fare was agreed upon, as she had left home today without sufficient money and was anxious, as she would not be able to draw any credit from her bankers. She need not have concerned herself; Mary appeared to be in funds.

The guard checked the time on his fob watch, noted it was precisely eight o'clock and mounted the front of the coach. The horn sounded the opening notes of Black-eyed Susan, as a few onlookers, braving the cold, watched and cheered the departure of the coach to Bath and Bristol. The service had been running for eight years but was still a subject of curiosity to many; only the wealthy could afford coach travel.

The interior was as cold as the exterior. Mary pulled the leather curtains tight to keep the air out and settled Annie onto her lap, with Helena taking the seat adjacent and opposite the other passenger who briefly introduced himself as Martin Hale, a banker from Bath, returning from a visit to Spain on behalf of his father. Evidently his travels had been tiring, as his chin soon slumped against his chest and he commenced to snore with a low sonorous tone. She settled a basket with the puppy at her feet, and covered him with a blanket, hoping he would endure the journey without disgracing her. The puppy whined for some minutes before curling up and falling asleep.

The coach rattled along the Old London Road leading north along the peninsula, initially making good progress along the dark and quiet road. It turned west, raising its speed to nearly ten miles an hour, making a rapid change of horses at The Dolphin in Southampton High Street, before heading north and west for Salisbury. At each halt during the cold night, the guard would sound a warning of the approach, raising the ostler from his room for fresh horses and the toll-gate-keeper from his sleep to record the toll in his account book for the next stage of the journey.

Mary slept little, Helena not at all, and the young banker, Martin, with some gallantry, exited the coach when the pull uphill proved too much for the team of horses. The horses were changed at *The Red Lion* in Salisbury, a little after the midnight hour. There, a halt enabled the coachman to offload a mailbag and take a pot of 'summat warming,' during which Mary and Helena took seats next to a tall Parliament clock for a late supper of toasted bread and warmed mutton broth, before returning to the coach to resume the jostling and pounding that was to be endured as the coach travelled the frosted, snow covered road.

The night wore on, interrupted only by the regular halts for change of horses; the coachman deciding to dispense with a change on the long stretch between Salisbury and Devizes, until eventually, the thin grey light of dawn crept into the carriage to stir the chilled, sleepless occupants within.

A brief breakfast was taken at The Woolpack Inn at Beckington, before the journey continued through the bustling spa city of Bath, halting at the *Three Tuns* for another change of horses. The young banker offered a polite farewell as he left the coach, which then took the road north towards Gloucester.

Helena slowly opened her eyes from a fitful sleep, and felt able to speak of their situation in the absence of an audience. 'Mary my dear, I make a poor travelling companion, I fear. Do we have far to go?'

'We can set down at Wootton-under-Edge. I have spoken to the coachman. From there I hope we can secure some transport to our final destination.'

Mary had no means of sending a message to her father-in-law, and her busy mind had been occupied during the night with thoughts of her husband. Quite what she expected Jack's father to achieve she was uncertain, knowing only he was a man of influence, able to offer a safe harbour, and above everything, a place of refuge, of safety.

* * *

Hamilton Smith could not suppress the anxiety rising within him. The imminent meeting of Royal Navy sailors, sent by Pitt to rescue him, was full of risk, and a risk he no longer controlled.

He was to meet them outside in the square in... he consulted his watch... just ten minutes. He drained the last of the wine, picked up his cloak and bag and silently crossed to the door. He listened for several moments before opening it, hearing the voluble sound of argument rising from one of the rooms on the ground floor. He had noted a door leading to the rear of the hotel, and with practiced stealth, made his way through into the night, his passing going unobserved. He paused to ensure he was not followed. Placing a white lily in his hat and keeping to the shadows, he walked slowly towards the church.

Thankfully, the town appeared quiet tonight. A drunken fisherman made his way across the square, with deliberate but inaccurate care until accosted by a prostituée, whom he embraced with patent gratitude. Hamilton Smith stepped forward, about to move from the security of the shadows, when a harsh command made him dart behind a wall. A patrol of citizens, four of them, had surrounded the couple; the leader, a large man, was remonstrating with the fisherman. An argument developed and the fisherman was viciously clubbed to the ground.

Hamilton Smith shivered. Such scenes had become too common in France. Revolution brought with it a rise in brutality in most towns, by a handful of violent men and women—self-seeking in the main, but intolerant of almost any who might challenge their self-appointed authority. From his window Hamilton Smith had noted two such patrols during the evening. He waited until the group moved away, taking the woman with them.

He moved to the west end of the church, with as much natural movement as he could manage. The shadows of two men appeared and then halted at the end of the Rue de Clieu, just to the north of the Place St Jacques. He watched them unobserved, until he was sure. The taller of the two he did not recognize, but that man was alert to any movement or sound. Smith's eyes scanned the roads and buildings with practiced efficiency. The second man was still in shadow until he moved forward and recognized his friend and assistant—Bontecou!

He moved half a pace, raising his hat, which the first man noticed instantly. The two moved quickly across the Place, toward him, until the Frenchman grasped his hands in a warm and affectionate greeting, pressing his cheek to that of Hamilton Smith. 'Mon ami. Je suis heureux de vous voir à nouveau et vous vous en sortez bien.'

Turning to Vizzard, he said simply, 'This is my friend Charles Hamilton Smith. This is the man you have come to rescue.'

Jack looked at the young man in some surprise, not expecting to see a fellow Englishman, or one so young. He extended his hand, 'Delighted to meet you, sir,' he said with warmth, 'First Lieutenant Jack Vizzard of His Majesty's Corps of Marines, to be at your service.'

'The privilege is mine, sir, I assure you. But I see no uniform to confirm your status, sir?'

'I thought it to be unwise in the circumstances. Our scarlet coats would be patently out of place in a French town. But come, sir, we must hasten. The road to the beach is now patrolled and my duty is to return you to England as swiftly as possible. Follow me, if you will.'

Jack turned smartly, noting Joe Packer and another marine were in the shadows some twenty yards behind. The sergeant took up the lead for the return to the landing beach at a smart pace. He glanced at the young man to his left, whose sang-froid unsettled him. Hamilton Smith caught his look and grinned briefly.

'This must be an unusual assignment for you, Mister Vizzard? Secret landings at night on the coast of a country embroiled in revolution? Rescuing a government agent? Not a service one might have anticipated perhaps?'

'Indeed not, but the Corps must now expect the unexpected I feel, Mister Hamilton Smith. This country's troubles are most likely set to continue, and I expect we will be at war afore long.'

'Have you not heard, Mister Vizzard? Paris issued a declaration against Holland and England yesterday. We are, indeed, now at war, sir.'

Jack halted. 'Are we, indeed? Well, now we must get you to London with all haste. I am instructed that your knowledge is of the highest value to the government.' *No price too high*; the Colonel's order continued to haunt him. With war now confirmed, he could not fail; the mission or his life depended on his actions over the next hour or so.

The question remained unasked and Hamilton Smith noted the loaded comment. 'My apologies Lieutenant, I can say nothing of my intelligence work, and it would be better for you not to know. Come, the roads are not safe and I will not be happy until I reach London. Even then, I may have enemies to confront, for I fear my information may not be entirely accepted by all. I know also,

Robespierre has his agents searching for me, and they are many, Mister Vizzard.'

The three quickened the pace as they left the town and sought the farm, to the rear of which Jack had left one of his men. He called softly to Joe Packer, instructing him to collect the man with the assistance of another private while he waited by the road. He instructed Bontecou and Hamilton Smith to hide behind a low wall as he stood guard himself. Another section of privates appeared from the gloom, with a corporal who informed Jack the advance party was on the beach with the signal lanterns made ready.

'Very well Corporal, get the lads assembled; I will be with you... ah, here's Sergeant Packer.' Joe Packer carried the injured Private Hannan on his back, panting heavily from the exertion, and then passing him to another private to carry to the beach.

'No sign of the French, Mister Vizzard,' he said. 'All the patrols have disappeared, although Jamie the Scot reckoned he 'eard something a while ago. Is this our spy then?' He nodded in the direction of Hamilton Smith, who snorted his disapproval at the familiarity.

'Yes Sergeant Packer. Now let's have the Navy here as swiftly as possible, to take us from this damned place.'

They followed the section of marines Packer had left to watch the road, having ordered the others to the beach. As they descended the track through the dunes, Jack saw the corporal set up the signal lanterns. He checked his watch, noting there were fifteen minutes before dawn, pleased the expedition was on time. Looking seawards, he thought he could detect the cutter *Nimble* beyond the surf, about five or six cables distant, but could not be certain. Yes, there it was—the pre-arranged signal he had waited for.

He felt, rather than heard, the musket ball as it whistled by his hat, striking a private on his right, shattering the man's left shoulder and sending him screaming onto the sand. Jack cursed and pulled his weapon from his shoulder.

'Embusche! Merde!' shouted Bontecou, rushing toward Hamilton Smith, who had drawn a pair of pistols.

'Corporal, make the correct response, quickly man.' Jack shouted to a section of men who had still to react. 'You four men - with me now!' More balls struck the sand as Jack raised his musket. He could now see some smoke but no clear target. Another section of four marines ran to stand to his rear as the first section fired an irregular volley towards the smoke blowing down from the dunes above them.

Hell and damnation, thought Jack as he fired, the weapon punching his shoulder. Swiftly he reloaded, tasting the powder in his mouth, a pinch into the pan, pouring the remainder down the barrel. He pulled his ramrod clear, having rammed the cartridge home and sought a target. A clump of grass moved and he fired. *The bastards were waiting for us—had been watching us all the time. They must know of our friend here.*

He heard shouts from behind and glanced back to see a ship's boat being hauled through the surf. *Thank God. If we can hold them off, we have a chance. How many of them are there?*

'Get them out of here, Joe!' he shouted to his sergeant. 'Leave a section and take care of him,' he jerked his head in the direction of the wounded marine. 'The rest of you stay with me!' Vizzard again prepared his musket with practiced skill and speed, repeating the preparation faster than the men beside him. He heard the crack of weapons from the grassy dunes and, seeing a hat above the grass, fired, taking satisfaction from the scream which followed. Behind him came more shouts, but he could not spare the time to look, for a ragged line of a dozen blue-coated infantry appeared from the dunes, advancing steadily, evil looking bayonets fixed to their weapons. 'Come then, you French bastards and taste British steel!' Vizzard bellowed. 'Stand firm with me, marines,' he said with more calm than he felt.

The noise of larger weapons was followed by small fountains of sand, as heavier shot buried itself in sand dunes to the right and in front of the French, spraying sand and seashells. John Lapenotière, with a keen eye to the scene unfolding on the beach, was throwing the weight of his guns into the skirmish. A few seconds more and they would be on him. *'No price too high,'* the colonel's words came to the forefront of his mind. *Is this what he had in mind? Is this where I die?* 'We stand and die here, you bastards!' he yelled at his marines, 'Not a single step backwards.'

He stood as a ball crashed into the road beyond, throwing up sparks and dust, which sparkled in the first rays of dawn. The gunners were firing too high; seeking to avoid hitting his marines, he decided. He thought he heard his name called from the rear, but all was shouting and noise and confusion as he readied to parry an oncoming bayonet. The man, in the vanguard of the French attack, fell as a ball pulped his face to splintered bone and blood. There was a familiarity about the face, but he had no time to think. Another man was in his place and he swung his musket, clubbing the oncoming bayonet away, spearing his own musket at another blue-coated figure and reaching for his sword as more shouts came to his ears. He slashed to left and right, keeping two of the enemy at bay.

A marine to his left fell to a sword slash that split open his skull as though it were no more substantial than a cheese. He had no time to even register the marine's name as he parried another bayonet away to his right, immediately lunging at the figure behind it, and feeling it strike bone. Another marine was at his shoulder—the corporal.

'They're away, sir,' the corporal panted. 'The navy 'as left us, sir.' The corporal fired at another target, and from the smoke another figure advanced. With a roar, the corporal swung his musket at a short, skinny figure in a blue coat, missing and taking a bayonet in the throat, his scream strangled with the blood spraying over Vizzard in a warm shower.

Jack realised he was alone and facing his imminent death. He glanced about him, distressed to see so many of his marines dead or seriously wounded. For each of them, there were several dead Frenchman. So this was the price. *At any cost.* This was his death; he thought of Mary; then a familiar voice called out.

'I suggest you lower your sword, Vizzard. I would hate to have you killed after such gallant resistance. You bring honour to the Corps, but your part in this escapade is known to the Committee in Paris and I fancy they will wish to talk to you.'

As Jack stared in surprise, the figure of Major George Squires appeared standing in front of him, a smirk across his face and a pistol levelled at his face.

'You bloody bastard! You filthy traitor,' he panted. 'Don't talk to me of honour, Squires. You have most assuredly sold yours. I should have known it was all too easy. You've been watching and waiting all night, haven't you?' He tried to spit but couldn't, and felt a great thirst and a growing rage.

'Why of course, Vizzard. This has been my enterprise from the beginning. Unfortunately, that fool Souter would not confide in me, else I would have intercepted you sooner. I have known of Hamilton Smith for several months and spent much time seeking him, but thanks to your resistance, he has slipped away. A pity, I would have enjoyed examining his bag and ah, questioning him.'

Jack lowered his sword, understanding he might not now be executed on this cold French beach, but would be taken to Paris as a prisoner. To be tortured, no doubt, before being shot as a spy. He controlled his breathing and his rage with difficulty. He wanted to shoot Squires in the face, wanted to attack him and slice his head from his shoulders. The betrayal, by a British officer, was, in Jack's mind, the ultimate crime; the man was beneath contempt and deserved to die.

'I imagine you have sold your soul for French gold, Squires. I hope you consider it worthwhile, for on my word, I will see you in hell for this, you traitorous worm. I swear I will see you—'

The butt of the musket struck him on the back of the head, instantly turning his world black as he slumped forward to the cold and bloodied sand.

CHAPTER 8

Sir Henry Vizzard sat in the old leather armchair and stared into the fire, waiting for his daughter-in-law to join him for supper. He sipped on a glass of sherry wine and looked at Caroline's portrait, wishing as he did daily that she was still alive and there with him as he slipped into old age. Mary and her friend, a plain but cultured woman, had arrived at Lampern House in a hired carriage drawn by a single horse, which was now sharing the stable block with Jack's hunter. The old man, now of rounded shoulders and aching joints, still retained his sharpness of mind. Grey hair formed a mane about his neck, which he let loose, eschewing a wig unless in court. Neave, his butler cum servant, had fussed over Mary as if he were her father before scuttling off to the village to pass the news to Fred George that his only daughter had made a sudden and unannounced return to the village.

Henry had learned only that the two women had warned him to expect some bad news. Jack, his favourite child, was likely as not, in France on some government business and, as far as was known, he was alive and well. It was cold comfort and his busy mind worked itself into knots seeking some clues. Mrs Neave, Henry could never recall her Christian name, had ushered the women upstairs to freshen and a change of clothes, and was now warming the remains of a substantial stew as she had seen how tired, drawn and cold the two women were when they walked through the entrance door with Annie, shocking Sir Henry.

Henry was a lawyer by profession, as his father had been. His great dream, his grand design had been for his two sons, George and Jack, or at least one of them, to follow him into the law. George, the eldest, had left home furtively, to go to sea, some nine years ago. Nothing more had been heard of him. His disappearance had come close to breaking Henry's heart. Jack, his youngest child and second son, had always been a favourite. Jack had studied law at Oxford, at Oriel, Henry's old college, and had been called to the bar of Middle Temple, but had forsaken the profession and taken a commission in the Corps of Marines. Sir Henry still did not understand why.

'And now he's in trouble too, I sense it. He is hurt or taken captive. Or worse. We are at war with France once more, and Jack is on service.' He shook his head and sipped from the glass by his side. Looking up above the fire, he saw her smiling down at him, those eyes she had given to their son Jack at her death; the hybrid blue and green eyes giving him reassurance, inspiration, endless love. As she had in life, so she continued in death. *It is not so simple, my dearest,* he thought to himself. Not a simple legal knot to untie or sever with an advocate's surgical knife. This was an intractable Gordian knot to which no immediate solution presented itself. He felt helpless and inadequate.

He raised his glass in silent salute to the portrait of his long-dead wife. Caroline Vizzard had died giving birth to Jack twenty-six years past. He thought of her daily, and spoke to her, silently or out loud if there were no others present. Neave heard him occasionally and shook his head.

Neave opened the door and interrupted his reflective state. He rose with some discomfort to stand, as Mary and Helena entered the room together.

'Please stay seated, Henry dear,' said Mary, walking briskly toward him and gently kissing his grey hair. 'We feel so much better; do we not Helena? Tired we are, yes, but now, at least, with a sense of safety and security. I have left Annie asleep in my bed.'

'Indeed,' said Helena, speaking properly for the first time since their arrival, 'and I must thank you for the hospitality of your home, Sir Henry. I am most grateful for the sanctuary it offers, and when you wish, I am ready to explain our presence here.'

'Please, do sit. My housekeeper will be bringing a simple supper, which I think we might take here by the comfort of the fire. The dining room can be too chill at this time of year. Neave, please see to a drink for our guests.'

Edward Neave poured two glasses of the best of old Harvey's sherry wine from a dark blue bottle, and proffered them to the two ladies; the first to Mary and the second to Helena. His wife, Madeline, entered with a tray bearing a large tureen holding a steaming beef stew and placed it on a small table, together with two bowls and silver spoons. A basket with chunks of bread completed the simple meal, which both Mary and Helena seized upon with as much seemliness as they could manage, although both were more than a little hungry.

Henry watched patiently as his two visitors quickly consumed the food, trying to maintain some idle conversation on local events and people Mary would not have known, but would nevertheless wish to hear of, without obligation to add comment of her own.

In the kitchen, Madeline Neave pressed her husband. 'You must have a word with Sir Henry, love. Or I must speak to Mistress Mary.

I have to know what's going on. It must concern Master Jack, an' I have to know he's all right. Please love.'

'I will of course, Maddie, but I think it right and proper Sir Henry hears of it first. He'll tell us as soon as he can, be sure of it, my dear. Fred George is in Gloucester, I am told, and will not return afore morning and he needs to be told too, my love.'

Following his mother's death, Madeline Neave was taken in as Jack's wet-nurse. She and her husband had simply stayed on at Lampern, so Madeline and Jack had a bond Sir Henry well understood.

'Now my dear,' started Henry. 'Travel weary as you both must be, you have a story to tell me, and I fully expect you are here seeking my advice. Tell me all, and I will try not to interrupt as you tell your tale, but I make no promise, as it is a failing of mine.' He smiled in the fatherly, perhaps patronising fashion he had.

The two women looked at each other, as if the question was expected. They had agreed between them to allow Helena to speak first. She told her tale steadily, without embellishment, and in a considered, dispassionate manner, having realised during the journey from Portsmouth that expending further emotion on her husband was a waste of energy. She knew this to be true. She recited a short history of her courtship and marriage to Major Squires, told of his absences, alluded to such facts as were within her own knowledge, including the discovery of secret coded messages and her discussion with the colonel of the Portsmouth Division. She concluded by detailing her suspicions that Jack Vizzard had been betrayed by her husband and was in danger.

Henry rose unsteadily from his armchair and walked slowly towards Helena. Taking her right hand he bent low and brushed his lips against it. 'I would like to thank you for making the journey to tell me this news, saddened as I am to hear it. You have shown great courage in doing so.' Straightening up, he continued, 'Jack is my son and I am so proud of what he has done, and I hope, will continue to do in the service of his country.' He crossed to the Adam fireplace, plucked a log from the basket nearby and placed it carefully on the flames, watching as it crackled and threw up a brief shower of sparks. Looking up at the portrait of Caroline, whose eyes seemed to follow his movements, he smiled. 'His mother would be proud, too, and would worry, as indeed I do, for his safety.'

He reached down for his glass. Raising it to the two young women, 'I thank you for coming. I will consider how best we can deal with this delicate and unhappy situation. We shall talk again in the morning.'

Mary and Helena took the hint with good grace and wished him a good night before retiring to their rooms. Henry Vizzard sat by the fire, and pulled the rope by the wall, which was, in fact, quite unnecessary, as Edward and Madeline Neave had entered moments after watching their guests ascend the stairs to the upper floor of the manor house. He looked at his two servants and, with a rising lump in his throat, said, 'It seems our boy is in trouble.'

* * *

Lieutenant Lapenotière helped haul the marines on board his cutter with his own hands, so anxious was he to learn news of what had happened on the beach. As soon as the last man was over the side, he called back to the midshipman, Dickie Bird.

'Right, Mister Bird, as quickly as you like,' he grunted. Take us away from this miserable coast.' Lapenotière felt miserable. He felt sure Vizzard was alive and he wished with all his heart he could get ashore and mount a rescue. His duty was clear and, as much as he struggled with his conscience, he knew what was required of him. He must return Hamilton Smith to England.

He stared at the French coast as it slowly slipped from view.

Lapenotière's silver monogrammed flask was thrust into Sergeant Packer's hand, as a surgeon's mate cut away at his bloodied breeches. 'Steady there mate, I'm not about to lose my leg, do you hear!'

'How is it, Thatcher?' asked Lapenotière. 'Can you deal with it man?'

'It ain't too bad, sir. The ball has but grazed him badly and it has missed anything important, as far as I can tell. Reckon it will heal well for a splash of brandy and a couple of decent stitches. P'r'aps cauterize it too. It'll hurt, but he looks a tough bastard.' The man peered deeply at the wound, and nodded to himself.

'Very well then, Thatcher. Do get on with it. No, leave him here, I wish to talk to him as soon as you are done. Be easy, Sergeant; Thatcher here is not a surgeon but knows his business well enough.'

'All I can say, sir, is he better, 'cos if he don't I'll have his guts for m'dinner!'

The man growled something incoherent in return and poured some neat rum over the exposed wound on his thigh. Joe Packer, a man used to pain, screamed, and a stream of curses poured out; 'You lobcock! Christ on the cross, man, that fucking well hurt.' He was venting his frustration and anger and shame and yes, a degree of guilt. Guilt, because he was safe on a British warship while his friend and commander was either dead or captive. He felt wretched. The sailor hefted him across his shoulders as though he were no more than a sack of wool and carried him to the tiny cabin aft. Lieutenant Lapenotière followed.

'I shall return once we are clear of this place.'

He returned to the deck as Joe Packer commenced another stream of cursing, directed at the luckless surgeon's mate. He laughed in spite of the sadness he felt. Looking aft, he noted the coast slipping away into the darkness so, in a moment more, it would be invisible. Looking forward, he saw his men busy bracing the jib-sail and Dickie Bird looking stern-faced at the helmsman.

'She can sail a point closer man; make it so.' He looked directly at his captain. 'A poor business, sir, don't you think so?' The midshipman had been the first to see the French amongst the dunes and had ordered the guns to fire a carefully directed salvo amongst them. He felt saddened it had not been enough to disperse the enemy and enable the boat's crew to retrieve the marines before several had died and Lieutenant Vizzard had been seen to fall.

'Yes, Dickie. I fear we have lost a good man this night. But I have my duty, as Mister Vizzard knew his. I must get our guests back to England with no delay. So much I do know.'

The commander of the *Nimble* paced back and forth across his small deck, constantly examining the set of the little ship's sails, feeling the wind and feeling wretched with the guilt of having failed another officer. He cursed the top-men for imaginary failings, made the helmsman so nervous that the man let the ship fall away half a point, and generally became such a nuisance that his midshipman, Dickie Bird, finally and with much trepidation, obliged him to go below and speak to the marine sergeant.

Joe Packer was lying in a hammock that Lieutenant Lapenotière had slung in his own cabin, a sailor's pipe issuing a spiral of smoke up to the blackened beams above his head.

'How is the wound sergeant? Are you comfortable?'

Joe Packer attempted to rise but was waved down by the tired officer. 'All things considered, sir, I ain't too bad. Least I am alive.'

Packer looked ill. His face was white but smeared with the dirt and gunpowder his unqualified physician had not troubled to clean. Around his right thigh, a clean piece of linen had been tied. A small dark stain revealed that the wound had ceased to bleed.

Lapenotière poured a large measure of rum into a small battered pewter tankard and offered it to the wounded NCO.

'Thank you, sir. I will if you'll join me. I reckon we need something to keep the ghosts away tonight. Sorry sir, but I think I lost a good friend on the beach. Mister Vizzard and I, well we've seen quite a bit together.'

'If you wish for my opinion Sergeant, it is that your officer is a prisoner of the French. I do not believe him to be dead.' He sat on a three-legged stool and swallowed a large mouthful of the spirit. 'There is another matter, though Sergeant, I would discuss with you. My vessel has a small crew, insufficient to have landed and attacked the French. It is my opinion, and I shall report it as such, that your party was betrayed.'

'You mean the Frenchman we brought with us sir? I know Mister Vizzard didn't trust him, sir.'

'Exactly so, Sergeant, exactly so. The force we saw tonight was a strong one, and suggests to me they were aware of our coming; they were prepared to wait until you had collected our government man, and then pounced. Damn them. I will report to my superior, of course, but my intention is to get the government's man back to England and see what we can do to rectify this situation; perhaps to find Mister Vizzard and bring him back.'

Joe Packer grunted, more from the pain in his leg than the lieutenant's words.

'Brave words, sir, but if Mister Vizzard is still alive, they bastards will have him in Paris afore we can blink and then chop his poor head off. If it weren't for this leg I'd ask you to put me ashore an' I'd be after them myself. I wouldn't say no to another tankard, sir.'

Lieutenant Lapenotière obliged with a half-smile and said, 'I will see if our intelligence man can cast some light on matters, and perhaps seek his opinion, but you should know, Sergeant Packer, if I can, I will surely return here and bring him back.

CHAPTER 9

He did not know how long the voices in his head had been at work and he did not understand much of what was being said. The occasional word carried some meaning, of course, such as *'Angleterre'* and *'Londres'* and later, *'Paris'*. Then a voice, obviously belonging to an Englishman, joined the two other voices, and this familiar one was an assault to his ears.

His first, his immediate instinct, was to leap at the voice, and crush the breath from the thin neck of the body to which it was attached, to extinguish forever the traitorous sound rasping across the room. He realised he was prone on the floor, a cold stone floor, littered with straw, and it reminded him of the stables at Lampern. As he listened, not daring to move a muscle, his rational mind began to work and he realised he should remain still, perfectly still, and simply listen. As he did so, the English voice moved about the room, not that Jack had any vision or comprehension of where he was. The smell was disgusting; an odour of rotting carcasses pervaded the darkened room, mingled with the odour of stale earth and the vomit-inducing smell of blood. Then he recognised it as a butcher's slaughterhouse; he was sure of it.

He waited until the English voice, the voice he once respected, moved further to his rear. He heard a footfall on a creaking wooden stairway and risked a brief view of his surroundings with one eye. He scanned the dim room and observed empty meat hooks suspended from the blackened beams. A wooden block was in his line of sight, a bloodied, dismembered animal spread across it, a cleaver embedded in its carcass. Two muskets hung by the door and a lantern cast a dim light across the floor. On the rough-timber door hung his sword. He could just make out the maker's name: John Knubley of Charing Cross. His knapsack was on the floor with two others of a different style. French, he thought absently.

His body ached but nothing immediately appeared to be broken or in pain. His brain mentally checked off the fundamentals; feet and legs, torso, arms. Nothing consciously damaged; the wound in his leg still sore and the back of his head was damaged. He sensed a matted patch of hair and he resisted an urge to explore it with his fingers. The merest movement would alert his captors to his conscious state. He moved his attention to his ears, trying hard to understand what was being discussed. Obviously, it concerned his immediate future` and could not be beneficial. The longer he remained a captive, the more difficult things would become; of that he could at least be certain. He anticipated brutal treatment at the hands of these Frenchmen, and then what? When they discovered he knew nothing of Hamilton Smith's enterprise? He then served them no purpose, had nothing to bargain with. They would simply shoot him and throw his body in the river. He had to escape before they had a chance to start their inquisition.

It was time.

With a sudden scramble, he was up, and in two fast steps, he was at the door. Grasping the sword, he spun around, noting the two Frenchmen were seated at a rough bench drinking wine, but his real foe, the man who, until yesterday—was it only yesterday?—had been his commanding officer, was standing on the stairs. As his eyes met those of George Squires, the Frenchmen reacted. With an oath, the first of them shot at his feet, reaching for his sword. It was the last thing he did, as Jack's blade pierced his abdomen, spearing the man's intestines and liver. The second man would have to be dealt with swiftly, as Jack could see Squires reacting quickly behind them. Pulling the blade free with a quick twist, he slashed, catching the man, a sergeant, across the throat, a stream of bright crimson pumping from the severed artery as he fell. Jack turned to face a pistol, levelled only three feet from his face.

'Clever work, Lieutenant Vizzard. I had heard tell of your skill with a sword. But, of course, you cannot escape, and for this you will have to die. I am so sorry.' Squires's voice and eyes carried no remorse, as he pulled the trigger.

The flintlock fell as Jack flinched and ducked, but there was no pain; no sound, no discharge of grey-white smoke as the pistol misfired. Squires stared at the useless weapon, disbelief and fear on his face.

Jack needed no other opportunity, but thrust with hate in his heart; he was disappointed as the blade caught the major high in the chest and struck bone. He kicked hard into the man's groin as Squires screamed in pain. Pulling the sword free, he used the hilt, smashing it up and into the major's face, breaking the left cheekbone and pulping the left eye socket. Squires fell with another scream, which died in his mouth as the back of his head made contact with the stairs behind him. He lay still.

Jack straightened up, breathing in short, hard bursts, staring down at his enemy, knowing the man was not dead. He could not kill him now. Instead, he took the belts from the dead Frenchmen, using them to bind the major's feet and hands together. He stuffed a rag into his mouth. It would buy him time; time to think and get away from this place. Where was this place, he wondered? He had no knowledge of his location, guessing it was in the town. His brow creased as he thought. Where to, then? The landing beach would still be under observation. All suitable beaches would be watched, he concluded. More troops would have been alerted, surely. Then he must find a sympathetic ship's master or a fisherman, willing to cross the channel in mid-winter with a hunted English officer. Perhaps he should make for a different port, one further along the coast. Dieppe had become a death trap, one from which he must escape.

A half-eaten loaf of bread caught his eye, and he realised he was ravenous. Grabbing it, he fell on it with passion and looked for other supplies. A bottle of brandy, its contents glowing by the lamplight, brought his search to a halt. He poured a large measure down his throat, enjoying the fire as it travelled; he nevertheless coughed. As he raised the bottle for a second time he froze.

'You will get used to it *monsieur*—but this house has only the poor quality.'

Jack spun around at the sudden interruption, astonished to see a tall, slender woman standing close to the stairs. He had failed to hear her approach.

'Hell and damn,' he said aloud. Why had he not searched the house?

'The major is dead, yes?' She asked, her voice soft as she examined the prone, motionless figure of George Squires.

'He lives, madam, although he deserves to die.' Recovering from the surprise intrusion, he addressed the lady more politely. 'I am Lieutenant John Vizzard of His Majesty's Corp of Marines. Perhaps

I may have the honour of knowing your name, mademoiselle?'

'Certainly, Lieutenant. I am Vanessa d'Aubusson. My father is an *avocat*, a lawyer, yes? He is a good man, one of the Girondin, you understand? A member of the National Convention, he seeks a peaceful change to our regime. Alas, *monsieur*, I fear for my country and the extremists these dangerous times seem to bring forward. I go to England because it is safer there, I think. Your Major Squires, I met him last summer in Paris and he promises to help me, so I meet him here, but yesterday I learn different. He tells he is an agent of your government, but I find out he is in the pay of the Jacobins. He argues for more extreme change, more violence. This I do not agree with, so I worry and listen to him and these men. They talked of an English spy to be captured. That is you, no?'

She was beautiful in an understated way, a crown of butter-coloured hair flowed around her face. Her eyes were of cerulean blue that drilled into his like narrow steel blades, a patrician nose and wide lips. She captivated him instantly. The timeworn cloak she wore hung from her shoulders, open at the front, displaying a diaphanous shirt which barely veiled her ample breasts. His eyes were too slow; she smiled, understanding his reaction, expecting it perhaps.

'No, *mademoiselle*. I believe they were referring to another, to one of us who escaped.' He moved closer. 'It would seem that we have a common purpose, madam; we both wish to reach England. I have been wondering how to achieve my object.'

She sat down on the stool previously used by one of her dead countrymen. Wrapping her cloak about her she shook her hair from her face. 'Perhaps I can help, Lieutenant. I have friends in the town. One might be willing to arrange a boat. But it will cost much money, I think.'

Vizzard looked down at the still unconscious form of George Squires. He fumbled beneath the major's coat and found what he suspected, a large purse heavy with coins. Pulling open the neck he saw the glint of silver: a good many Constitutional Ecu. They would support a peasant's family for many years.

'The expense should present no difficulty, madam. We need only locate a willing fisherman and he will be well rewarded.' He smiled, a fleeting trace of triumph crossing his face.

The dim light in the room seemed to glow brighter as he gazed on her face. She returned his look, and he sensed a spirit in the room, as though another presence had entered. Vizzard shuddered. 'We cannot stay here; wherever *here* is.' He had no memory of his movements since the disaster on the beach. Hamilton Smith had got away, that much he knew; the marine had told him so, just before he died. What was his name? Corporal Todd. He recalled the man now. Poor bastard. With his last breath, the man had confirmed Vizzard's duty was done.

'We are in a farmhouse to the west of the town. You and your men passed it earlier yesterday, *monsieur.*' She looked down at the straw-covered floor. 'We... he and I, watched as your men went by. He laid a trap for you and was boasting about it, about how stupid and proud you were.' She stood, at once decisive. 'I am sorry, but I believed and trusted him. Come, I will take you to a friend.'

She spat at the inert body of Major George Squires.

* * *

Sergeant Joseph Packer was solid. The men all thought so. He commanded respect from all he encountered, private soldier or officer; he could be relied on. He never wavered in his duty, never allowed anything other than what his orders or conscience required of him. He never neglected the care of his men or the good of the Corps. He had never left a wounded man behind; until now. Now his record was tarnished, blemished and dishonoured. It was an uncomfortable, unfamiliar condition, and Sergeant Packer was angry.

Lieutenant Vizzard was more than his commanding officer. He had become a friend, as unlikely as would have been thought between men of different ranks, backgrounds and circumstances. Or perhaps it was because of their differences. He recalled the day Jack Vizzard had first walked through the archway into the barracks all those years ago. Well-dressed, although dirty from a long journey, Packer had him marked as another 'nob', one of the gentry, a younger son who had to find some occupation because an elder sibling had the father's estate. It was common to find many in the same situation, in both the Corps and the Navy.

But he had soon realised Second Lieutenant Vizzard had the right qualities to be an officer in *his* Corps. Slowly, almost begrudgingly, Joe Packer admitted his 'new officer' would be sound, would and could make decisions, could and did use initiative, led men, did not push them, would never ask a marine to do something he wouldn't do. Perhaps most of all, Sergeant Packer had witnessed him stand up to a bully. He had been with Vizzard through the voyage to Botany Bay with the first fleet of wretched criminals sent to the other side of the world. When none of the men had known where they were bound, it was Mister Vizzard who had taught them. He was their officer who trained them, guided them and showed them new and novel ways of doing things. He had set an example and set the standard for the men to reach.

Then, on a warm, misty morning at dawn, overlooking the sparkling waters of Sydney Town's expansive harbour, Vizzard had beaten the bully, had settled a matter of honour that finally sealed Joe Packer's respect. That morning he had watched from the cover of shrubs as 'his officer' had given a display of supreme swordsmanship, and defeated a bully. The bully had been their commanding officer, Major Robert Ross, and Mister Vizzard had displayed more moral courage in that one act, than in the other escapades in which they had become involved.

But now, his officer, his friend, was caught by bloody revolutionaries and trapped on the other side of the English Channel, and he could do nothing to help him. The colonel had made that clear. His first act on returning to the barracks had been to march into the colonel's room and demand, yes he had demanded, and now smiled at the memory, demanded the right to lead a rescue party back across the Channel to find the lieutenant.

'No Sergeant, I cannot, would never sanction such foolhardy a thing! Why man, we are at war with the bloody French again. I respect and admire your loyalty and courage but I cannot countenance such nonsense.'

The colonel had made his views quite clear. Vizzard was almost certainly dead; if not, then he was a prisoner and as good as dead. He would not be found, not by a squad of volunteer marines, however loyal and courageous they might be.

Joe Packer had marched from the colonel's office in sour mood, swearing at the first marine he encountered as he strode to the barracks. *As good as dead.* Not Jack Vizzard, it just could not happen, he thought.

It must not.

* * *

The fog had settled, lying low in the fields, and Jack could see the sharp relief of the woods etched against the night sky to his right as they moved with the protection of the wall. The clouds ahead were paler, a discernible grey against the darkness of the night. Trees by the road, their branches like spectral fingers, blown in one direction as if by some superhuman force, pointed the way inland.

His companion kept close to his side as he made for the town for the second time. He was uncomfortably aware of her presence, and aware, too, that the town was plagued by self-appointed guardians of the state, by brutal men who would not hesitate to cut him down and only later enquire as to his identity and business.

A rasping cough from the bushes ahead halted him instantly. His hand instinctively went to his sword. Vanessa d'Aubusson dropped to one knee and listened. She placed a finger to her lips, quite unnecessarily.

His motionless body started to ache with tension as he strained to detect any further sound while his eyes peered into the thin fog. He saw and heard nothing for a long minute. His heart sounded so loud that he thought it must be heard. Again, that sense of fear encroached. *Keep your fear to yourself; you have nothing to fear from a Frenchman. It's the French woman you must guard against*, he told himself. Forcing his muscles to relax, he looked at Vanessa and signalled her to follow him as he stepped forward, his boots crunching in the frozen mud. The sword slid from the scabbard as silently as he could manage, but he was still unprepared for the slash of another blade as it cleaved through the wisps of fog, some instinct causing him to pause as the blade whistled past his face, followed by a roar from a face, appearing only a few feet from his own. Reaction was immediate and effective as his own blade shot forward, piercing the man's chest and turning the roar of attack to a gurgling cry of fear as the Frenchman died.

Were there others? His muscles strained and ears remained on full alert, poised for another assault. A whimper from his rear acted as a reminder.

'Do you recognise him, Vanessa?' he asked, panting heavily.

She nodded. 'He was with the major yesterday,' she answered. 'One of his thugs, I think. He was sent to the town to watch for strangers.'

'The bastard very nearly killed me,' he grunted. 'Are there any more of his henchmen?'

'None that I know of, Lieutenant,' she said. 'We should make for the port, *monsieur*. The fishermen will be making ready to leave with the tide,' she whispered. 'My friend will be with them. He has business with the English in... how you say it? Corn Wall? Is correct, yes? My friend sells cognac and makes much money. He will help us.'

Jack Vizzard grunted. He did not share the lady's confidence. It would take little for him to be betrayed. Frenchmen would do so willingly, as soon as his nationality was revealed. His diffident use of the French language would instantly identify him as English. His lack of uniform would merely mark him as a spy of the British government, and spies received no sympathy, here or in England. This was a pretty kettle of fish, he thought. How to escape? The question dominated his thoughts. If the lady's friend was as co-operative as she believed him to be, then perhaps it was possible. What must be in Mary's mind now? She would surely know of his capture. She would be worrying, and there was not a thing he could do about it. He failed to suppress the feeling of helplessness intruding into his tired brain.

The enterprise had been foolhardy in the extreme, he thought. Oh certainly, the government's agent had been found and returned to England. At least he had performed his duty; he had served his king and his country. He had been wrong to abandon the king's uniform; perhaps it had been a mistake. Now he was committed to assisting a French woman, about whom he knew nothing—except that she was one of the most beautiful creatures he had ever seen—but could he trust her?

He thought not.

* * *

Charles Hamilton Smith lounged in the chair, his right leg draped across his left knee as he studied His Majesty's First Lord of the Treasury, Mr William Pitt. His eyes became fixed on the politician's face as the documents, now removed from his bag, were devoured with hungry eyes, each word and phrase consumed with the insatiable appetite for language the young politician displayed in the Commons.

'You are quite certain in your mind of the authenticity of these documents, Charles?'

Hamilton Smith raised an eyebrow in disdain at the question. 'Need you ask, sir? I am, indeed. The documents were signed and sealed in the presence of an impeccable source, one whose word and integrity cannot and should not be doubted.'

'They are remarkable, Charles. I am in your debt and so is the country; I do not exaggerate. So in point of fact and revealing, but you know this. There will be a sea-change,' said Pitt.

'Sir?'

'Shakespeare, Charles. The Bard of Avon, as Mister Garrick named him. *"Full fathom five thy father lies; of his bones are coral made. Those are pearls that were his eyes: nothing of him that doth fade but doth suffer a sea-change into something rich and strange. Sea-nymphs hourly ring his knell...*" and such and such. There will be a change on the Continent, Charles. You have my word on it.'

Yes, sir, I am familiar with *The Tempest*. I am then heartily pleased to have been of service, sir. You will be directing appropriate action to manage the situation, I trust?' Hamilton Smith asked.

'This will be a naval matter, Charles. We cannot send an army to the continent at this time. I must consult with His Majesty and my fellow ministers, but in all conscience I must acquaint the first lord of this intelligence. You understand?

'Indeed I do, sir. I have yet to have the pleasure and honour of your noble brother's company, but would be delighted to discuss the circumstances and implications of this intelligence with him, should it assist in his deliberations.'

He stood slowly, stretching his legs unobtrusively, as he contemplated another long coach journey. 'With your leave, I shall continue my journey, Mister Pitt. I have some people to visit in Gloucestershire.' Head inclined, he left the room as silently as he had entered.

Pitt watched him leave and returned to his chair, reading one document with studious care. He slapped his thigh; 'Good God,' he whispered. 'They are starving and will be forced to buy from the Americas. A year from now or less, they must, or the country will revolt again.'

He pulled twice on a braided cord by his side. An official opened the door, raised an enquiring eyebrow.

'William, thank you. Please draft an urgent letter to the

commandant of the marine garrison in Portsmouth if you would be so kind. A copy to the Admiralty, yes the first lord. I want the officer responsible for my visitor's safe return to be recovered from France. He must be rescued and there is not a moment to be lost. And I wish to meet him as soon as practicable. See to it immediately, please.'

CHAPTER 10

The lack of any word was a concern. There had been no message from the barracks, nothing at all from the colonel. As Mary walked with the dog, which trotted erratically from clumps of grass to a rabbit scrape and back again amongst the bare trees, the frosted ground snapped and crackled beneath her feet. She felt the cold through the soles of her shoes, come damp with the dew. Her mind was oblivious to the cold; it was across the Channel in France; with Jack.

As she traversed the rising ground leading to the escarpment, Mary glanced back at Lampern. It was large house, part covered in creeping ivy with several carved brickwork chimneys causing smoke to spiral into the clear light air. Leaded lights to the rear sparkled as the sun slipped away from a veil of morning cloud. The original house, dating from the time of Elizabeth, had been extended but then left to deteriorate by the previous owner of the estate. Sir Henry had invested large sums of his and Caroline's money to make it a habitable home for their family. A new roof of clay tiles had been added, an oak staircase installed with new wall panelling to replace the rotted timbers. 'New hat and new boots,' Henry had said about it when they talked, years before; before the nightmare of her

114

trial and imprisonment and the voyage to New Holland. She shivered, not because of the cold air. Two wings had been added to enclose a parterre, with steps down to the Ewelme, the stream that wandered lazily through much of the village and had powered the mills further down the valley, from which the village had derived so much of its life force. It was a house greatly admired in the district, and Mary, as a young girl, often wondered about the family who occupied it, never imagining that she would one day act as *de facto* mistress of the house, as Sir Henry wished. The mellow Cotswold stone looked pale in the morning light, but in the evening, with the dying sun washing the stone, it glowed like creamed honey. The realisation that the house would one day pass to Jack gave her a sense of wonder. The humble weaver's cottage in which she spent her early years would fit entirely within Sir Henry's drawing room. She resolved to visit her father after luncheon.

She watched as a squirrel paused, stared in her direction, directly at the puppy, eyes innocent but alert, before it bounded for the closest tree, the puppy oblivious to the woodland animal. Smoke drifted across her nostrils from the cottage at the edge of the woods. Nausea made her retch and bile rose in her throat; she bent as her breakfast disgorged itself onto the whitened grass, discolouring the crisp, virgin frost. She coughed. Again and again. The taste assaulted her tongue. It was simply dreadful.

Whatever was wrong with her? She was never ill, not since Sydney Town, but now she felt a stream of nausea; such a wretched sensation in her stomach she had never before experienced. Only, she had... oh yes she had! Once before in the leaking, crude log hut in Sydney. *Oh no, surely not*, she thought. She sat, shaken at the realisation, on a fallen tree, its bark cold and rough. *Oh Dear Lord, why now?* She was pregnant. She was convinced of it. The realisation that Jack's child grew within her—his dream—and he was not with her to share it. She pulled the woollen cloak tighter around her.

In her dreams she had wondered if this time would ever come. Then she smiled; he would be ecstatic. It was time to tell Sir Henry. After all, he would be the child's grandfather. Good heaven, no. What was she thinking? Heavens no, that was not right or proper, she reasoned with herself. Jack must be the first to know.

'Oh come here, Charlie, do,' she called to the puppy, who was still hard at work sniffing the grass, leaving an erratic trail of prints in the frost-coated grass. 'It is time to return home.'

Dutifully, the dog stopped her investigation and bounced toward Mary, eyes bright and wide, and they walked together across the field, back to Lampern, to the sound of a horse pulling into the yard and Neave's voice greeting a visitor.

Ed Neave nodded in her direction as a young man in worn and unfashionable clothes was dismounting from a large grey horse, similarly mired in the stains of travel. He removed his hat and, turning to Mary, introduced himself with a polite bow. 'Madam, I am Charles Hamilton Smith. I owe my life to your husband and have come, uninvited, to tell you so.'

'How do you do, sir? I have not heard my husband speak of you but if you have news of him then you are most welcome and must come inside and speak with us. His father and I are most desperate to learn any news of him.'

'I would deem it an honour, madam. I thank you.' He allowed Neave to walk the animal into the stables and pass instructions to the village boy who worked there.

The puppy led the way into the house as Neave made to announce the unexpected visitor to Sir Henry.

'Pray do come into the drawing room, Mister Hamilton Smith. I know there is a fire set there and Neave will find you some refreshment. Will you take tea?'

The puppy scrabbled on the tiled floor of the entrance hall as Neave pushed open the doors to the room, wearing an intrigued expression on his face. 'I'll inform Sir Henry, Mistress Mary.'

'Do take a seat, Mister Hamilton Smith. Not the green one though, if it appeals, as it is Sir Henry's favourite. The one opposite will prove just as comfortable, I am certain,' Mary said apologetically.

'Too kind of you, dear lady. I see your husband is unquestionably a most fortunate man.

'Oh no, I do assure you I am the fortunate one. Lieutenant Vizzard did me great honour in taking me as his wife,' said Mary.

'Fiddlesticks and fiddle-faddle, my dear,' interrupted Sir Henry Vizzard, entering the room with the aid of a stick. 'It is yourself has brought grace and beauty to the dusty life of the Vizzards, for which I will ever be indebted to you.' Henry beamed at his daughter-in-law, extending his hand to the visitor as Charles rose from the armchair.

'I am Sir Henry Vizzard, young man and I am delighted to have the honour of your acquaintance. How may I be of service?' Henry lowered himself into his armchair and sighed audibly.

'Sir Henry, the pleasure is mine and I do hope I may be of service to you.'

'Neave, Neave,' Sir Henry bellowed, 'some claret if you will. Bring a bottle of Harvey's best, would you please.' The demand had been anticipated by the long-suffering servant, who appeared clutching a decanter, as Sir Henry's last words left his mouth.

Henry Vizzard dropped uneasily into his chair by the fire,

extending his legs and looking at Mary's puppy in a silent invitation. The dog, requiring no further bidding, bounded onto the old man's lap and rolled its head into the crook of Henry's elbow. 'This is really the most affectionate of animals, Mary. What did you name it again?

Smiling patiently, Mary replied, 'I have named her Charlotte, Henry, to honour my sister-in-law.'

'Hah. Indeed, you have told me so my dear. Well, no matter, the puppy is still a delight.' Henry fondled the dog's ears, smiling and making noises such as a nurse would to an infant.

Neave returned with two glasses carefully balanced on a tray, setting them down on a small mahogany table, he poured some of the contents of the decanter into the glasses and offered the tray up to the guest first.

'If you will permit, Sir Henry, I should like to offer a toast to your son, who I am pleased to report is alive, or was to my eyes, when I last saw him four nights ago.' Hamilton Smith stood and turned his back to the fire, enjoying real warmth for the first time since leaving London. 'For it is entirely thanks to his sense of duty that I owe my liberty, indeed my very life. For I venture to say, had I been taken by my enemies I would not be alive today.'

Henry Vizzard beamed at Mary. 'There, my dear girl. Did I not tell you so? Now, sir, I am delighted to hear your news, although I am curious, I confess, to learn more of your acquaintance with my son.'

'He does you great honour, Sir Henry. He is working on the most secret and direct orders of His Majesty's minister and assured my safe repatriation to England, escorting me safely from Dieppe, so much I can say, and into the safe custody of the King's Navy. Without his courage and example, I fear I would have been taken by a villainous traitor,—one of his own senior officers, so I now understand—a Major Squires.'

The sudden eye contact between Mary and Sir Henry did not escape Hamilton Smith's keen observation, but he continued as though it had.

'Lieutenant Vizzard was ambushed at the last moment. We had escaped the town without apprehension or challenge and had returned to the beach where we were to be collected by the Navy. As I walked to the sea, indeed, my boots were in the water, we were fired upon.'

'Where was Jack?' Mary could not help the interruption.

'He was to my rear, my dear. I believe the enemy had not immediately been aware of our arrival, as the marines were quiet and were not in uniform scarlet coats or wearing their white cross-belts. Your husband had taken the curious and most unorthodox precaution of using non-standard clothing for his men—we were quite invisible until we reached the landing point. Quite ingenious, I thought, and something I have observed in nature; I shall investigate Lieutenant Vizzard's ideas in a more scientific manner, I believe.' Hamilton Smith held the glass of wine to the light and gazed through the windows with his mind on other matters, in particular the animal kingdom and how certain creatures had evolved to remain hidden from predators.

'Jack has an imaginative and inventive mind.' Sir Henry brought him back to the conversation. 'Always did have to try to do things differently.' He smiled at her portrait.

'Be that as it is, Sir Henry, ambushed and surprised as we were, his first action was to ensure my safety and then, in as calm a fashion as if he was on a field exercise on the South Downs, he had his men form up and return fire. With remarkable accuracy, too, I may say. I watched this from the boat as the Navy rowed me to their ship, or cutter, as they reminded me. A ship is a ship, ain't it?

'I know nothing of the world of ships, Hamilton Smith, or the Navy for that matter,' Sir Henry concurred.

'Sadly, he lost some men; I saw one unfortunate man die at his side before he gave up the fight. Oh indeed, I did see him lower his sword at the moment of his capture by the Major Squires I referred to earlier.' Hamilton Smith sipped from the glass. 'I should very much like to meet that officer and see him dishonoured and preferably, hanged. The major, I hasten to say, is not known to me, but I have gathered more knowledge of him since my return. None of it provides any comfort or pleasure, I regret to say.'

'Alive?' Henry's voice trembled. 'You are certain he is alive?'

'I have every reason to believe so, Sir Henry. He has been taken prisoner, I feel sure of it. They will believe him to have valuable information and, if I slipped through their treacherous net, they will wish to....' Hamilton Smith left unsaid that which he feared; that Jack would receive little mercy, once his enemies realised what little intelligence a junior officer of marines actually held.

'Then there must be the prospect of an exchange. I have heard of this before.' Henry failed to keep the note of desperation from his voice.

'Before I left London, I sent word via my servant to a friend in Paris who might be of some assistance.' Hamilton Smith could not tell this kindly old man or the beautiful, distressed woman opposite him, that such a thing was unlikely in the extreme. Lieutenant Vizzard was a junior officer of little importance or value, and the more probable outcome was torture and a painful death as an English spy, incarceration in The Paris Temple, or at best, a swift end under Madame Guillotine in the Place du Carrousel. Hamilton

Smith suppressed a shudder at the memory. 'Certainly, Sir Henry, it is a possibility and I sincerely hope an achievable one.'

'Ah, Mister Hamilton Smith, Charles, if I may, what in truth is the prospect for his safe return? I have been going half out of mind with worry for him.' Mary's face was composed; she kept the turmoil inside concealed.

Hamilton Smith, the government man, gazed at her, quite moved by her gentle, quiet dignity, at the composure when faced with extreme anxiety. 'Madam, Mary if I may, I will not deceive you. He is in a dangerous country and probably in the hands of a traitor who is now a desperate man. I have taken some measures to assist him, but in truth, I do not know his present circumstances or situation. Those who know your husband inform me he is a resourceful and capable officer. He will need those resources to survive; so do not abandon hope.'

Mary swallowed hard and knelt down to gather up the puppy, as the door opened to Helen Squires, who strode forward and announced with evident anxiety, 'I am told we have a visitor from London who may have news of Lieutenant Vizzard.' She moved to the centre of the room and stood directly in front of Hamilton Smith. 'Sir, I am Helena Squires, a friend to Mistress Vizzard and I presume you are he? What news do you have, sir?' She glanced sideways. 'Sir Henry, do we have good news?'

Hamilton Smith bowed to Helena and said, 'I have acquainted Sir Henry and Mistress Vizzard with such knowledge as I possess.' He sipped from his glass, the better to view the wife of the man recently condemned, in his mind, as a traitor and a spy. 'I take it Major George Squires is your husband, madam?

'You are correct, sir. I am ashamed to admit it.' Helena's eyes moved from Hamilton Smith to Sir Henry and back once more to the visitor. 'I have placed myself under Sir Henry's protection, having faithfully informed him of all I know of my husband's activities, sir.'

'Then, madam, I wish to converse with you. You may unwittingly have information of immense value to our country,' he spoke gently. 'Perhaps you would allow us to withdraw, Sir Henry?'

'Hmm? Oh yes, certainly, my dear sir. Please avail yourself of my study. Mary, if you would be so kind as to show them the way, my dear.'

A minute or more passed as Henry Vizzard stared absently into the flames dancing in the hearth.

'Well, and what do you imagine this private tête-à-tête is for, Henry?' said Mary, re-entering the room.

'My dear, I deduce Mister Hamilton Smith, as an agent of the king's minister, knows more than he is presently willing to divulge. He also wishes to interrogate Helena, in the gentlest manner I am sure, to determine if she has other knowledge of benefit. I believe him to be an intelligent young man.'

'I simply wish for his help in obtaining Jack's return. It is what I pray for nightly.' She slumped into the chair opposite her father-in-law and sobbed.

* * *

The old woman shuffled into the room, back bent, eyes darting. She spoke no English, but signalled she had come to clean the rooms and prepare a meal. Jack had not left the room for two days, other than furtively, for necessary reasons of hygiene. He and Vanessa d'Aubusson had no contact during those days and nights, leaving Jack confused, anxious and troubled. He was in a small cottage close to the port—that much only did he know. Mlle d'Aubusson had slipped away on the first night, before light, with a hurried word to stay hidden and a brief assurance she would return when all was arranged.

Jack was grateful; he had not thought much of food, but was now ravenous. Only some dry bread and water had he consumed today. By crude signing, he indicated he wished to shave. Understanding lit the old woman's eyes and she poured water into a blackened kettle, hastily gathering a handful of small logs, thrusting them into the range in the corner of the kitchen.

Then he realised his pack was still in the farmhouse. He had the gold concealed in his belt and hat, a notebook and a crude sketch of the town, but his supplies and field-kit were lost. 'Hell and damnation,' he said to the wall. Then he laughed.

The old woman looked up from the eggs she was beating in a bowl, a note of alarm in her brown, kindly eyes.

'I have no razor,' he said to her. Another hand gesture and she understood.

'*La bas, monsieur*,' she said, pointing to a drawer of the stained chest behind him.

A French-pointed straight razor with an ivory handle was revealed when the drawer was opened, alongside a matching brush.

The old woman brought a small bowl of water to him. '*Voilà, monsieur.*'

With the residue of a well-used piece of soap, Jack shaved; the water was hot, the stubble on his chin thick and tough. He washed and used his fingers to comb his hair. The simple act of hygiene improved his humour.

A wooden plate of beaten eggs appeared before him adorning a crust of poor quality bread and he forked the food into his mouth, careless of the mess created by his haste, taking pleasure in pacifying the gnawing pangs of his stomach.

He moved to the armchair, thanking the old woman in halting French. She smiled at his clumsiness, a broken row of carious teeth protruding from thin lips. He thought she would just as readily slit his throat if called on to do so.

A hand on his shoulder woke him; it must have been many hours later, because darkness had cloaked the small window and filled the room, a flickering oil lamp dying slowly on the table.

'Lieutenant, we must go quickly. We have a boat waiting.'

She stood with a glass lamp in one hand, his knapsack in the other.

'What? How did you come by my pack, mademoiselle?' He was awake now. Questions filled his mind. 'Where have you been?'

'The bodies, *monsieur*, have been disposed, yes? The major has been taken away. I know not where he is. Now we must be gone. A boat is ready for us.'

The old woman was nowhere to be seen, so Jack followed, buckling on his sword and ducking as he passed through the low door.

It was colder as once more he followed Vanessa d'Aubusson along a mud-clogged lane, downhill, he noted—toward the harbour. The odour of the port mingled with the salt air and caused his spirits to rise higher at the thought of a ship home.

Then Vanessa paused by a wall and slipped into its shadow, pulling him behind. 'Hush, *monsieur. Regardez*—look.' She nodded towards an untidy squad of French sailors, striding along the cobbles toward them.

He pushed closer to the wall; finding a recess, he pulled her behind him, his hand on the hilt of his sword, his mind working fast. How many more of them? Where to go when, or if, he disposed of these men? The odds were against him, he realised, but hell and damnation, I'll not be taken again. His grip tightened as the shapes drew nearer. Only fifty paces now. Forty... thirty.

Perhaps they will pass by. He pushed further back into the darkness.

Twenty paces... ten.

He held his breath and prayed.

The last man stopped, grunted to the others, turned, opened his culottes and steamed piss into the cold shadow. Jack felt it on his boots and could not tolerate it.

The Frenchman, aware that something or someone was close, raised his head. Jack's sword skewered the man's throat, allowing a stream of blood to leave the Frenchman's dying body; his last sight on earth an English officer's bared teeth, set in a silent, open mouth.

It was if the hounds of hell were loose as the street exploded with noise and light and shouts and screams. A musket ball struck the wall behind Jack's head, sending stone chips and dust into his ear. He realised Vanessa had disappeared. His mouth clenched in a silent curse.

If he were to die, then he would do so fighting. He wished for a musket but must make do with the sword. He glanced along the cobbles and slumped as the stock of a musket struck his back, sending a flash of pain across his shoulders.

He rolled, grasping for his fallen sword, but a boot smashed his side, adding fire to his side and he retched. Shaking his head, full vision returned and he saw a pair of bayonets inches from his chest.

'*Monsieur* Vizzard, I believe. I am so delighted to meet you.'

He stared up at the strong, haughty face of a French officer.

'You are a difficult fellow to apprehend, *monsieur*. But, I regret, you are in a good deal of difficulty, for you have compromised one of our agents. I think you will be welcome in Paris, yes? But do not expect a prolonged stay.'

'Your English is very good, Lieutenant...?'

'Charles de Bruin at your service, Lieutenant. Now please, I have little time.'

Two gendarmes hauled him roughly to his feet and pulled him along the street to a waiting coach with a pair of Breton horses and he was pushed into the darkened interior, where he saw Vanessa d'Aubusson smiling at him.

'Madam, I wish I could say it was a pleasure; alas, I succumbed to your charm and, fool that I am, was deceived by you.'

A finger raised to her lips silenced him. 'All may not be as it seems, sir,' she whispered, pulling a cloak tighter around her shoulders.

Jack narrowed his eyes and half-opened his mouth, but lay back against the padded leather bulkhead and just looked at her.

The carriage crawled along dark roads, its ultimate destination unknown; a prison in Paris probably. He felt a wave of despair. Once more a prisoner, he was constrained to ask no questions; to do so was only to become a hostage to fortune.

But a prisoner he could not be. It was anathema to his soul. Therefore he must force himself to be patient and await an opportunity to escape. He had not offered, nor had he been requested, to give his parole. There was a guard on the carriage in addition to the driver, he discerned. What of the French officer, he wondered? De Bruin, was he in attendance?

He listened. Yes, there it was; the distinctive sound of hooves to the rear. So, he had an escort. He would have to find a way of dealing with the guards before he could attend to their officer. Or should he deal with the officer first? He decided de Bruin would be the greater danger and therefore should be the first target. How to achieve it? The coach would have to stop for a change of horses. A halt on the journey might present an opportunity. They would be watching, naturally. He must be alert to any chance.

'Mister Vizzard, I 'ave decided I must flee to England.' Her voice was low, she leaned toward him. 'You can 'elp me do this, yes?

He hesitated. Escape would be hazardous alone, but accompanied by a woman? She might prove to be a help or a hindrance. He nodded.

'First we must remove our escort,' she said, echoing his thoughts. 'The guards are loyal, *monsieur*. It is their officer we must...' The intention was unspoken but understood. 'You must do this if we are to escape. I 'ave a weapon, it is small, but will be of use.'

From beneath her cloak she produced a small pistol. Jack took it from her outstretched hand and recognised it as a muff pistol of some quality; a handle of engraved ivory and a brass barrel. *Probably by Bunneys*, he thought.

'Is it primed? Do you have powder?'

'I loaded it this evening, Lieutenant. It is reliable.'

Vizzard concealed it beneath his jacket. 'It is light, madam; neither is it a powerful weapon. It may suffice, however. We will see what may be possible.'

An odorous leather curtain flapped as the vehicle rumbled slowly along a worn road, the dark sky showing traces of light as the dawn signalled its arrival. There would be a change of horses soon. A chance, if he could count on surprise and boldness. His head ached and his mouth was dry. He would need more than a lady's peashooter. He wondered about his sword. He missed the reassurance of it by his side.

As he searched the surrounding countryside, a village came into view in the valley to the right of the road. A malnourished and neglected dog barked as they drew past a farm, along a road twisting its way around an empty, dilapidated barn standing guard over unploughed fields, dressed with a surfeit of weeds, signalling a lack of husbandry by the local community.

The horses, steaming in the morning air, came to a noisy halt outside a shabby roadside tavern, the walls and windows covered in mud and grime, the studded door at the front denuded of paint. A young boy—he was no more than twelve, Jack thought—strolled out without enthusiasm and held the bridle of the lead animal.

The driver spat at the boy's feet and demanded water for the animals and wine for himself. He dropped to the muddy road, stretched and shouted at the guard, '*Venez, vous malotru gros, je veux mon petit déjeuner!*' The guard lowered his bulk slowly to the far side of the carriage.

Lieutenant de Bruin pulled up alongside and stared into the carriage as Vanessa d'Aubusson stirred from a disturbed sleep and Jack Vizzard returned the hostility in the officer's eyes.

'Come now, *monsieur* Vizzard. You may be our prisoner but we are both gentlemen; *sommes nous, non? Nous mangerons ici et echangerons les chevaux.* We will eat something and exchange the horses, yes?

Slowly Jack eased the door open, bending down to exit as de Bruin's horse sidestepped, its shoes clattering on the cobbles as he stepped down from the carriage. At the same moment, de Bruin swung his leg to ease out of the saddle. The shot was good; the weapon as close to de Bruin as Jack could place it, the ball passing through the Frenchman's right eye, snapping his head backwards.

The blood poured down his face. He was dead before his crumpled body hit the earth and Jack was on the motionless body in a moment, reaching for the man's pistols, and yes, Jack's sword was on the Frenchman's horse. His silent prayer was answered; both pistols were ready.

Spinning around to the rear of the carriage, he came up behind the guard, who was still peering to his right, any understanding of the action during the last few seconds eluding him. The hilt of the sword struck the back of the man's skull, the crack of bone audible, rendering him unconscious.

Good enough so far, Jack thought.

The carriage driver appeared at the door of the tavern, saw the prisoner armed and ready to fire, and quickly ducked inside; the sound of a bolt sliding home was clearly audible.

'Come, madam,' Jack shouted to Vanessa, 'I should like to return to England. And I fear I will be even less welcome in this country after today. However, I know not where we are, nor in which direction to travel. But first things first; we need transport and these horses are done for.'

'They may be, sir, but there must be fresh ones to the rear. Let us look.' She led the way to the rear of the building, Jack keeping a wary eye and a ready pistol, facing the door.

The stables, four of them, were occupied. Vanessa d'Aubusson found saddles and bridles hanging from pegs to the side of each and, with practiced hands, secured two chestnut mares and led them from the stables.

'You are a resourceful lady, madam. I believe these will do quite well.' Jack carefully tucked one pistol into his belt, keeping one in his right hand for instant use, as he took the reins of the larger mare.

A foot in the left stirrup and he slowly lowered his aching body into the saddle, gaining a measure of respect from the animal. With a soft squeeze of his knees into the sides, she moved forward. Jack thought instantly of the rides with Mary along the escarpment above Woodchester many years ago, becoming melancholy at the memory.

'Lieutenant, this way, I think,' she said, heading north along the road recently travelled. 'Are you forgetting?'

Jack shrugged and smiled, pulling the animal around gently. A ball passed his head as he did so, the wind of its passing breathing against his left ear. The mare snorted disgust as he levelled the pistol at the window from which the shot was fired. His shot shattered the glass, covering the innkeeper with lethal shards and sending him ducking, which suited Jack well enough.

'Come, madam, we must ride.'

He squeezed its girth and moved the animal into a canter, copying Vanessa, and within a moment they were out of range of anything other than a skilled sharpshooter.

As the sun rose higher the night's mist slowly disappeared, the muddy road emitting wisps of vapour as they continued, eyes scanning ahead and to the rear. Miserable sights were all he saw. Itinerant peasants, seeking work or food or shelter, some too tired and hungry to walk, slumped against tree trunks, in ditches, against farm walls, their clothes torn and dirty. Faces grimed with sweat and some with the faces of the walking dead. The fields they passed were untended.

Vizzard had rarely seen such evidence of total poverty, such images of hopelessness and despair. Then he remembered; yes, he had seen sights such as these before, in the transports to New Holland.

His mind meandered, as it was wont to do, thinking of the journey to England. How it was to be achieved, what his chances were of surviving and wishing he were not so alone.

They rode until the horses required resting, finding a slow-moving stream heading north. He and Vanessa d'Aubusson sat on the bank of the stream, as the animals drank. It appeared too fouled for Vizzard to risk drinking and he pulled a bottle from his valise, sitting next to Vanessa and taking a large swig before speaking. 'They will be watching the roads into town, madam. If we can pass their sentries, do we have a boat?'

'Yes, I believe so, Lieutenant. My friend will have sailed, I think, but there is usually a boat at, how you say, ready. It may be small, but you can sail, no?'

Vizzard knew he was no sailor. 'I could manage something modest in size, but an experienced hand or two would be a blessing, madam. Perhaps you know of someone who could be trusted?'

'We shall see, *monsieur*. We shall see. First we must reach the port, *oui*?'

'Before we go further, I wish to know what you were doing while I was in hiding. You were missing for, what, two days? Why?'

A tinge of colour emerged on her cheeks. 'I had to see to the bodies. They had to be removed and I needed 'elp with that. I also had to see Georges. You wish to return to your England, I need to find Georges.

It was unhelpful and unconvincing. Her explanation, with all the innocence of the fairer sex, did nothing to allay his suspicions.

* * *

The first sentry was intoxicated in the day's waning sun, a pike sprawled across his lap, as they walked past his snoring form, the horses having been left to graze in a field some distance from the town. A patrol of two men glanced without interest as two tired and shabby travellers walked slowly towards the port. There were few citizens abroad at this time of day, and they were not approached before they reached the quayside.

'Ahead of you, *monsieur*; the dark green boat with the big man at the front. He is the friend I talked about. He is Georges, a man who frequently is delivering wine and cognac to people in England. He will help us. But you must reward him, as I have no means to do so.'

If the civil authorities knew him as a smuggler, the man was not to be trusted. Vizzard was wary and cautious as, with Vanessa on his arm, he approached the vessel. It resembled a hog-boat, used by Sussex fisherman from the south coast of Sussex and Kent. Vizzard did not know it, but Georges de Castelain, the owner, had purchased it in Shoreham before the Revolution.

An ugly tub of a craft, flat-bottomed and blunt in the bows, only thirty feet overall, Georges loved her. The craft had earned her price many times over in the last ten years. He was not a skilled fisherman, but Georges was a discreet and successful smuggler. He'd spent so much time in the coastal towns of Kent and Sussex that his English had become acceptable. The citizens of the port all knew of his activities and it concerned them little, earning for some of them modest incomes. Georges worried the new regime would interfere with his trade.

A hurried, whispered conversation, a nod from Georges and half a dozen gold coins from Jack and the bargain was agreed. With a growl at the curly-haired youth sitting cross-legged in the bows, a hatch was opened and Jack and Vanessa disappeared into the hold. The vessel edged away from the quay and caught the ebb as the offshore evening breeze took the small craft out into the Channel and comparative safety.

The hold stank of stale fish with an odd hint of spirits; Vizzard sniffed and crawled along the decking until a bulkhead halted his movement. Tapping his way around, he found what he was searching for—a concealed compartment in the stern.

'Deck there,' said Jack, 'how do we access the...'

'Lift the ring in the floor—it will open the bulkhead. You know of these craft, *monsieur*?' He edged the tiller and the cold easterly breeze filled the foresail, pushing the vessel onto a course to the northwest.

'I have heard of them, yes. There are vessels in these waters I have no wish to meet. However, should you see a king's ship of any description, you will call me immediately. Understand?'

A grunt sufficed for the smuggler's answer and he pulled a clay pipe from the pocket of his woollen jacket, sucking noisily on its emptiness as the dying sun slipped into the oily and cold, cold sea.

CHAPTER II

William Pitt was at his desk in the drawing room, methodically reading his way through a pile of papers, the quill dipping silently into the well to his right before scratching a note in the margin of each paper in turn. Should a longer note be required, he annotated the lower right corner and completed his commentary or instructions, as the case required, on the reverse of the document. He had already written several letters of his own and his wrist was aching.

The firelight cast dancing shadows across the room, adding to the spectral scene. The candle at his side sputtered, the ruby liquid in the glass flashed and his eyes ached. He sighed, a slow exhalation of air through his nostrils as he regarded the pile of paper in front of him, which appeared no lower than when he'd commenced his labour—he glanced at the clock—three hours since.

The day had been spent inspecting the castle with a clerk making pencilled notes to aid his dictation later. Walmer was a castle, and might be needed as such once more, though its cannons had never fired in anger. As the new warden, he had decided to change the ancient buildings and make a home of them.

He frowned as he read. The news, it seemed, deteriorated daily.

The people Grenville had deployed to garner information had failed to deliver any intelligence of value. A disorganised network of informants throughout France, Prussia and Austria were not earning their corn. And His Majesty's government was expending a vast sum on corn, he felt. He needed sound intelligence and he needed it quickly. Now he had to grapple with more correspondence from the Prussians and Austrians. The coalition of disparate states was vexed and fragile. And expensive, excessively so.

Turning papers aside he spotted a note from his secretary, confirming that the officer in whom he had taken an interest had been identified: the man who had ensured the safe return of Hamilton Smith. It was a cause to celebrate, in which to rejoice. Hamilton Smith was a promising young officer and a resourceful, talented spy. It was as well he was safe in England. And now there was the intriguing lawyer-turned-marine responsible for his agent's safe return. The note informed him that the fishing boat the man had boarded to escape from France was intercepted by the same vessel used to land him in France at the commencement of his mission. Vizzard had returned to Portsmouth. Two days ago. Pitt grunted.

The prime minister was not a naval man, but he knew England had need of its navy once more. Pitt took a deep swallow of the ruby liquid, realised the bottle was empty and rang the bell for his servant.

'Sir?' the tall figure of Williams stood at the door.

'Another bottle, Williams; if you would be so kind.'

'Indeed, sir. There are two officers arrived to see you. I have them awaiting your pleasure in the gatehouse. They claim to have an appointment, sir?' Williams had no knowledge of this but was accustomed to late-arranged appointments for friends of the king's premier minister. It was rare for officers to simply appear unannounced at Walmer, hence the servant's scarcely concealed curiosity. 'They are accompanied by a lady, sir. She appears to be a French-woman, sir.' His expression remained as unchanged as if he were announcing the arrival of rain.

'Ah. Good. Excellent. Have them brought right along and have the dining table ready in half an hour, if you will. Well-stocked mind, Williams. I fancy my guests will have need of a bottle or more! Wait; a Frenchwoman you say. How very interesting, William.' His brain, always keen, worked with more speed than usual as the tiredness fell away and his eyes gleamed.

He poured from the bottle Williams had brought in response to his summons, scratched a note on the memorandum he had been reading, and stood in anticipation, quickly donning a dark purple velvet frock coat and straightening his neck-cloth.

The door opened once more, a minute or two later, and Williams announced, with suitable gravitas, 'Your guests, sir. Mademoiselle d'Aubusson and Lieutenants Vizzard and La... Lapenotière.' He inclined his head, as the two men entered, either side of Vanessa.

'Good evening, sir. My apologies for the intrusion and I am honoured to meet you,' said Lapenotière. May I present Mademoiselle Vanessa d'Aubusson and my particular friend, Lieutenant Vizzard, of the Corps of Marines?'

'The honour is all mine, er... mademoiselle and gentlemen, I do assure you. England has need of its officers... and its men. Especially, I do believe, its sailors. These are dark days, gentlemen, but I fear there are darker days ahead of us. Do, please, be seated. A glass?'

'I am delighted to be your guest, *monsieur*,' said Vanessa, inclining her head. 'I regret my unannounced visit and trust you will forgive the intrusion.'

Jack sat, awkwardly pulling his coat turn-backs aside, a little awed to be in the presence of the king's premier minister. He sipped at the claret wine to cover his confusion.

'Now, gentlemen and, er... mademoiselle. Welcome. This is an unexpected but timely visit. First order of business, I suggest, must be a toast. To the king... and the destruction of his enemies!'

The officers remained seated, as was their custom for a loyalty toast, although Pitt stood. Draining his glass, he stood with his back to the fire and looked hard at his guests.

'You will, I trust, be curious as to your presence here.' It was a statement not a question. 'I would have wished to avert this present war; the American one was absurd and barbarous, and, I'll wager, this one with the revolutionaries of France will only be worse. You may depend on it.' Pitt poured another glass for each and continued. 'You may explain your presence here, mademoiselle,' he coughed, 'for I have no knowledge of your interest.'

Vanessa candidly described her relationship with Major Squires, giving a remarkably full and detailed account of her travels with the major, of the people she had met, places visited and explaining her desire to escape France. She received a cool audience from William Pitt until she described how she had assisted in Lieutenant Vizzard's return to England, at which Pitt allowed the trace of a smile to animate his mouth. 'Then I will arrange for a friend to provide you with assistance and suitable accommodation, miss.' He turned to address the officers. 'I have consulted with the seniors of your service and orders are even now being carried to your immediate commanders.' His blue eyes sparkled as his audience showed surprise. 'My late father, in the last war with our neighbours, often advocated taking the battle to the enemy's homeland. We have a fleet blockading her ports, but that is all. I wish for more, gentlemen. It is my opinion that actions such as your recent expedition demonstrate that we have the capability to be more... offensive in our dealings with the revolutionaries.

Both men understood the prime minister's meaning. He meant to distract the enemy while planning alliances and building the nation's forces. Jack glanced at his friend, who returned the look and smiled.

'You take my meaning. You will stay the night? There are rooms for you all in the gunners' lodging.' It was a directive, not a question. 'Good. Now, gentlemen, we should dine. I trust you have an appetite, as our kitchens here are as fine as any in London!'

They walked through the door to the adjacent anteroom before passing into the dining room. A large mahogany dining table was laid for four, but could comfortably have seated a dozen. Pitt rarely entertained on such scale. He disliked large social functions, preferring the greater intimacy of good friends and supporters. He gestured to the cane-seat chairs and bid his guests to be seated, as he took a dominating position at the head of the table.

'Gentlemen,' he opened when the glasses had been filled, 'we face difficult times ahead. Britain has pushed to its utmost our system of temperance and moderation, but we are now slighted and abused by our old enemy. Such is the conduct which they have pursued; such is the situation in which we stand. It now remains to be seen whether, under Providence, the efforts of a free, brave, loyal and happy people, aided by our allies, will not be successful in checking the progress of a system, the principles of which, if not opposed, threaten the most fatal consequences to the tranquillity of this country, the security of our allies, the good order of every European government, and the happiness of the whole of the human race.'

'The Navy stands ready, sir,' said Lapenotière, taken aback by the man's eloquence and passion. 'You have, through your industry, made it so.'

'And I have little doubt, undermanned as the Corps is, the Marines will acquit themselves with equal merit, sir,' Jack added.

'I have every confidence in your Corps, Vizzard. That is not my chief concern at this time. My government faces difficult tasks; our very prosperity is threatened; merchants all beat a path to my door, banks are inhibited from advancing credit and Grenville has much to do to achieve an alliance with our continental friends. Our army is in no fit condition to take to the field, alas, and must be grown swiftly if we are to mount any expeditions to contain the Convention's expansionist policies.'

'If I may enquire then, sir, what do you propose to remedy the present situation?' Jack asked.

'The Admiralty will become increasingly active, gentlemen. I have alluded to the fact that orders are in course to implement some of my ideas. You are both now acquainted with the French coast, are you not?

Lapenotière nodded. 'Indeed, I am, sir. M'friend Mister Vizzard has only a passing knowledge, however.' He smiled at his friend.

'Then his new orders will remedy the situation,' Pitt replied quickly. 'I wish to have regular and frequent knowledge of what the French are about. To such purpose, Lieutenant, you—and others of your service—will keep me and my office informed of changes in the northern ports; I wish to know all activity which happens along the cursed, Gallic coastline. I wish to know of troop movements, shipbuilding, constructions or additions to their harbours. In short, gentlemen, I am asking you to become my agents across the

Channel and provide me with all intelligence possible concerning our enemy.'

The officers' reactions were interrupted by the arrival of dinner, delivered by a pair of immaculately attired servants. Further conversation was paused until the food was distributed and the servants withdrew.

'You wish us to become spies, sir?' Jack could hold back no longer. 'To put ashore in France and spy for you?'

'Yes, as agents for me, Lieutenant... and for the benefit of Britain. Is my request unreasonable?' Pitt asked. 'If my lord's commissioners are to conduct an effective war, they will have need of reliable, frequent and informed intelligence, will they not?'

Jack Vizzard listened as the prime minister expanded his ideas: to gather information, to cause disruption and divert the enemy's resources, while at the same time building for the campaigns, which would surely follow as the war developed. The unfolding conflict would continue far longer than he ever contemplated.

Jack's mind turned over the prospect; now he would have all the opportunity for glory and promotion he could want. The question he now had to consider was, could he meet the challenge and survive?

'If I... we... are to do this, sir, will I have a degree of autonomy with respect to my preferred methods? What I mean to say is, will I be bound by divisional orders as to uniform? I have every pride in my uniform, sir, but hold the view that, for operations on French soil, an absence of conspicuity might be preferred.'

'Lieutenant, I am a politician. I cannot, rather I should not, interfere in military matters, but one must be active in this. However, one of the reasons I had desired to meet you was to seek confirmation of your suitability for the type of work I have in mind.

By your questions, I am satisfied you are precisely the type of officer the service requires! Your services, in whatever guise you choose to discharge them, will have my support—conditional only on the results you achieve. I trust we have an understanding.'

'Indeed we do, sir.'

'Lieutenant Lapenotière, you will have an understanding of your part in these operations, I trust?' Not waiting for an answer, Pitt continued, 'You are to provide Lieutenant Vizzard with the means of observing the various ports and facilities and, in the manner which seems appropriate in your judgement, to render all practical assistance in reporting his findings to me. I wish you to support him in any land operations that seem to assist our efforts to confuse and injure and divert the enemy. You will both be on detachment from your current posts with orders to report directly to me and my specific ministers; principally my Lords Wyndham and naturally, Dundas.'

'I daresay, it will prove more diverting than playing escort to convoys, sir, which is tiresome work, if I may venture.' Lapenotière said.

'Good. Then I am encouraged. It is my desire we cause the enemy serious harm. Their resources must be stretched, their ships destroyed, stores and supplies burned, crops razed. I need time, gentlemen, time to build our army. Time you must find for me. Now, your glasses are in need of replenishment.'

'Mister Pitt, I have listened carefully to all you 'ave said,' Vanessa d'Aubusson spoke for the first time, 'and it grieves me to hear these things of my country. But, sir, if I can assist you and your king in removing the vile people who have over-run my country and executed my dear King Louis, then I gladly offer myself to your service.' She smiled, stirring thoughts amongst the gentlemen at the table.

The servant crossed the room in silence and, with accustomed speed and a deft turn of the wrist, filled the prime minister's glass first, before moving to the guests.

'The Revolutionaries are even now equipping and mustering armies which will become powerful. What they lack are leaders, but I do suspect some bold men will emerge from their ranks and cause us great harm. Mark me well, gentlemen; we must do the same, if our beloved country is to survive the coming conflict.'

'Now, I suggest you take to your homes in the morning and say farewell to your loved ones, gentlemen, as you will, like as not, have little time to do so in the months ahead. Your orders will be delivered to the admiral at Portsmouth in the morning.'

* * *

'The prime minister was quite clear, Mary. I am to be independently employed as one of his agents. Not simply a spy—the Corps would not wholly approve of such work for one of its officers —but as a combatant. We are at war with France.'

Jack and Mary Vizzard were sitting in Henry's study three days later, taking tea as the wintry sun slowly faded and dipped behind the escarpment, the fire in the grate in need of refuelling.

Jack Vizzard rose, collected a pair of large logs from the basket and, with care, dropped them onto the fire, watching as the sparks spat and crackled, as though mocking him. He stood with his back to the flames, staring into the garden, thinking of what may be asked of him in the months to come.

'I understand, beloved, but this is too dangerous; it is simply too much. You will be caught and executed by those evil people.' Her initial tears had dried but the feeling of dread remained tight in her chest. 'I worry so, my dear man. You know I do. However, there is another reason I am fearful. I... um, you should know I am with child! There, it is said. I had wished to keep this from you for a while, but my heart is bursting today.'

Jack crossed to her and, kneeling at her feet, clasped her hands to him. 'My dearest love. What wonderful, completely wonderful news. Fear not, beloved, I shall not perish at the hands of our enemies. I have even more purpose to life now than to permit that to happen.' He kissed her hands, then sat on the arm of the chair and held her tightly.

'My sweet Mary, never forget how much I love you and need you. I will never hazard us unreasonably or unnecessarily. I will though, I must, do my duty and serve my country. You do know I must.'

She cupped his face in her hands, smiled and said, 'Oh, Jack. I do understand. Naturally, I understand. I am so fearful this war is to be so terrible and so dreadful to our country that I feel you cannot survive it. And to place yourself in the heart of it, taking on so much. You must come back. My heart would break if I were ever to lose you.'

The opening of the study door caused Jack to disengage and stand, an embarrassed expression lingering a moment too long, which Henry Vizzard, even with his failing eyesight, was able to observe.

'Now what is to do with the pair of you?' he asked, smiling toward his daughter-in-law. 'Has he distressed you, Mary? If he has, I'll have him horsewhipped! No sooner does he arrives home and, bless me, he has you in tears. Come, come now; what's amiss, child?'

'You should take a seat father; it is after all, your study,' Jack answered. 'Make yourself comfortable and I will tell you; but only that which I feel I can, and even that may be too much.'

Henry Vizzard remained impassive, with difficulty, as his son recounted the events of recent weeks.

* * *

The wood-smoke drifted across the low, beamed room, blown from the inglenook by a down draught. The wool merchant in the corner coughed and clutched a handkerchief to his nose and blew with vigour, and continued in low tones to his neighbour, exhorting him to accept the price offered, met with a slow shake of the head by the seller. The latter understood the demand for wool would rise in the coming months and was not about to sell cheaply.

Lieutenant Vizzard observed them over his tankard as he waited for his friend to join him. *The Ram* was a second home and he and the landlord, Bill Brice, were old friends. Brice had watched and aided as the two Vizzard boys had grown to become men. George, the eldest, had not been seen nor heard of in nigh on a decade and must now be thought long since perished at sea. Jack thought of his lost brother with great affection and sadness, tinged with chagrin that his mentor and childhood companion had simply left the family home with not a word.

A small roadside tavern at the lower end of the village, adjacent to The Old London Road, The Ram was popular with villagers and travellers alike. The thatch was worn in places, but still waterproof. The ridge displayed a pair of peacocks, skilfully fashioned from local reed, harvested from nearby Sharpness, the trademark of the local master thatcher, Will Peacock. Tendrils of ivy covered most of the walls.

A chimney poked impudently from the centre of the roof, the mellow yellow brickwork spalled and flaking, the mortar in need of re-pointing.. Wisps of wood-smoke wrapped around the wrought iron weather vane fitted to the top—a long-horned ram, cleverly made by the village blacksmith when the inn was his property, some years ago.

Bill Brice had bought the inn on leaving the Navy many years before and had turned his hand to brewing. He called his beer 'Old Spot' after the popular local species of pig. The Ram had a large room, used by the men of the village on a Saturday evening, where they would stand and drink his cider and home brewed ale until the landlord threw them out, or when they became too drunk to stand, or when the coins in their pockets were gone. Bill was not a man to give credit to mill workers. A smaller room—Bill called it 'The Gunroom' and kept it in a more comfortable state—was for the use of some of his more 'genteel' customers. A large blue ensign decorated one wall, and a miscellany of naval artefacts gathered dust on shelves and sills around the room.

The mellow golden sandstone walls, extracted centuries before from the local Cotswold Hills, displayed the staining of smoke of many years. Traces of straw on the flagstones forming the floor gave evidence of the farm hands who had been drinking earlier. A thin layer of tobacco smoke hung beneath the beamed ceiling, swirling each time the door opened, allowing the chill, damp air to swoop in.

A captain, tall and commanding in the uniform of the 28th regiment of foot, filled the doorway as the evening sun sank behind him, throwing a long shadow into the room. A pair of old heads, grumbling in a corner, smiled as two younger men slipped discreetly from the room to the door at the rear.

'Vizzard! You wretched dog! Stand aside and let me chase the rabbit. Brice, Bricey - a bottle of Harvey's and large glasses, if you will,' he growled with a smile. 'M'friend and I have some time together at last and I have a ploughman's thirst on me,' he said, as he slapped his arm around Jack's shoulder and walked to their table by the window.

Bill Brice muttered an oath and bent under the counter to lift a large blue bottle from a case he kept for his own consumption. Mister Vizzard, as he now knew him, was the son he'd never had, and he was fonder of him than he ever let on. He had cuffed him about the ears as a boy, paddled his arse with a cricket bat when the boy had raided his cider press, but had also aided and abetted him when he had turned off the evil vicar of the parish; this was before Vizzard had escaped to New Holland and none in the village knew of it, either. Never would know of it from Bill, who swore to keep the secret safe that night. The captain, Mister Mountjoy, the heir in all but name to the Lucie estate, also knew the truth, Bill suspected, but never had there been any talk between them. But Bill had seen it in Mountjoy's eyes all those years ago. He knew, but he had protected Jack too. So Bill said nothing, chewed on his baccy and continued brewing and serving ale and cider.

'So good to see you again, m'friend. How are things with the Corps? I must say, Jack, I had not expected to see you again. Fully expected you to be at sea or hear you had been murdered by the natives in Africa, old chap. And what of this war? Should be good for promotion, don't you think?'

'We are kept busy enough, Giles. I have leave of absence before joining the fleet and 'tis good to see you, old friend.'

Giles Mountjoy was a good friend from childhood and Jack had cause to be grateful for his friend's loyalty and discretion. He was possibly the only one who knew the truth of Jack's crime, besides

Bill Brice. Giles had shadowed him from Gloucester on the wild night so many years ago, when he had taken the law into his own control and disposed of an evil man—a cleric who had raped Mary and engineered her trial on false charges, ensuring her transportation to New Holland for seven years. His father's determined intervention had eventually brought about a Royal Pardon and Fate had reunited him with his beloved in the penal colony.

'I am well, Giles, quite well, I thank you. A minor scratch or two from which I am recovering with no complications, but in truth, as fit as ever.' He lowered his voice against eager ears. 'We have been busy in France, Giles, and I believe there will be more warm work in the weeks and months ahead.'

Mountjoy's eyebrows lifted a notch. 'What are you about, my lad? God's teeth, you are up to something; I see it in your eyes. Never could keep a secret from me, now could you?'

'The government, by which I mean Pitt, has seconded me from the Corps to do some dirty work for him, Giles.' The glass in his hand wobbled imperceptibly as he related in scant words the briefing he had received at Walmer Castle.

During his friend's discreet confessional, Giles' mind was working. It was rumoured the regiment would be marching to the south coast soon. He was of a mixed mind; the estate needed him, the family—he and Louise now had three sons and two daughters—but he was restless. If his friend was to be taking the war to France, he wanted to be involved.

'If you are to take the war to France, Jack, then I want to be with you,' he said. 'The regiment is likely as not to move south and it should be possible for me to persuade the colonel to allow me some freedom from duty. Do you think your political masters could be persuaded to er... allow a keen fellow to participate? To mind your back, as it were; Lord knows your appalling fighting skills demand it, dear chap.'

Jack laughed at the joke, knowing well that in their youth, Giles presented little challenge in the wrestling games or shooting contests they arranged in the hills and woods above the village.

'Perhaps best if I do not consult them, Giles. If your colonel will agree, who am I to raise objection? There is the matter of my sergeant, however. He has no time for officers, especially those from line regiments and I fear he long ago appointed himself as my personal guard!'

'Hah, I look forward to meeting the man. I shall delight in showing him how a Gloucester officer behaves and fights the French. Consider it a bargain, my friend. My colonel is an obliging sort.'

'The Corps is not for every man, Giles. We look to recruit the best men; they need to be healthy, strong and with some learning. I question if you have the required attributes, my friend!' Jack laughed.

'We are no longer children, Jack. You may have bested me when we played in the woods above the village but we are men now. I have trained and studied and have learned a thing or two, you know.'

'I have no doubt my dear man. I sincerely hope you have the opportunity to demonstrate your prowess soon. Now, drink up and let me tell you what I have been doing since last we spoke.'

* * *

Summer came and slipped into autumn, finding Giles Mountjoy

variously at Littlehampton and Portsmouth with his regiment. Colonel Prescott had proved obdurate and refused Giles's repeated applications for secondment.

CHAPTER 12

Hamilton Smith was sketching. It was a compulsion he could not avoid, never did want to give up. Drawings of flora and fauna filled his rooms, as did sketches of buildings of both antiquity and contemporary construction. His travels on the continent had allowed him to visit many of the capital cities, which he had explored intimately, sketching and painting his way from country to country. He had become fascinated by colour. For half an hour or more, he had sat on a camp chair, observing, waiting for the light to come right, before ever lifting a pencil.

Horse guards he had drawn many times, but now it was one of the more recent additions to the northern end of Whitehall he was studying—the first lord's house, built recently by Cockerell and much admired by Hamilton Smith. Sunlight flashed on the windows, sending secret signals, as might a heliograph, to the disinterested populace intent only on journeying, usually to or from Westminster or Saint Margaret's. His pencil moved across the paper—short, neat strokes and soft, broad infilling, adding shadow as the piece took form. Eyes lifted frequently to measure structure and perspective and his left hand danced around the paper. He was pleased with the progress of his work and enjoyed the leisure time, which had become a rare thing of late. He felt the sun's warmth overhead and smiled with the pleasure it brought.

Presently, he observed a servant leave by the front entrance and, with practiced skill, manoeuvre his way through the busy traffic that was rumbling and snorting north and south along the broad, muddy avenue, littered with equine droppings. He was a mature man, who walked with purpose and with an unusual gait, as though somewhat affected by alcohol, as indeed, he was.

The odd thing, thought the artist, was that the man appeared to be generally following a path that would bring his journey to a conclusion directly in his line of sight. Three or four minutes or so later, it did. The man nodded to Hamilton Smith by way of obeisance and, in a voice more accustomed to shouting orders at seamen said, 'Good day to you, sir. Do I have the honour of addressing Charles Hamilton Smith?'

'May I enquire as to the originator of your question?'

The servant, bemused at the response, pulled at his neck-cloth, a garment he found uncomfortable and novel, grinned a seaman's grin and inclined his head over his right shoulder.

'I am correct though ain't I, sir? His Lordship, Earl Chatham, the first lord hisself, commands me to request your attendance upon him; if convenient for you at this time.'

Intrigued as to why the first lord should seek him out, he stood, collecting his camping chair and placing his paper and pencils in a valise.

'I should be most honoured to attend on His Lordship. Please, lead the way.'

Navigating the carriages and horses with a helmsman's skill, Hamilton Smith was guided across the thoroughfare by his escort. To the west side of the entrance hall there was a small, all but concealed entrance into the building. The stairs led up to the vestibule on the first floor. The servant turned right, into the library. It was a large room, the largest in the building, with three windows along the west elevation overlooking the mews in Spring Gardens and filling the room with natural light. It had been Howe's favourite room when he was first lord.

Hamilton Smith had never met Chatham previously. He saw a man in his late-thirties, handsome in appearance with a confident visage, a long chin between prominent cheekbones, dressed in fashionable but not ostentatious clothing; a deep navy blue coat with a high collar over a white linen shirt. Intelligent, blue, almond-shape eyes beneath dark brows looked up in greeting as he entered the room, behind the servant.

John Pitt, Second Earl of Chatham, Knight of the Order of the Garter and First Lord of the Admiralty, was comfortable in a leather chair adjacent to the fireplace, *The Times* spread across his knee and a tall cup of coffee in his hand, which he promptly placed on the table to his left. He played with a heavy, red ring on his left hand.

'Ah, Hamilton Smith, thank you for accepting my invitation; most kind in you. I do hope I have caused no inconvenience? Will you take coffee? Or something...'

'Coffee will be most welcome, m'lord.'

Chatham waved him to a matching chair.

'See to it please, Walter,' he instructed.

'You will be wondering why I wished to meet with you, no doubt, Hamilton Smith. M'brother mentioned you recently, in connection with some business in France. Pointed you out at *The Cocoa Tree* the evening afore last. in point of fact, but you vanished as we made to approach you.'

Hamilton Smith took the chair opposite the first lord, hooked his ankles together as he stretched in the comfort of the soft leather. It was unfortunate Chatham had seen him at *The Cocoa Tree*. One of the lesser-known clubs and wagering dens, he felt more secure within its walls than at *Boodles* or *Whites*. It was a source of information, the life-blood of his clandestine work for His Majesty's government.

Yes, indeed he was curious at Chatham's polite and informal summons. Smith had not met Chatham since his appointment to The Admiralty by his younger brother, William Pitt, the King's prime minister, some eight years previously. He was aware of the elder Pitt brother's reputation, however; with a reported tendency to indolence and extravagance, he was not universally regarded as an effective administrator, all but openly described by a few envious members of the nobility as a lacklustre member of the family. Chatham had refused to serve in the Americas against the colonial forces as a matter of principle, which suggested to Hamilton Smith a principled man of firm views who would not be anyone's puppet. Instead, he had been despatched to Gibraltar for years of tedious garrison duty. Hamilton Smith was not a man to carry prejudice; Chatham alone of the cabinet was a professional and experienced soldier, with a soldier's eye for detail and opportunity. For that reason, if no other, he was happy to meet his lordship with an open mind.

'The prime minister gives me to understand you are... er, of assistance to his administration of foreign affairs in matters pertaining to our friends on the continent. I, that is, m'brother, requires of me to devise plans and ideas to damage the damned Frenchies and to divert them from their intentions in the United Provinces. We, er I, had hoped you could be prevailed upon to assist me in this matter.'

Lord Chatham sometimes felt the burden of his title with the weight of opinion in social circles, comparing him to his father, the First Earl of Chatham, a distinguished leader of the nation during the Seven Years' War, and also to his younger brother, William, the king's prime minister.

Poor John Pitt, thought Hamilton Smith. Often seen as living in the shadow of his precocious younger brother, William, who had always outshone, had always been the favourite of their late father. Now the first lord was looking to him to help him with his ministerial duties, indeed, with the conduct of the naval war.

'M'lord, my business with the government is not something that should ever be discussed outside these walls, and never with any other party, save for the king and his premier,' he cautioned the first lord. 'It is true; I am occasionally in a position to render some service to our country of a discreet nature. I have travelled much on the continent and have some knowledge of engineering and artillery; and some have spoken kind words of my work, which may be of help to His Majesty's forces, perhaps to the Navy in particular.'

'Yes, yes, indeed it is the Navy of which I speak. I wish to use it wisely in this war, but am of different minds as to the best means to direct it in these troubled times. We are so scattered, it vexes me to decide how best to use the squadrons.'

Chatham's initial air of confidence appeared to slip momentarily, and he made a conscious attempt to regain a dominant presence. For a moment or two, Hamilton Smith felt a degree of sympathy for the first lord. But only for a moment.

'The king's prime minister has charged me with seeking out enterprising officers amongst the fleet and the Marine Corps,' said Hamilton Smith. 'He believes the country needs time to build alliances and increase our strength. He therefore seeks to take the war to the enemy on their shore. The army is in a pitiful state, m'lord. Fortunately, the Navy is better equipped to defend our interests, due, in no small part to the efforts of your noble predecessor, Lord Howe, who is a naval lord of many fine qualities.'

'Yes, yes. A fine officer, indeed, but he no longer has the responsibility—the responsibility has been mine these last eight years, sir, and I am most anxious and determined to make a success of it in this war, Hamilton Smith.' Chatham spoke tersely. 'And you can help me achieve... you will not find me unthankful, I can assure you. What's to do? How can we best cause confusion and discourage our enemy? Hm?'

Hamilton Smith thought it questionable that Chatham could have the force of character to manage the admirals, officials and politics of the office. Neither did he care, for the man was not best positioned in this war and would not last long in this office, he decided. The office of first lord required a more dynamic, visionary individual than the one before him now. The Admiralty should be served by an experienced administrator who was also a distinguished sea officer, in his opinion. However, Chatham had, he reminded himself, argued with cabinet colleagues, successfully too, for the Corps of Marines to receive pensions. Perhaps there was more to Chatham than he and the public presently understood.

'There are a number of tasks which, if performed well by those selected to perform them, will reflect great credit on the service and on the Admiralty. m'lord. I have a number of ideas for modest goals; the chief object must be to cause the French to suffer losses in ships, in materiel, of personnel and of supplies of every description. M'lord, this war will become ever more brutal and, mark me sir, ever more widespread. We must fight our enemy with total resolve and with total ruthlessness if we are to survive and prosper. For most certainly, France will endeavour to destroy us.'

Hamilton Smith's passion had carried him beyond what he might have said in other circumstances. His colour changed imperceptibly, not because he regretted his words, but his too-obvious display of patriotism.

'My Lord Chatham,' he continued, 'Robespierre is in a precarious position. For many months past he has sought to conscript Frenchmen, in the hundreds of thousands. The country is exhausting stocks and has, I am liberty to tell you, found a new partner with which to conduct trade; I refer naturally to the United States of America, as we must call the former colonies.' Hamilton Smith rose from his chair and slowly paced. 'Sir, France is even now transacting business across the Atlantic. They are moving gold clandestinely and bargaining for grain and beef, sugar and other goods.' He paused to see the effect of his words and drained the coffee from his cup. 'There will be a convoy, the size of which we have not seen before, and it must be found and taken, m'lord. My estimation is, it will gather in the Chesapeake; however, it is the destination port I am more interested in. My information is poor on this but my belief is the convoy will make for Brest. It is the logical, indeed the only practical choice Robespierre has.'

'You wish to lay a trap, Hamilton Smith? Is that what you are saying? Chatham's eyes drilled into those of his guest.

'Indeed, m'lord, It will be a prize to make many men as rich as Croesus,' he said. 'Come, m'lord, let me show you on the map, something of what I propose.'

<h1 style="text-align:center">CHAPTER 13</h1>

The November waxing moon was nearing its final quarter and the temperature of the sea had fallen to near freezing. Flakes of snow floated from the land, swirling about the masts and sails of the ship, dusting the rigging with a crystalline sheen. The sea frothed from the bows as nervously they approached Pointe Sainte-Mathieu. The task before them involved both obvious and latent danger and required intense concentration. It was to be preferred to the monotony of fleet duty or convoy shepherding.

The schooner was now less than ten miles from Brest; they were sailing down the enemy's throat and all on board knew it. Every man felt the tension, realised muscles had contracted, was aware that danger stalked in every mile they advanced; from the forts and batteries along the granite cliffs, from the possibility of an encounter with a French frigate or privateer, but chiefly from the danger of a lee shore, should the wind change. The waters through which they sailed concealed a confusion of wicked rocks, any one of which could tear the ship to matchsticks in minutes.

Jack made his way aft to where the schooner's commander, John Lapenotière was standing, now more relaxed than he had been during the slow and cautious approach through some of the most hazardous waters in Europe.

Lieutenant Lapenotière navigated with extreme care, sensing the run of the tide through his well-planted feet on the deck timbers, feeling the wind on his cheeks. Now they were running south-south-east and a half east along the Chausée des Pierres Noires, to the south of the notorious Black Rocks, lining the course into Brest like shadowy sentinels of death.

'Alter course to east by north and a half north, now, if you please, Mister Almy,' commanded Lapenotière to the ship's master. 'Do you see the rock to the south, Jack? It's the Parquet Rock and has claimed many a fine vessel. Ahead is Pointe du Toulinguet, there are a number of batteries there, and beyond are the village of Cameret and your destination, Jack.'

The entrance to Le Goulet, the channel leading to Brest, acted as a tunnel, along which snow and sleet lanced at Vizzard's face like needles. Salt encrusted his hair, where it hung from beneath his oilskin cap. His eyes stung and he felt chilled to the bones. 'It is a fine night for an excursion, John,' he grunted.

The coming landing held more trepidation for Vizzard than those of the summer now past. The several landings he had made with Lieutenant Lapenotière had, in the main, been uneventful affairs. Gathering information and preparing sketches and questions of the occasional Royalist supporter; only once had he had to fight his way from zealous guards. That was at Saint Malo, two months ago. Now, Giles Mountjoy and he had been ordered by Lord Chatham to do more, to damage French installations and to survey the French naval vessels in Brest. The words of his latest order were, *"My Lords of Admiralty judge it of benefit to the service to reconnoitre the Vauban Tower and, should you find it practical to do so, to seek to destroy the building and any appurtenances.*" His men were carrying more of Faversham's finest powder, packed in stout paper sacks and stored in knapsacks. None had been heard to complain at the extra burden on previous excursions ashore.

'Ease her off, Mister Almy. I'd like to anchor behind the point to starboard—Point Toulinguet, according to the chart,' Lieutenant Lapenotière ordered in a quiet manner. 'Make it half a cable's length; there is good holding ground and depth, as best I recall.' He had been here only once before, when the world was a more peaceful place. 'The tide hereabouts has a marked rise and fall, so anchor well.'

It was at the approach to Brest where *HMS Childers* had been attacked, nearly a year past. The Admiralty needed to know of changes to the defences since the last attack and the number and nature of vessels presently in the harbour.

Captain Mountjoy stood huddled behind Lapenotière, a comforter wrapped around his neck, as Jack nodded to Lapenotière and took up position by his side. 'So happy your colonel was persuaded to release you at last, Giles. I merely hope you have no cause to regret joining our expeditions. They become decidedly... well, bloody dangerous at times!'

'Hah. You have no idea just how tedious life in barracks can be, my lad. T'will make a refreshing change to have some excitement to face, let me tell you,' said Mountjoy, pulling a fisherman's rough cap tighter on his head. 'However, my dear, this manner of fighting a war of yours is contrary to all I know, I don't mind saying. But let me show my worth and who knows, mayhap *your* colonel will find a vacancy for me.'

Jack smiled, rubbing on his right ear lobe as he did so. 'It is a means to an end, Giles, a means to an end.'

'Sir, your orders 'ave been completed, sir. The men are ready.' Joe Packer grunted, approaching the officers. He relaxed the leg, which, though now well healed, remained a source of discomfort to him.

Giles and Jack had formed a plan to take a party of men ashore with the intention of causing maximum damage in the attack on the Vauban Tower at the entrance to the Goulet at Cameret, timed to take place before *Nimble* had to slip away on the ebb tide, just before dawn, if the wind was kind. If it were not, Lapenotière and his beloved vessel and his crew would be in hot water, for which Jack would be entirely responsible. He shivered.

'Do you judge our disguise as a Dutchman will deceive the French, Jack?' Mountjoy whispered. Lieutenant Lapenotière had attempted to camouflage his craft and had hung the appropriate ensign to add to the deceit.

'We have a chance, Giles. If we anchor in the lee offered by the cliffs, we may even escape observation entirely,' Jack replied, with more insouciance than he felt.

In near total silence, the small vessel hove to and silently slipped an anchor into the freezing water, as men moved in response to orders issued earlier in the day and rehearsed during half a dozen similar excursions along the French coast in the last six months.

Jack hoped to add to the information Lapenotière would collect from his position. Midshipman Dicky Bird would take a boat and take soundings to add to the chart, which was deficient, while masquerading as a guard boat.

'Away with you then, Jack. We'll have the boats ready to take you off at six bells in the middle watch. That's ...'

'I am by now quite familiar with the Navy's system of announcing the time, John, thank you,' Jack said with a broad smile. 'Be sure you watch the fireworks. I hope they entertain you as much as the French. I fervently pray we get out of here alive.'

'God speed, Jack,' said Lapenotière, clasping Jack's right hand in both of his. 'Make the devils pay, and we'll get away as fast as my *Nimble* will allow; and that is speedy, have no fear, my friend.'

Two boats, carried aboard for the purpose, slipped into the night, rowlocks muffled with rags and tar, the marines' faces dirty with slush. Again, on his express orders, uniforms were not worn. His men had come to terms with Jack's odd ways: Vizzard's Vandals, they were being called by the sailors. Regarded as undisciplined, dirty, surly and insolent, they had nonetheless become feared as ruthless, efficient fighters. Trained by Packer and Jack Vizzard, they now cared little for the spit and polish of garrison duty, for field days with immaculate, regular lines advancing on defended positions. Vizzard was unorthodox, and Packer, always the smartest soldier in the Portsmouth Division, was now one of the unkempt when on one of the 'Guvnor's Frolics' as he now termed them.

But they respected him. Trusted him to bring them back from wherever they landed on the enemy's coast. From Dunkirk to St Malo, they had caused damage and disorder, chaos and fear among the populace. And Jack was fiercely proud of them.

The cold, cruel sea slapped against the rocks as Jack shelved the boat on the spit of shingle beach, urging the ten men of his boat ashore with a whispered, 'Out and take up positions.'

The Irishman, Michael O'Farrell, was the first ashore, leaping cat-like onto the wet sand before scrabbling uphill to take up his favoured position at the head of the platoon. Joe Packer, in the second boat with Giles Mountjoy, dropped to one knee beside him, as others joined and spread along the edge of the beach, which shelved steeply up to a rocky outcrop. Vizzard strode through them all, lying prone next to the big Irishman. 'Hear anything, O'Farrell?'

'Thort I heard a faint voice, if the wind's roight, sor,' he whispered. 'Over yonder.' He pointed with his nose to the left. With his head motionless, Vizzard extended his right arm, calling the men forward.

'To the left, Joe,' he said, instinctively knowing his sergeant was by his side. 'Paddy thinks he heard a voice.'

Packer and O'Farrell slid forward into a ditch and disappeared within seconds, the night all around silent, save for the gentle lapping of the sea against the shore behind them.

A hoot from fifty yards ahead and Jack rose and moved forward, the remainder of the men following in an extended straggle, either side of the track. A minute later and the grinning Irishman whispered, 'Just two of 'em, sor. The sarge an' I did for 'em.'

'Very well, Paddy. Let's not loiter—scout ahead for any others. Where is Sergeant Packer?

'Come with me, sor, if you'd be so good,' he addressed Captain Mountjoy. 'Sergeant Packer is going after them Frogs like the clappers and I best get him back, afore he kills every Frog for miles. He's fricking melancholy as a gib cat, an' likely to get hisself in trouble without Michael O'Farrell to watch his back.'

The large Irishman loped forward, wolf-like and exuding power, his bayonet, edged in glistening crimson, gripped hard in his right hand. Mountjoy followed tight-lipped and eyes wide. The rest of the platoon followed, the men in a loose formation along the track, as heavier snow followed them from the rear.

A hundred yards further on, a low hoot alerted Jack. He halted the platoon and edged along a ditch on the right side of the track. Hidden under a clump of bushes, he found his sergeant.

'The patrol is about fifty yards ahead, sir, moving towards the fort. They must be posting piquets. Might be expecting us, d'you think?' Packer kept his voice uncharacteristically low.

'Possibly, Joe,' he whispered, 'but the French will be cautious hereabouts. Brest is the largest harbour they have and will be well guarded now we are at war. And that is why we're here, don't forget. To make the buggers sweat and keep them wondering where we will hurt them next.'

Two French soldiers were pacing and muttering in the dark, making enough noise to identify their location.

'Looks as though you and O'Farrell will have more bayonet practice, Joe. We must reach the fort unseen and unheard. Surprise is our key weapon.'

A nod to the Irishman and the two marines crawled as silent as snakes along the ditches, ignoring the brambles and icy, brackish water as they hugged the freezing earth.

Jack waited as a muffled squeal reached his straining ears. It was quickly followed by another low hoot and he closed up with the platoon. He reached the body of one within a minute, the neck still bubbling with a trickle of blood, unseeing eyes staring to the night sky. 'You're getting clumsy, O'Farrell. I heard that one die.'

'Sorry, sor,' said the big Irishman. I'll do better with the next.' His teeth shone from his oily face.

A half-moon slipped from the clouds, illuminating Jack's target. The three-storey tower was hexagonal, built in the previous century by Vauban as part of a network of defences for France. It was surrounded by a low bastion wall and was positioned at the end of a spit of land overlooking the Le Goulet, the strait of water giving access to Brest roads.

The platoon moved forward with practiced stealth, not even

glancing at the bodies, taking up offensive positions as the remainder of the French patrol reached the entrance to the tower's drawbridge, already lowered in readiness. 'That's obliging of the Frogs,' whispered Jack. 'Are the grenadiers in position, Joe?'

'Just there now, sir.' Joe Packer answered, as the four designated men from the grenadier company reached their selected positions.

The entrance to the polygonal tower was via a double-door gate, which opened lazily, the returning guards not expecting the explosions that sent body parts screaming as the marines used their limited supply of improvised grenades with deadly effect. The hours of practice on Southsea Common that Jack had demanded of the men now paid dividends as the stunned defenders died at the gates.

Marines tore through into the central courtyard, the modest force dividing as Jack had planned and practiced with them. Half made for the tower and its three stages, led by Giles Mountjoy with Sergeant Packer, the other half making for the dozen guns, their barrels poking seaward like fingers of Black Death.

'Fast as you like, Corporal Todd,' he yelled, quickly glancing about. 'I want them all disabled within two minutes. Captain Mountjoy and Sergeant Packer and his men will have dealt with the remaining guards within the time allowed. Or have died in the trying,' he added to the marines' backs as they set about the task of hammering barbed spikes into the touch-holes of the dozen 36-pounders lining the outer wall. 'And don't forget those charges, Todd. Keep them hidden under the carriages as I showed you.'

Musket fire resounded through the tower, a blood-curdling squeal as a man died on a bayonet. 'Please, God. Not one of mine,' he muttered, checking to see the guns being disabled, one by one.

The ground at his feet exploded and he flinched as stone chips spattered against his lower legs. Instinctively, his musket came to the shoulder and, through the swirling snow, he saw a white face at the open window on the uppermost level of the tower. He fired and the face disappeared as his shot splintered brickwork, a foot from the man. 'Hell and damnation!' he shouted, quickly working through the reloading of his weapon, a task he had spent hours perfecting with a blindfold.

Another scream as Giles Mountjoy reached the room and dispatched his would-be assassin in the act of loading for a second attempt; a raised thumb on an extended arm confirmed the tower had been cleared of Frenchmen.

Shouting from his left spun him around and he dropped to one knee as four French guards ran into the courtyard from the accommodation building. 'To me, corporal - on the double!' he bellowed. Corporal Todd with three privates were at his side in seconds, muskets levelled as the Frenchmen lost their confidence and hesitated. The volley fire crashed out, sending smoke rolling back into the marines' faces, bringing flakes of freezing, stinking air into their nostrils. As his vision returned Jack saw one Frenchman standing, white faced, alone and terrified. 'Forfeit your grog ration, Todd, unless you drop him now,' Jack shouted. The man turned and ran, seeking the safety of the building he had just left. The Frenchie reached the door as two muskets beside him fired again, their balls striking the man in the back and left leg, transforming him from a running coward to a dead hero. The entire time taken was less than two minutes, he felt sure, as the corporal's remaining men ran to his side.

'All guns spiked, as ordered, sir,' the corporal panted. 'They will have their work cut out to fix 'em buggers now,' he said, his chest heaving. 'The bags all fitted with short-lengths of slow fuse, sir.

Should 'ave a couple of minutes to get away, Mister Vizzard, no more.'

'Our work here is done, Corporal. Time to be away from this place.'

'You might like to see this, sir,' interjected a breathless Sergeant Packer, handing over a leather satchel. 'Found it with a Frog officer who seemed rather unwilling to part with it. I've had a quick squint and it 'as a bundle of important-looking paper. Lists of what looks like ships and dates and whatnot; pages of numbers, too. God knows what they are; more your thing than mine. Was going to put 'em on the fire I lit up there.' Packer jerked a bloody thumb over his shoulder towards a glow now appearing in a lower window.

'Time enough for that later, Joe. Now we must make an orderly and rapid withdrawal to the boats. Take the rear and watch the back door, will you.'

The platoon left over the drawbridge, Sergeant Packer dropping a bag with a burning fuse behind him as, in Indian file, the marines ran along the track.

The return to the boats was accompanied by loud shouting and screams and the sound of explosions as the cannon within the fortress exploded amidst sporadic musket fire, while the troops stole away and the wind picked up. Freezing sleet stabbed at their faces and Jack grew troubled; worried the exhausted men would find the return too difficult.

'Come on lads,' he called cheerfully. 'Keep your heads up. That was good work tonight. We've dealt the French a punch and I'll see you have a double tot of pusser's rum once back aboard the *Nimble*.'

The platoon reached the beach without incident and quickly collapsed into the boats, Dickie Bird grinned in spite of the cold, 'Good morning, sir. You have fired 'em up; there's sounds of firing everywhere. We need to get back to the ship, Mister Vizzard. The captain is becoming agitated.'

Vizzard looked around and made certain there were no stragglers and that all his men were in the boats. 'Very well, Mister Bird. Shove off,' he ordered, climbing into the boat. The oars rose and fell as the boats crawled with agonizing lack of speed, the slap of water interrupted by a shout from beyond the sleet, '*Qui va là?*'

Dickie Bird pushed the tiller to larboard with one hand, raising his free arm to halt the second boat to his rear. 'Oh shit, a French guard boat,' he whispered. '*Patrouille de la Tour Vauban,*' he muttered through his woollen comforter. 'Best prepare for an encounter, sir,' he said to Vizzard. He pulled his dirk from his belt as Jack slowly drew his sword.

The guard boat bumped into the starboard gunwale, catching the marines off-guard—all but Joe Packer and Michael O'Farrell, who levelled weapons and fired a volley into the French boat, sending two of the Frenchmen into the stern sheets of the craft. Two other guards shouted and fired their weapons too hurriedly, the shots going wide and high. Before the French could recover, a second pair of marines turned and sent another lethal discharge into the boat; one guard was thrown backwards and swallowed by the rising swell. The shouting ceased.

'Good work, Joe,' Jack grunted. 'Now let's get away from here before another of the bastards catch us.'

The air temperature was lower, turning pale skin raw. Within minutes they were back aboard *Nimble,* her captain watching the low, leaden clouds scudding by as the small and crowded vessel that had become his life slipped silently and unseen through Le Goulet, aided by a fast-flowing ebb tide of five knots and chased out into the welcome solitude of the Atlantic by flurries of snow.

* * *

Three glasses of brandy were poured by a smiling Silas Matheny, captain's steward and general factotum, the heat of it welcome in the cold, damp atmosphere of the cabin.

'Christ on the Cross, that's what I needed,' said Mountjoy. 'I was shaking so much I reckoned on my teeth falling out.'

'Hah, dear man, I was startled at the ease of the thing. They simply were not expecting any assault, which is in truth an oddity, considering the history of the place. I truly expected greater resistance.' Jack appeared more relaxed than he felt. 'We could have achieved more, I feel. Pass the Frog satchel would you please? I think I should see what intrigued Joe Packer so much.'

He pulled at the straps and opened the bag, extracting a slim bundle of loose papers wrapped in waxed paper and spreading them on the table.

His knowledge of the French language remained poor and he passed a couple of letters to John Lapenotière. 'Take a look at these, would you, John. You likely understand the language more readily than I.'

Beneath the letters were two other documents, but they were not in the French language. The plain sheets were covered in clusters of numbers; hundreds of groups of three, four, five and six integers. It made no sense to Jack at all.

'These are coded correspondence, damn and damn again! I cannot even tell from whom they originate nor the recipients. They must be delivered to Pitt. He will know what to do with them, I have no doubt.'

'The Alien Office has some ability in such matters I hear, Jack,' said Mountjoy. 'That or the Post Office. Documents taken from

French prisoners are invariably sent there, according to my colonel.'

'That's as may be, Giles, but I report to the king's minister and only to him, so I must ask our host to see we are returned to London with as much speed as possible.' He raised the glass to Lapenotière.

'Alas, Jack, the same wind that fetched us out of Brest will provide a challenge to our up-channel swim! I will do the best with the wind we have, but may have to put you ashore at Falmouth and leave you to overland to Whitehall.'

'So be it, John. But with Pitt I must speak, and as soon as possible, as I fancy these papers will contain news of which he will be eager to know.'

The weather was against them. For the next two days *Nimble* made little progress, beating her way east, only to be pushed down channel again and again. Her captain rarely left the deck, save for brief spells to eat or to snatch ten minutes of spare and light sleep.

On the third day, Falmouth Bay opened before their raw faces and crusted hair.

CHAPTER 14

The birth of a boy was celebrated in Woodchester as the leaves turned from vibrant green to yellow and gold and multiple shades of brown, falling from the beech trees as the fields hardened with the first of the winter's frosts and as the village children pushed barrows laden with effigies of Guy Fawkes stuffed with straw and paper. They gathered firewood, all manner of combustibles, food, drink and pennies from wealthier neighbours.

Mary, her adopted daughter Annie and Helena Squires had been walking home after attending church at St Giles, as a troupe of excited children skipped along, chanting:

> 'Don't you remember
> The fifth of November,
> 'Twas Gunpowder Treason Day...'

They both smiled and, delving into purses, produced several copper farthings and halfpenny coins, which sent the children whooping with excitement. As they climbed the hill to Lampern, Mary stooped, clasping her belly, and groaned. She breathed deeply and sat quietly on a low, dry stonewall, recognising it as one that she and Jack had shared so many years before.

'Oh Mary,' said Helena, 'has your time arrived?' The talk had been of little else during recent weeks, as Mary's belly swelled and as the ladies continued to enjoy the peace and security offered by the Gloucestershire countryside. They felt safe at Lampern, and had made friends with several families in the Stroud area.

As she spoke, one of the new scullery maids arrived following slowly behind with a basket of meats from the local butcher. The girl, no more than thirteen or fourteen, hesitated to speak, but smiled shyly. 'Megan, oh Megan, what a relief to see you here, girl. Do run to the house, child. Leave the basket. Mistress Vizzard is... very near her time. Pray hurry and tell Neave. He'll know what to do.'

'How my back aches, Helena. I do believe my child is preparing to enter this world. Ow, ooh I should stand, perhaps that will ease me.'

'Oh Lord, I have no experience of these things, Mary. Pray, tell me how I may assist you, please,' Helena implored her friend.

'Goodness, I have no idea. In our time together, Jack and I have lost one; in New Holland, but we believed it to be due to our poor diet. We near starved to death there, Helena. It has taken Jack all this time to regain his vigour. Now he has... he is away playing soldier once more, when I need him here!' she cried. 'I am sorry, I do not mean to be self-pitying, but I do so miss him, Helena.'

'Then as soon as we are back at the house, I will write to their lordships and urge them to release him from duty, Mary. There are many others to do the government's work.' Hooves thudded, as from the bend ahead, Neave, the family's butler and general factotum, appeared driving a cart behind one of Sir Henry's horses, anxiety furnishing his reddened forehead, with his wife, Madeline, next to him. They pulled up and the old man slowly lowered himself to the ground, hands extended. 'Now then, mistress, step here and we'm be taking care of you. I sent young Megan to fetch Doctor Steele and Mrs Bidgood from the village to aid thee. Careful now, here's the step. And Sir Henry is mathering around the house in a right muddle, not knowing what to do or say! May be a fine lawyer, but... well, make thee comfortable and we'm have you home in a trice.'

The boy—Mary thought to name him Henry Frederick John, thus joining her father's name with that of her father-in-—was born on Guy Fawkes night. The children of the village were enjoying apple-bobbing and hot pies and bowls of warming soup, much of which was due to the beneficence of Sir Henry, who enjoyed the annual celebrations with the same enthusiasm as the children. The night sky above the village was showered with coloured lights and explosions, sending the younger children screaming and the older ones shouting with excitement, as a full-size effigy of the Catholic traitor burned on a magnificent pyre in the middle of the village green.

Mary watched from the nursery room at the top of the house, and felt a sense of immense peace as she nursed the infant at her breast. She had provided her man with the son he secretly craved. She fell asleep smiling.

* * *

The horses pulling the Salisbury Flying Machine finally succumbed to fatigue as they snorted and stumbled into the yard of the *Red Lion Inn*, at Basingstoke. Jack, too, was travel weary and in need of refreshment. The journey had already involved a dozen or more stops and changes of horses. Bodmin, Launceston, through

Devon, Dorset and now Hampshire, the post inns en route already fading memory. His bones ached from the constant bouncing and shaking. He longed for a hot bath and a hearty meal. His eyes were red and his face dark with growth. He scratched at his cheek. After two days and a night of travelling they still had another fifty miles or so before he could present himself at the Admiralty with the documents captured at Brest. They did not hear or see the lone rider slowly following them, and who disappeared into the shadows of Wote Street.

'Come, Jack,' said Giles, 'I believe we have earned an hour of peace, a shave and some of May's Ale.'

The coachman, making a note in his log, looked askance, spitting into the street and said, 'You'll have twenty minutes, sirs. Not a minute more nor a minute less, as this is the king's mail and can wait for no man!'

Giles Mountjoy, with aching limbs and eyes half-closed, could only nod in assent and followed Jack through the door of the old inn. Candlelight danced along the panelled walls of the hall leading to the interior of the inn.

'Landlord, two tankards of May's Ale and a room to freshen and shave afore we continue our journey,' Jack hailed the proprietor as he stepped forward from the gloom of the shadows.

'Yes, sirs, please make you comfortable aside the fire and Bessie here will prepare some hot water. Make yourselves free with the room at the top of the stairs on the left, at your leisure, gentlemen. Bessie will call you when all is ready.'

Jack slumped in a worn leather armchair, enjoying the warmth generated by the logs in the inglenook, as the innkeeper produced two large foaming pewter tankards of locally brewed ale.

'By God, it tastes good, Giles,' said Jack. 'Does it not?'

'I declare it the finest ale outside of Gloucestershire, m'friend,' replied Giles, seated opposite in an identical chair. 'Lord, I am so damned weary, yet we have more than fifty miles to go, and for what? I do hope those French despatches mean something to Their Lordships. I fear they will prove to be not worth the exertions of delivering them.' He spoke quietly as he rubbed the sleep from his eyes.

'We will know more once they have been decrypted, Giles,' he retorted, 'and the sooner we can ensure they are in the right hands, the happier I will be. Now, I see the chamber is prepared, so I suggest we shave the whiskers and freshen ourselves in readiness for Their Lordships' receptions.' Jack rose from the chair, stretching the tiredness from his arms.

'Before we do, Jack, I seek your counsel on a matter that has exercised my mind of late.' He paused as Jack returned to his armchair. 'I have an offer of an exchange of commissions. I wish to join a more er... shall I say a more energetic, distinguished regiment. I mean the Corps, he added carefully. 'Jack, damn it, I'm of a mind to join the Marines as you know, but have a contract waiting to join a proper line regiment, the 29th. Have a chap willing to sell me his commission; the militia is not for me now we are at war. But damn, I've found nothing short of a captaincy at an extortionate sum of four hundred pounds. What say you, old chap? Would you speak up for me, do you think?'

'Certainly, Giles, you know I will. A formality, I assure you. The Corps is seeking to enlarge its establishment and there will be a place for you. You will not have to purchase a commission. We will arrange matters on the morrow. Now, we must wash the dust from our faces and sharpen our wits. Then we'll take a modest repast and be on our way to London with not a moment to be lost.'

In the room ten minutes later, Jack was freshly shaved and washed, changed into a fresh shirt and pulling a brush through his hair, as Giles pulled his boots on after replacing his socks.

A gruff, incoherent voice accompanied a soft knock at the door, 'Got some vittles and wine for you, sirs; master's orders.'

'Oh come in,' said Jack, irritated at the intrusion.

The door opened swiftly with a creak. As Jack turned to speak to his friend, the explosion of noise in the small, dim room seemed to close his ears. A shadow moved across his vision of the servant entering the room, not with a platter of food and drink, but with a pistol in his hand. Then he realised the shadow was Giles's body, leaping across the space and falling in a crumple at his feet, blood pumping from a hole in his chest. All this appeared slowly, as life itself slowed to a heart-stopping, dread-filled motion.

He reacted slowly to the unbelievable, feet leaden, hands heavy until the awful reality registered in his numbed brain. The intruder had shot his closest friend and was about to discharge the second pistol, but it didn't fire. The man was staring at the inutile weapon, as rage tore through Jack's now mobilised brain. With the roar of an aggressive lion, he snatched up his sword from the table, the scabbard flying on a journey of its own. In the dim light he recognised a scarred Major Squires, but he did not hesitate. The blade, always kept sharp, nearly severed the man's head, sticking instead in the left side of his neck, opening muscles and the left carotid artery, creating a pulsing fountain of blood as the man fell dying at Jack's feet.

He pulled the sword free, threw the weapon aside and dropped to his knees to speak to his friend.

'Oh, Christ on the Cross, Giles, why? Dear God in Heaven, for what did you do this thing? He held Giles's face between his hands.

'You gallant man, you fool, you damned fool....'

'It comes dark now, Jack. My life is ending, I fear, and... it grows cold. So cold... Jack... there is one thing... it has been on my mind for many a year and I must... must speak of... Barnfield.' He coughed blood onto his crumpled shirt. 'You know of what I speak. I did deduce what you did the night you fled. The day Mary was convicted...You knew I would... I never... never spoke of it... not to a soul. Take care of my Louise, I beg....' He coughed more blood and wheezed as his life ebbed away.

Desolate, Jack wept.

* * *

'They are starving, Mister Vizzard. Such is the content of the correspondence you have brought us. I had suspected as much,' said Pitt, 'but what comes as a matter of some surprise is the lengths to which the rogues will go to manage their parlous state. They have courted the Americans, who will provide for them, for their own ends I have no doubt.'

Jack Vizzard took the glass proffered by Williams, the Prime Minister's servant, and sat in the easy chair in his rooms in Downing Street.

'We have some clever gentlemen in a secret office near Abchurch Lane, Vizzard. They produce quite marvellous intelligence from various sources; the documents you liberated from Brest, and the information on the contents of the harbour there, have been analysed and deciphered. The rogues have been negotiating with the Americans for months; they have laid plans for a substantial merchant fleet, a convoy, to carry corn and other foodstuffs. An escort and the Brest fleet are to accompany the convoy.'

'Then there will be work for the Channel Fleet, sir; and the prospect of battle.'

'I believe that to be a necessity, Vizzard. We simply must find and capture the convoy, or see to its destruction. Thanks to you, we have the knowledge to ensure our success. The commander of the Channel Fleet, my Lord Howe, has the information now.'

Three days had passed since Giles's murder in Basingstoke. Jack had stayed to make arrangements with an undertaker to prepare and store his friend. Letters had been written and despatched, arrangements made for his friend's return to Gloucestershire, and his own, as soon as Their Lordships of the Admiralty granted leave to do so. The letter to Louise was especially painful to write, the paper tear-stained. The note to Mary all too brief, scratched in a shaking hand, heavy with grief. To the undertaker engaged to attend to the late Major Squires, he left instructions to send a bill to the Admiralty, with a copy and a brief note addressed to the commandant general of the Corps.

'Sir, the country cannot engage the Americans, too. We will be pressed hard to fight the French, as you are too well aware. What will you do with this knowledge, sir?'

'That is a matter for my government, Mister Vizzard. You are here to receive my thanks for the performance of a dangerous duty. However, I can tell you I intend to do all in my power to prevent the French being supplied with grain from the Americas. I will have discussion, and no doubt protracted debate, with my colleagues and see how best to counter this threat. I dare say you will find you are involved in some manner, have no fear.'

'What of the Frenchwomen, D'Aubusson, sir? Do you have word?'

'Ah, yes. She has returned to her own country, Lieutenant.' Pitt's eyes drilled into Jack's, the unspoken question evident there. 'She works for me, Lieutenant. Did you not know? Even now I receive messages from her and her acquaintances. She is a most valuable ally of ours. I hope soon to receive more news of the French plans. That convoy must be destroyed, Vizzard.'

Jack realised his mouth was open and he closed it rapidly. Pitt's explanation was plausible, likely true indeed, but Jack was incredulous. 'I trust you will relay my thanks, sir,' he nearly stammered, 'the next time you have occasion to communicate with her.'

The images of former occupants of the house stared accusingly at William Pitt, challenging him, exhorting him to follow their example for better or worse. The simple truth, as Pitt understood clearly, was Britain had at her disposal only one strategic fleet; the Channel fleet commanded by Richard, Earl Howe, and presently it was under-manned and almost certainly insufficient to meet the new French threat. He was acutely aware of the fact.

'However, since you have performed your country such valuable service,' Pitt continued, 'the Channel Fleet must prevent the French from landing their imports; I will have their fleet destroyed first. I would see them burned or sunk or taken captive. It matters little to me, but the evil that is the new French nation must not be permitted to flourish. We owe our present happiness and prosperity, Mister Vizzard, which has never been equalled in the annals of mankind, to a mixture of monarchial government. Not the invidious, atheist domination of a people such as we now witness across the Channel. Thank God those waters keep our country remote from such evil.'

Pitt leaned forward in his chair, the determined gaze lighting up for a moment. 'Now, Lieutenant, I understand you grow tired of my game of espionage and seek a return to er, more orthodox duties. I have a meeting with some naval officers who may be willing to assist you. Where are you lodging? Would you care to join us at m'club? Make up a four at a table?

'Sir, I would be most honoured. I will stay at The Turk or Evans Hotel, I have used both before.' Many years ago now he thought. 'Who are the officers?' he said aloud. 'You refer to White's, sir?

'Indeed I do, White's is where I take some leisure, although less frequently now, and pray, patience, Mister Vizzard. "*How poor are they that have not patience.*" May I suggest we meet at eight? I shall leave word at the door you are my favoured guest.'

Jack accepted the polite dismissal with grace and left the decaying building, hailing a cab once he reached Whitehall. As in years past, Jack was awed by the bustle and noise of the city. Rarely had he seen so many animals and people in congregation before, and he longed for the tranquil green rolling pastures and streams of Gloucestershire.

The cab crawled along the hardened, rutted road, conscious of the falling temperatures, as the city business life drew to a close and gentlemen returned to their homes or their clubs or their favoured bagnio.

The cab halted outside the Evans Hotel in the north-west corner of Covent Garden. The fine red-brick building amused him. The frontage resembled the forecastle of a ship, which is what Jack now wanted. He had wearied of stealthy landings on alien soil, of spending too long slithering in ditches and watching ports and harbours for endless hours.

'A room for two nights, if you please,' Jack said to the smartly dressed man who approached, 'one to the front, if you will.'

'Yes, sir. Please follow me, Your Honour.'

The man escorted him to the first floor, a wide, sweeping

staircase rising slowly around the periphery of the large entrance hall. Jack heard the voices in the dining room rising as more and more joined the throng, seeking supper and musical entertainment for the evening. His head ached after the strain of travel and interrogation by the king's prime minister. Now he faced an evening of cards with some naval officers. He played, one had to, but he hated losing, which he did rarely.

The room was comfortable if compact. An iron bed was set against a wall, a chair neatly positioned by the solitary window and paper lining the walls—a neo-classical style with Grecian urns and goddesses in a flock finish.

Jack sat at the window and stared out into the evening, thoughts of Giles's death filling his mind. As ever, he questioned his actions, or his failures. Could he have known of the assassin's presence? Should he have observed him en route? The enemy was everywhere, it seemed, and his lack of awareness, his inattention, had led directly to the death of his best friend. In that moment he vowed revenge on every Frenchman he encountered. The anger burned within him.

* * *

Two hours later, rested but melancholic, he climbed the steps to the entrance to *White's*, the club popular with Billy Pitt, as members of the public often referred to the king's minister.

The gaming room was already filling as the master, Griffin, first approved Jack, with a distinct air of obsequiousness, before pointing him in the direction of Pitt's table, in the far corner, behind a heavy draped curtain.

Jack walked slowly, with as much nonchalance as he could muster, regretting his acceptance of the offer as he realised the extent of wealth and personage occupying the room this evening. It had been said that as many as eight dukes could be found dining in the club, and one or two of the bewigged old men could pass for such eminences; Jack had rubbed shoulders with minor aristocracy since boyhood, but the gentlemen members of *White's* were known to be amongst the most wealthy and influential in the kingdom. He could not remove a small sense of awe. Almost before he realised it, he was standing behind Pitt, facing a naval officer of ruddy complexion and greying hair, with eyes that narrowed at Jack's approach.

Pitt placed the cards face down and turned his head. 'Ah, Vizzard. So good of you to come! Harvey, Berkeley, I have the pleasure and honour to introduce Lieutenant Vizzard of His Majesty's marines. Vizzard—Captains Harvey and the Honourable George Berkeley. I forget their ships; no doubt they will apprise you of their respective commands. Gentlemen, this officer is largely responsible for the plans m'brother and I have been developing with My Lord Howe.' Pitt slowly consumed the contents of the claret glass by his cards and continued. 'And the thing is, gentlemen, the fellow seeks an appointment afloat. Seems little enough reward for the trials he has endured on our service. Pray, do take a seat, Vizzard.'

'I'm obliged, sir,' Jack said, nerves pulling at his brain as he sat on the spoon-back chair next to two post captains of the Navy.

'Vizzard, d'you say?' said Captain George Cranfield Berkeley, pouring from one of several bottles on the table. 'Not related to the lawyer in Woodchester, are you? Sir Henry Vizzard?

'My father, sir,' Jack replied.

'I see. I met him last year, as I recall. Your father was of help to my cook when she was... well, no matter. Wouldn't take payment for his work, which struck me as odd behaviour for a lawyer!' He laughed.

Jack smiled. 'Father will work *pro bono* on occasion, for a worthwhile cause, sir.' He relaxed. A little.

'I thought it most decent in him, so I sent him a brace from the castle and a case of Warre's port. Least I could do.' Berkeley was the owner of a castle in Gloucestershire, close to the banks of the river Severn, which had been in his family since the twelfth century. Captain Berkeley continued to gaze on the younger man before him, wondering exactly what it was had brought him approbation from such a person as the king's premier minister.

'Didn't realise your people were of the legal sort, Vizzard,' Pitt said. 'I read at Pembroke, you know.'

'Indeed, sir, I am aware of your family's preference for Cambridge. I followed my father to Oriel and was called in '84. I practiced for only a short period, I have to confess, before taking my commission.'

'A most curious... how would you gentlemen say... a change of wind?'

'A tack, sir,' said Berkeley, 'we change tack in order to alter course, depending on the direction of the wind and the desired course.'

'Alternatively, sir, we are known to wear; but only should a change of tack be impossible or impractical,' said Harvey.

'All Greek to me, I'm bound to say,' said Pitt. Now the reason I am here, gentlemen, other than the conviviality of your company, is to seek your support for m'friend here. I am in his debt. Indeed, England will owe him too, should his recent endeavours and ahem, the intelligence he has gathered, prove accurate. The Admiralty will increase the establishment of the Corps of Marines, and will dispose of officers as they deem necessary, but I did hope one of you fellows would find room for an officer of some resource?'

'Sir,' said Captain Harvey, 'it appears I lack sufficient lobster-backs, but I am given to understand I could have a Captain.'

'Fiddlesticks and nonsense, Harvey. Another officer, of whatever rank, will be welcome on your ship I have no doubt. I will pass a note this evening and we may consider it arranged. I trust the arrangements are satisfactory, Vizzard?'

Jack inclined his head in acknowledgement. 'I am obliged to you, sir, should it meet with Captain Harvey's approval.'

'As you gentlemen will soon learn, I mean to cause the French good reason to pause and reflect on the aggressive position they have adopted.'

'May I enquire how it is to be achieved, sir?' enquired Harvey.

'You will learn soon enough and through your Commander In Chief, Earl Howe. Plans gentlemen, take time to formulate and implement. Suffice it to say you will be back with your ships sooner than you may believe at present.'

Two pairs of eyes raised slightly, the news welcome to their owners' ears. As captains in the Channel fleet, they had spent too long cruising the waters around the French coast with nothing to show for their labours, save tired crews and wear to the fleet's ships.

They now wanted to prove the superiority of both.

CHAPTER 15

'I have a week, at best, Mary; that is all. Then I am required to report to Portsmouth. I join the *Brunswick,* after all.'

'Oh Jack, it is so unfair. You have been in so much danger of late and now you choose to go to sea and... I know, I hate it. I simply loathe the service at times. I see so little of you as it is, my dearest.'

'My darling Mary,' he said, handing his son back to his wife, 'we are at war with our ancient enemy, and the threat to our nation is patently real. I have learned much this last twelve-month. This revolution is as brutal and despicable as anything history has shown us. Johnny Crapaud is building a fleet of invasion vessels across the Channel. I know this to be true, for I have seen them and, indeed, on one occasion, destroyed many of them.' He stood up and paced the room in his anxiety. 'Would you wish to see the French invading our England and young Freddy here being taught the French at his school?'

He thought back to the night with the fires burning and barrels of powder exploding with fearsome power. Two men had been lost that night and three more injured, never to fight again.

Mary huffed and exclaimed, 'I certainly would not!' She

continued in a softer voice, 'Mister Brice sent a note for you some days ago, in the hope you would have some time at home. He is devastated by the news of poor dear Giles, and asks if you would see him on your return.' She passed a note to him, the black ink in a shaky, unpractised hand.

'Yes, he will be grieving, as are we all. I had half-forgotten Old Brice. He was a sea-daddy to us when we were young. I should see him.'

'You should, my love. Go this evening before dinner. But do not stay late. I know how you can be distracted in his company.'

* * *

Within a few minutes he had saddled his old horse, Humbert, donned a woollen cloak and was gently riding down the hard, rutted lane to the inn of fond memory.

Brice's glum features opened and a thin, sad smile appeared on his face as Jack strode through the room, arms extended.

'My dear friend,' he said, as the old man held him close, breathing heavily and smelling of ale and cider, a heady mix that caught Jack's nostrils in an instant memory. He felt at home here.

'Master Jack, my dear boy. So happy I am to see you again.' The old man took him to a corner table, nodding at the barmaid, who noted the silent order and poured a golden liquid into two large pewter tankards. 'Here we are at your table, Master Jack. You and he always sat here in the old days.' His eyes moistened and he casually knuckled the corner of his left eye. 'Here's young Sally with ale. I'll let thee have a pull or two, then I needs to 'ear the story, or as much of it as you can tell me.'

Requiring no further instruction, Jack drank several large gulps of the light, honey coloured ale, licked his lips and sat back in the chair.

'He died saving my life, Bricey. A nobler friend a man never had.' He spoke softly, swallowing a lump rising in his throat. 'We were followed by a traitorous spy, a former comrade in the Corps and my superior officer, but a spy in the pay of the French, nonetheless. I had tried to kill him before, the bastard; I discovered his treachery in France, when he would have had me executed in Paris, handed over to Madame Guillotine.'

'When you were in France,' said Brice. 'What were you doing in...?'

'I cannot answer you, Bricey. It was on government business, is all I can tell you. I miss him greatly. He was planning on joining the Corps, as he wished to see more action.'

'Well I dunno about you lads muckin' about in France, but I hopes you caused 'em a headache or two. It were them bastards did fer me leg,' he said, rubbing the left knee. 'I remember the two of you and your brother George...' Brice hesitated at the sharp look thrown at him.

Jack shrugged, dismissing the thought, chasing the ghost of his missing brother from the conversation. 'Now, here is the thing, Bricey, I'm worried that Major Squires, for such is who he was, indeed my company commander, did not work alone. A French woman who escaped from France with me, but whom I fear I cannot trust, aided me. We parted company at Deal and I have not seen her again. By extraordinary circumstance, she even met our Billy Pitt.'

Jack pulled a small tin from his pocket, extracted a cigar and lit it from the candle on the table. He explained, briefly, the events of the night he was captured at the beach and how Vanessa d'Aubusson had saved him from Squires.

'You see, Bricey, Mr Pitt confides that the lady is one of his agents. But perhaps I ain't as convinced of her loyalty as he. We parted with Mr Pitt taking it upon himself to assist her, but I fear she may now be searching for me and I am uneasy in my mind. Even now, I cannot be certain as to her true allegiance, her intentions or motives. She may be what she claims and Billy Pitt believes; but then, she is also capable of duplicity and if she should discover my whereabouts, Bricey... well, you understand my anxiety, I am sure.' Jack glanced around the dimly lit room, as if half expecting the subject of his anxiety to appear.

'Indeed I can, but why... if she shot your Major Squires?' Brice reasoned.

'Because, my friend, I now believe she had decided he was compromised and with his identity known, would be of no further use to her; so I have reasoned in my own mind, as I offered her the opportunity to travel to London. In truth, I do not know the answer. She may be entirely authentic, yet... yet there exists a doubt, something intangible, perhaps no more than the mystery that enhances any woman of beauty; for my friend, she is certainly a beautiful woman.' He blew a circle of smoke toward the ceiling.

'Master Jack, no French sounding woman would go un-noticed in these parts. The county is nervous as buggery at the thought of a fleet of Frenchies swimming up the Severn, never mind a foreign talking lass. Do not fret on it now; I will keep my eyes and ears wide open and spread the word in the right quarters, have no fear of that, boy.'

He stole a casual look around the room, as if also half expecting to see the object of their conversation walk boldly into his beloved inn. 'Beg pardon, Master Jack. Should call you sir now, you holding the king's commission an' all.'

'We must be prepared, Bricey. We live in dangerous times and the enemy may be in our midst even now. Be alert to any strangers, old friend; all may not be as they, or she, might appear. Her English is good, with barely a trace of accent, so we cannot be fools and expect her to arrive with a tricolour flag and singing La Carmagole!'

'Singing what, Master Jack?' said Brice.

'Never mind, Brice, never mind. It's a song of the Frog's revolution; it's a sailor's song from Marseille and the sans-culottes sing it their taverns—and we will not hear it in England. Not if I have any say in things.'

* * *

The parish church of Saint Mary in Painswick was very old. Jack recalled from his studies at King's, the church having been recorded in Domesday. The spire, weathered as it was from its exposed position and pointing the way to heaven, was pockmarked; Cromwell's forces had occupied the church against those of Royalist forces during the siege of Gloucester, and the damage had never been repaired. The spire laid a shadow across the churchyard as the sun failed to warm the congregation, stepping with lowered heads through the gallery to the north aisle.

A large gathering of family and friends had collected at the ancient church where the body of Jack's oldest and closest friend had been planted in the cold earth, the bluebells around the graveyard bringing a splash of welcome colour to what had been one of the darkest of days. Members of the South Gloucestershire Yeomanry provided a guard of honour. Jack and Mary and the children were dressed in black, which suited Jack's mood. The anger burned within him like a gunner's slow match.

'Grant this mercy, O Lord, we beseech Thee, to Thy servant departed, that he may not receive in punishment the requital of his deeds who in desire did keep Thy will, and as the true faith here united him to the company of the faithful, so may Thy mercy unite him above to the choirs of angels. Through Jesus Christ our Lord. Amen.'

The priest intoned the final ritual and Jack and Mary led Lady Louise, Giles's widow, to the carriage, where her tears flowed, after being held at bay throughout the service. Her father, Lord Ducie, took her in his arms and comforted his daughter, not having words to do so.

Jack and Mary's daughter, Annie, stood holding her mother's hand, as Mary and the wet-nurse examined the latest addition to the Vizzard family, 'Baba Freddie,' as he had come to be called by Annie, and who, oblivious to the solemnity of the occasion, was gurgling with pleasure.

Bill Brice, unashamed, wept like a baby.

CHAPTER 16

Captain John Harvey, in command of *Brunswick*, was a prime seaman. He thought so. His peers amongst the captains on the Admiralty list thought so. His men thought so. After nigh on forty years at sea, he knew as much of war as his sponsor, Richard Earl Howe, the admiral in command of the impressive fleet in which he now served. Harvey had fought in the Seven Years War, the American War, and had been Robert Duff's flag captain during the Great Siege of Gibraltar.

Highly regarded by Earl Howe, Harvey held his present command at Howe's particular request. He loved the ship as much as he loved his wife, Judith. She often teased that his greatest love was his ship.

But my, she is a beauty, he thought as he paced his pitching quarterdeck. He momentarily thought of his wife as he looked at the standing rigging, the full sails and the men about the tasks, wondering if he would be back in Kent in time for his birthday next month. A strong, well-built man of fifty-three years, he had been in the Navy since turning thirteen years of age. Bushy, dark eyebrows set in a rounded face surmounted kindly grey-green eyes, and his thick grey hair swept back, revealing a high, broad forehead, stained by exposure to salt and sunlight. Having lived well, he had developed a double chin beneath his full mouth.

'Mister Bevan, I'll thank thee to keep the fore-course under control; I noted a shiver this instant.' He spoke quietly and not unkindly to his second lieutenant. A good man, he thought, but it would do no harm for him to think his captain was checking on his work. The lieutenant acknowledged the comment with a nod and a hand to his temple, with a barely audible 'Sir.'

Seventy-four guns and a crew, albeit short-handed, but a crew trained to use them. Yes, she was a smart ship. He took a few paces around the deck enjoying the stiff breeze while keeping an eye on the flagship, *Queen Charlotte*, in the centre of the line, waiting for Howe's signal flags to break out into the breeze.

'There it is,' he said aloud, trying to decipher the code. He had spent several hours studying his admiral's 'Signal Book for Ships of War'; a distillation of Kempenfelt's earlier studies, which reduced the number of signal flags to a mere ten, but providing the fleet under Howe's command with 10,000 pre-determined orders and instructions.

Try as he might, he could not discern the command. 'Mister Bevan, your assistance please, if you would be so kind. Your eyes are younger than mine. What does Lord Howe say?'

'If I read it right, sir,' he replied, a large telescope to his right eye, 'His Lordship makes our number and wishes us to make more sail. I believe he feels we are losing station, sir.'

'I will be damned. Very well Mister Bevan. Please oblige His Lordship and me, by issuing the necessary orders.' He scowled at a midshipman, causing the boy to jump.

Harvey continued his pacing across the canting deck as the second lieutenant shouted a rapid sequence of orders to the watch on deck, bringing *Brunswick* swiftly back on course. 'I have no desire to see such a signal directed at my ship again,' he growled at the men at the helm. He was angrier for his own momentary inattention. The wind drew from the southwest, obliging the fleet to alter course only five minutes later.

Harvey reflected on the days since the Channel fleet had left Spithead on 2 May, escorting a convoy out of the Channel under the lee of Montague's squadron, before heading for the cruising station off Brest. He was pleased and proud of his ship. He commanded it with a firm grip on the crew, and even more firm hold on the officers.

Harvey knew every inch of her and loved her for the powerful warhorse she was. A third rate of seventy-four guns, *Brunswick* had been built at Deptford in '90. Her main gun-deck mounted 28 thirty-two pounders with a similar number of eighteen pounders on the upper gun-deck. Lighter armament was distributed about the forecastle and quarterdeck.

But he was short of men. Seamen he had, although few enough good top-men, and even fewer able seamen, but his gunnery was good, too. One hundred short, all told, he'd reckoned from his muster book. And he lacked marines. Yes, he had some of the 29th Regiment, but they knew little of the business of a ship of the line. He corrected himself; they knew nothing whatever of the business of a ship of the line. It appeared to Captain Harvey that they barely understood their own business of soldiering. They could not serve his guns, nor could they work the running rigging, other than lend some weight when required. They were there to form boarding parties and to be his marksmen in battle.

The marine officer Pitt had introduced had brought a platoon of tough and rough-looking men, who might prove useful. He thought the lieutenant to be zealous. Vizzard had exercised his men daily and was doing so again, now. He watched the lieutenant drilling them about the foremast. Loading, priming, presenting. Each day making them work and move faster, with more cohesion. But damn the man, he was unorthodox. None of his men wore redcoats, but dirty, grey jackets with a colourful variety of headgear. Vizzard's response to his rebuke on the subject of uniforms had been bordering on the insubordinate. 'Yes, sir,' he had said. 'You prefer toy soldiers who look the part but cannot fight, to my fighters, who do not look the part but who can. Understood, sir,' had been the marine's response, with no agreement at all.

But now, watching the manner of their fighting, watching their energy and their speed of action, he wanted more of them. They were different, and the sailors silently acknowledged them, wary and watchful of these barbarian-like men, who shouted and screamed in war-like fashion and raced and fought each other around the deck.

'Mister Vizzard is a most curious officer, do you not think, Bevan?'

Taken aback, the second lieutenant could only agree. He watched Vizzard practice loading with a sea service musket, each time performing faster and more smoothly. 'He is certainly zealous, sir. His methods are not of the accustomed variety, but one has to admit to their effectiveness. If I may say, sir, should we fall in with the French, I feel a certain sense of reassurance. He has them throwing round shot at each other, and one of them, that young corporal, is a juggler such as one might see at the Royal Circus in Lambeth. They are all of them first-class shots, sir. Have you seen that rough sergeant of his? He shot a gull yesterday; the range must have been over fifty yards and he took its head off, clean as you like.

In flight too; it was quite remarkable.'

'I heard tell of it, Bevan. Vizzard is also said to be an excellent shot with a musket, though I have yet to see evidence of it,' said Harvey. 'He is well placed with the government, d'you know. Introduced to me personally by no less a personage than Billy Pitt himself. Seems the man has been conducting clandestine… activities in France. Came close to losing his head, I hear. Be kind of you to have him join us for supper this evening, unless Black Dick has other plans for the fleet, naturally.'

'His Lordship is not entertaining on this cruise, sir. He is keen as mustard to get on station and intercept the French. As are we all.'

* * *

'Mister Bevan approaching, sir,' Sergeant Packer grunted from the corner of his panting mouth. 'I reckon I've earned my grog this evening, sir. You've pushed us all uphill and down dale most of the watch, an' that's no error.'

'Quiet, Joe,' Jack muttered from the side of his mouth. 'Good day to you, Bevan. How goes the cruise?' He addressed the lieutenant with a smile.

'Very well, Vizzard. You have impressed my lord and master this afternoon and I am instructed to request your company at supper. You should feel honoured, as the captain infrequently invites officers to dine.'

'I shall be delighted, naturally. Why now I wonder?' he said.

'Oh some nonsense I expect. Seems to think you and your men will be of value when we come to have our scrap with the Frogs!' Bevan said. 'They do appear a fearsome lot, Vizzard, you must admit of it.'

'They may appear a rough-house gang of thieves and villains and cut-throats, Bevan; indeed that is precisely what many of them are. Or they were. However, I would prefer to have them behind me when I meet the French than those pretty lads from the 29th of Foot. My lads enjoy a good fight and are bloody damned good at it.' His white teeth grinned at the naval lieutenant.

'Dinner should be an enjoyable occasion, Vizzard. The captain is in good cheer and anticipating the coming engagement, for it would be a disappointment to all should we miss the French.' Bevan smiled back, feeling Vizzard's enthusiasm, sharing in it.

'If one must then, I shall endeavour to present a more or better groomed appearance for your lord and master. Uniform coat to please him, I suppose? He impresses as a skilled sailor. Is he a fighting man, though?'

'Oh, upon my word, Vizzard. You will not find a more vigorous and determined officer in the fleet,' replied Bevan. 'Saving, of course, Black Dick. He cannot wait to catch 'em and pound 'em to pieces.'

* * *

'Vizzard. Welcome lad. Take a seat.'

Captain Harvey pointed vaguely at the table, laid with plain linen cloth and common seamen's fiddles, with pewter and wooden mugs in place of the crystal he used when in port. Patched canvas covered the floor, with screens removed to create greater space. Jack noted the following ships in orderly line astern through the stern gallery, the sea a darkening, oily grey, broken by the broadening wake as *Brunswick* sailed the admiral's course. Reassuring sounds of routine activity echoed down from the skylight above.

A number of officers were at the table, some of whom Jack had not yet become familiar with. Harvey bade them introduce themselves, clockwise. He instantly forgot most of them, but noted the token middie, James Lucas, and also the officer commanding the ship's infantrymen, the 29th Regiment of Foot, Captain Alexander Saunders. Rowland Bevan, the only ship's lieutenant he'd had any contact with since coming aboard, sat directly opposite him.

'Good evening to you, Vizzard,' said Captain Saunders of the 29th. 'I'm delighted to have you and your men with us.' The voice was cultured and polite; Saunders was pleased to have another officer under his command. For his detachment of seventy-six private soldiers, he had only a young ensign and two sergeants to assist.

'I am pleased to be aboard, Saunders. Odd to see foot soldiers on a king's ship, but I dare say, we will have need of them afore long.'

Vizzard knew of the shortage of trained marines and the use of line regiments to supplement the shortage aboard the king's ships. He thought them of little use but kept an open mind until they were tested in action against the enemy.

'I will certainly have need of you and your men, Vizzard, if they can shoot as well under fire as I observed this afternoon,' said Saunders.

'They are tested and true, Saunders,' said Jack. 'I have trained them and fought with them. On French soil too!'

Captain Harvey's head jerked up. 'So, it's true, is it, Vizzard? You have been busy in France?'

'Indeed, sir. We have been conducting certain, ah, activities to discomfort the French, sir,' said Jack with a smile.

'A damned sight more than mere activities, Vizzard, as I

understand your recent, er... new acquaintance put it to me when I was last in town.' Harvey's eyes quickly scanned the table as though inspecting the set of his sails. 'Gentlemen, one of the reasons we found ourselves in this fleet is due, in some measure, to the efforts of this officer of marines. I learned from the highest and most reliable of informants that the French plans to purchase grain and other necessities from the Americas became known to His Majesty's government through a combination of documents obtained during Mister Vizzard's various excursions to France.' He beamed at the curious faces to his front.

'From his labour, enterprise and the duty he has performed, we know an extremely large convoy of merchantmen will soon be approaching. Yes, a force commanded by Admiral Vanstabel will escort the fleet. It will be joined by the Brest squadron under Villaret de Joyuese, about whom we know little. Before their revolution, I suspect he was a mere petty officer; their belief in equality, fraternity la-la, seems to ignore experience and seamanship.' Harvey paused to drink from a large glass.

'I offer a toast to Mister Vizzard, the latest addition to our happy band; and confusion to our enemies!'

A murmuring of assent rippled around the table. Eyes looked afresh at the young marine officer, his cheeks now tinged in crimson.

'You must respond to the toast, Vizzard. Come now, let us hear you.' The demand came from Lieutenant Bevan. He thumped the table, rattling the cutlery and glassware.

The ship rolled and Jack grabbed his glass as it slid across the mahogany table towards the young ensign of the 29th, whose name escaped him. 'I thank you for the honour you do me, sir,' with a nod to Captain Harvey, 'which is ill-deserved, and to you gentlemen for your warm welcome.' Then he drank deeply from the glass. 'In truth the honour belongs to my sergeant, for it was he who found the papers. On a Frenchie who was rather reluctant to part with them, I understand!'

Laughter ran around the table as the captain's servants brought a succession of covered tureens and dishes.

'Salomungundy to start with, gentlemen, as the people call it,' Harvey said, 'followed by a beef stew with suet dumplings. 'Tis a favourite o' mine. Take the spoon and use it generously, youngster,' he said to the midshipman. 'I still remember the hunger of the gun-room.' He smiled kindly at the most junior of his guests, a boy of twelve or perhaps thirteen, he thought. 'When is your birthday, Mister Lucas?'

'Next week, sir,' the boy replied in a soft, anxious voice. 'I shall turn fourteen, sir.'

'Then God willing, lad, you shall see a battle of a scale not seen by many in this fleet. I trust you will do your duty and serve our king.'

'Sir,' the boy said, 'I will gladly die to serve my country, sir.' his trembling voice in earnest.

'I fervently pray such sacrifice will not be necessary, my boy. Do your best and obey the officers put above you, and I will be happy.' Harvey smiled at the boy as if at one of his own children, as, in a sense, he was.

'Now Mister Bevan, the wine appears hove-to at your station. Kindly bear down man, and pass it along, there's a good fellow.' Harvey's right arm reached out to gather the bottle and then grinned at his favoured lieutenant. 'I thank you, Mister Bevan.'

'Sir, apropos your comments to our honoured middie, do you care to speculate on when we will meet the French?' Bevan made the enquiry. 'Do we know if they have left Brest?'

'Ha, there's the rub, Mister Bevan. I venture within the week, but who can say? We will take a look in at Brest Roads and see what we shall see. Rear Admiral Montague is hunting for the convoy now and His Lordship has detailed his ideas for attacking them when found, in several circumstances; that is to say he has an open mind as to how we deal with them. However, deal with them we shall, and most thoroughly, mark my word, Bevan.' He spread his hands wide. 'I am confident of a glorious victory against the French fleet. They are revolutionaries, so will fight with vigour, I have no doubt, but we are dealing with a foe much weakened by Robespierre, who has surely decapitated the best France has.'

Jack Vizzard cleared his throat, 'Beg pardon, sir, but as I perceive the purpose of our cruise, we should chiefly consider the grain convoy the French admiral has been sent to protect and escort into safe harbour, should we not? It would be a great and glorious thing to defeat his fleet in battle, for certain, but our prime purpose is to capture or destroy the grain and beef that the Americans are sending to feed the revolutionaries. It must be the chief object, in my humble submission.' Jack smiled at the captain.

'Hah, a lobster-back with a mind to fleet tactics, hey?' The captain chuckled, others joining him. 'Well, Mister Vizzard, may I counsel you to leave such matters to Earl Howe and his captains. We do know our business here.'

Jack felt the bemusement of the officers rather than the argument he anticipated. Tension was absent from the room. 'I intended no disrespect, sir, and Earl Howe is rightly regarded as our finest admiral. I merely wished to suggest that as a matter of national strategy our efforts would be better directed to intercepting and capturing the grain convoy, rather than engaging in a bloody and uncertain encounter with a sizable fleet of Robespierre's warships.' He paused to fork buttered potato and deliver it to his mouth. Swallowing quickly, he continued, 'I am aware the fleet is undermanned, sir, and a fight with the fanatical French might prove a costly affair, do you not think?

'We shall have both, Vizzard. As I stated, Rear Admiral Montague has been detached with a force to deal with the convoy, and we have a fleet powerful enough to deal with the Brest fleet, of that I am confident.'

'Whichever of them we meet then, sir, it appears we are in for a fight,' Jack replied.

* * *

The ensuing days and weeks passed all too slowly, with tensions rising at each report of an unknown sail, which never proved to belong to the enemy. Intelligence gathered from passing merchantmen was sparse and confusing. No word came from Montague's detached squadron, and the endless drill began to pall with even the best of Jack's men.

Eyes were constantly straining, seeking a focal point on the horizon in every direction, but chiefly to the west. Seamen blinked away salt tears as they stood braced on decks, wondering who would be the first to detect the other's fleet. Eyes reddened staring at the eternal, wavering liquid horizon; was that a sail or a surge of foam on a distant wave-top? Was that the hull of a ship or a cloud? If a ship, is it a friend or a foe? What is her course? Would today bring death or glory? Or worse; maimed for life from the loss of limb.

Then, on the morning of Wednesday 28 May, a sharp-eyed

lookout on *HMS Phaeton*, one of Howe's scouting frigates, spied a sail.

The fleet was four hundred thirty miles west of Ushant, according to Lieutenant Rowland Bevan's estimate when he came on deck at three bells in the morning watch. He checked the slate and noted the fleet's course as west of south west, as the flagship, *Queen Charlotte*, threw out a signal sending a powerful charge through the entire British fleet as soon as it could be discerned: signal number one—enemy in sight! The word spread throughout the ship in a moment. All those permitted on deck, and several who were not, found themselves staring ahead and estimating when the battle would commence. The chatter flew about the *Brunswick* until silenced by the captain's appearance on deck. He scowled them into a watchful calm, waiting for battle to be joined between the two fleets. It was not that day, to the frustration of all, the hours passing with agonising lack of progress until the admiral signalled, at ten that morning, to tack in succession, followed quickly by signal number seven: general chase.

'Oh Lord,' said Bevan to nobody in particular, 'this is to be a drawn-out business today.'

'Why is that, sir?' asked Midshipman Lucas.

'Because, dear boy, the admiral cannot position the fleet to best advantage. We will spend the day chasing their tail and be damned lucky to see a Frenchie afore nightfall.'

'We have to follow the flag, sir,' said Lucas.

'Oh yes, indeed, Mister Lucas. We must follow the flag. The difficulty is, we will never get within range of even the rear of the Frogs. If we could but cut their line in several points at once... now, that would see us in a pell-mell, only-the-best-will-succeed kind of fight. That is what I suspect Howe seeks, but it will take us hours in this weather to even touch their rear.'

'Why so, sir?' The young man asked.

Lieutenant Bevan paced to the weather side, followed meekly by the midshipman and said, 'smell the wind, Mister Lucas. What do you smell?'

'Is it cook preparing breakfast, sir? I swear I could eat a horse this morning.' The middie licked his lips to emphasise his point.

Midshipmen were always hungry, thought Bevan. 'Midshipmen are always hungry,' he said aloud. 'I was and all in my gunroom were too. It improves only in modest degree once one obtains a commission,' he grunted, taking up his glass once more, to study the flagship as she glided through the silver sea. He thought he picked out gold lace on the quarterdeck, wondering if it were Howe or his flag captain, Sir Roger Curtis.

'Admiral is signalling, Mister Lucas: preparatory. Let us see how quickly you can decipher it, please.'

Lucas pulled himself monkey-like up the larboard ratlines and onto the mizzen's fighting top as the signal flags whipped open, where he had a good line of sight. He held onto a shroud, pulling a small telescope to his eye for half a minute. Then, tucking it away, a notebook and the stub of a pencil appeared from his jacket and made some rapid notes.

'To *Bellorophon*, sir. Admiral Pasley is to take the flying squadron and reconnoitre strange sails to the south. It has to be the French, sir!' He shouted down to the deck, made his way to the backstay and slid down in a few seconds, leaping to the deck nimbly, just as Captain Harvey announced his own arrival on deck.

'Have we found the enemy, Mister Bevan?' Harvey could not contain the excitement he felt, his eyes sparkling with anticipation.

'It does appear so, sir. I'll send more lookouts to the main and foretop to keep a particular eye on the flagship and His Lordship's manoeuvres, sir,' he replied. 'Shall we bring the people to quarters, sir?' he asked.

'Not yet, Mister Bevan,' Harvey answered in his cultured voice, 'let us wait on developments, shall we. There is plenty of time to get the men ready.' Harvey pulled his own telescope from under his arm, a four-draw instrument by Benjamin Martin that his brother had gifted him on his taking command of *Brunswick*., The ship slowly rolled beneath his feet. 'Mister Lucas, your shoulder, if you will; I need a support.'

The midshipman obliged, allowing the captain to rest his telescope on the young man's left shoulder, as he gazed along the line of the British fleet. 'Ain't that a sight, sir?' The youngster grinned, enjoying the moment and the wind on his cheek.

'A rare sight indeed, Mister Lucas. One I may never see again in my lifetime.' Harvey grunted in approval and pulled the telescope close with a smooth, slow movement. The great line of canvas cathedrals sailed onward, the tension rising in the hearts of the men who drove them.

* * *

Later, John Harvey watched as the French fleet came into view, and there they remained for some hours, with the French hove-to, while a large three-decker sailed along the length of their fleet, perhaps relaying orders or encouragement. Hours passed as the enemy struggled to form their line, slowly, interminably, being blown slowly toward Howe's hungry fleet, as a shoal of fish to the waiting British net. The British, for their part, took the opportunity to have lunch after Howe signalled, with inappropriate courtesy,

'The people may have time to dine.'

As the order was passed through the ship, tension turned to humour. 'Time to dine?' said Sergeant Packer. 'What is this, a bloody society dinner! Let's get at the buggers!' he said through gritted teeth, to be greeted with a roar of approval from his men.

From the quarterdeck, Captain John Harvey smiled appreciatively. Signal number seven, with two guns: "General chase to the whole fleet." *Now the hunt is on*, he thought. 'Mister Cracraft,' he shouted to the first lieutenant on watch, pausing to enjoy the moment, 'clear for action, if you would, please.'

With those few words *Brunswick* became, in an instant, a disturbed anthill of activity. A marine drummer beat a raucous rhythm on his drum. Below him he heard screens being knocked down, above furniture hauled into the upper rigging, splinter netting strung over the decks and several barrels of water taken to the fighting tops, to aid in the event of fire aloft. Seamen ran up the companionways and fanned along the deck to their allotted stations, yelling at shipmates and grinning like demons, eager to be the first to reach the positions at which death or glory were to be found.

'Now we shall have a fight, Mister Lucas,' Harvey smiled kindly at the youngster, 'are you ready to do your duty?'

'Ye... yes, sir.' The young man stuttered, taking control of his emotions. 'Of course I am, sir.'

'Admiral signalling again, sir,' Lieutenant Cracraft interrupted, lowering his glass, 'Number forty one, sir: "Engage the enemy's rear." It will be our turn soon enough, I fancy.' Cracraft spoke with more sangfroid than he felt. 'We simply have to wait for our part of the line to—'

'I am a patient man, Lieutenant, but this waiting is always the worst part of it,' Harvey spoke sharply. 'Black Dick wants a melee, Cracraft, and by God, so do I.' Harvey could now all but smell the glory he sought. He could hear the roars from the seamen below decks and thought he could hear also, the shouts of Frenchmen across the narrowing space of rolling sea.

The state of excitement was palpable; the people thought now of nothing more than to perform the duty their captain expected of them. Their cheering and huzzas moved him.

He raised his glass again; there, now he saw a glimpse of the French, just ahead of *Russell,* the first of the British fleet, commanded by his friend, John Payne. There also he could make out *Bellorophon*, the Greek god who slayed the Chimera; there too was *Marlborough, Thunderer* and *Leviathan*—with all her sail spread, majestically cresting a wave and proceeding like the sea monster for which she was named.

Russell opened fire and the waiting game was over.

The battle had begun.

CHAPTER 17

'If oid a known it would all come to nought, I would have stayed abed, mates.' Michael O'Farrell spat a plug of tobacco into the bucket under the mess table, as the order to down hammocks was beaten on the drum and audible through the entire ship. 'Oi bin standing in the mizzen top all bleedin' day and not had even a pot at a bluidy Frog.'

'Aw pipe down, Paddy,' said Packer. 'You'll have the chance to get your bleedin' 'ead blown off soon enough.'

'I'd like to meet the French bugger dat tinks he could, Sergeant Joe,' O'Farrell retorted, reloading his mouth with another plug of tobacco. 'Cold enough to freeze the balls off a brass monkey, it is. Got any rum, Sergeant?'

The weather had become squally as the afternoon progressed. Reports from the flagship provided only little information to the rest of the fleet. Harvey learned *Bellorophon* had received a mauling from a large Frenchman. Word had spread, as it did in a fleet on a high state of readiness, of how *La Revolutionnaire,* one of the enemy's major ships of one hundred ten guns, had fought alone against several British ships for many hours, inflicting much damage on *Bellorophon.* The British warships *Thunderer* and

Audacious had both acquitted themselves with honour, with *Audacious* retiring from the scene, severely mauled. The news had a sobering effect on many of the lower deck.

With the wind blowing hard, the onset of nightfall had brought an end to the inconclusive action. Night signal-lights, grouped as triangles, were suspended from the rigging of British ships, another order from Earl Howe, with ships' lookouts straining every nerve to follow the flickering, dancing lights during the blustery night. Sailors in both fleets found little sleep, lying or crouching by their guns, ears alert to the slightest sound, nerves as taut as the marines' drums.

The following morning, as the middle watch came to an end, Howe issued another order even before the sun spilled its fragile rays over the battleground, requiring the fleet to form line of battle ahead or astern of the flagship and to leave off the chase.

The French fleet formed up in disciplined fashion, as Captain Harvey had noted in his log. He lowered his telescope. 'Humph,' he grunted, 'Monsieur Frog appears to be competent in manoeuvring his fleet, Cracraft.'

'Yes, sir, but can he fight as well as he swims?' the first lieutenant answered. 'Our gunnery is certain to be superior.'

'One hopes we have the chance to find the answer to the question, Mister Cracraft.' Harvey scanned the mainmast. 'I think we'll shake out a reef; we are making heavy weather of it in this growing swell.' He steadied his legs as the wind, gusting from the south-west, delivered another sheet of salt rain into their reddened faces, filling their boots and chilling them all to the inners.

'Keep a close eye on the flagship and the admiral's signals, Mister Cracraft,' said Harvey, heading for his cabin. 'I'm in need of some breakfast. His Lordship will most likely be moving us closer to the enemy. We are still a league or more from them, in my estimation.'

The admiral had challenges to contend with first; the French were on the western horizon, heading south, close-hauled against the strong south-westerly. To force an engagement from his leeward position, Howe would have to have the fleet tack, more than once, within sight and even cannon range of his enemy. He had to handle his fleet with some skill. and that depended on the skill of his captains.

And they were all to be tested.

* * *

Howe signalled his first manoeuvre at 7 a.m., requiring the fleet to tack in succession. Now he was on course to intercept and cut the French line.

'Oh hell and damnation,' said Jack Vizzard to Lieutenant Bevan, as they watched from the foremast. 'This looks wrong to me, Rowland. It must be we have tacked too soon, or the enemy is faster than His Lordship estimated. At this rate we shall pass to their rear. Tell me I'm in error, will you?'

'Keep them in view, Jack. You may yet be proved wrong,' replied Bevan. 'There you have it, our turn to tack in just one minute; then you shall see.'

From the quarterdeck the order bellowed from the first lieutenant's speaking trumpet; his hands positioned at the braces sprang to action and the efficient *Brunswick* turned sweetly to starboard and into the wind as the main course crackled and flapped briefly, directly in the wake of *Montague,* commanded by James Montague, who had requested the command for no better reason than the commonality of the ship's name.

'Hah, there, did I not tell you so, Jack? There is your enemy. Now we shall be among them afore dinner and a mêlée we shall have.' Rowland Bevan's eyes appeared to glow at the prospect of battle.

'You are a bloodthirsty devil, Rowland. I do believe you have no fear of death. I, on the other hand, now have a family to sustain and worry for my wife and children.' Jack's appearance grew wistful, unlike the terrifying warrior he could become in the heat of action.

'You are wrong, Jack. I am no madman, simply a humble officer anxious to do my duty—and destroy the French!'

'I cannot help but feel we are in the wrong place, Rowland. Our chief purpose is to prevent the convoy from America reaching port. Find that convoy, capture it, destroy it if necessary; but prevent the French from having the supplies they need to sustain their armies. Surely it is what we should be about, and this cat-chase-mouse game of ours is not going to do. The French admiral is laying a false trail for us to follow; in my opinion.'

'Mister Bevan,' the strong rising voice of Captain Harvey from the quarterdeck, distorted by the speaking trumpet, 'the admiral is signalling, but we cannot decipher all. Can you assist from your perch?'

Most of the signal flags were obscured by drifting smoke, mixed with the lighter mist from the bubbling, frothy sea. Bevan spent a long minute staring through the opaque lens.

'Sir, I fancy it is an order to tack in succession, but regret that it is not entirely clear to me,' he shouted back.

'Are any others preparing to tack, Mister Bevan?'

Again, Bevan steadied the telescope, twisted to focus on the straggling line of British ships. 'It does not appear so, sir,' he bellowed, shaking his head in emphasis.

'Then we shall maintain our course. So be it.' shouted Harvey.

* * *

Below decks men were growing tired and restless. A fight broke out between a marine and an infantryman of the 29th Foot. A bayonet was drawn by the soldier, but dropped when Sergeant Packer intervened with his musket, 'Now son, your toothpick will not stop a ball. You best drop that afore I blow what you call your fucking brains out!' The soldier stepped back into the shadows and disappeared, amid a torrent of lower-deck language from the handful of the marines gathered around.

'Thanks sergeant,' said Tom Clutterbuck. 'Sorry, but it turned a bit grim too bloody quick. I weren't looking for to pick a fight, honest.'

'If you want to lose them stripes faster than you earned 'em you found the right way to do it, young Tom!' Sergeant Packer liked his junior corporal, not because he was Vizzard's former servant, but simply because he had brought the boy on in the Corps, taken him under his wing and taught him soldiering. The boy Jack Vizzard once knew was now a man, a useful man to have in the platoon, who had earned the respect of the men. 'What was it all about, anyway?'

'Something and nothing, Sarge. Just a bit of banter about how marines can shoot better 'n faster than the infantry!' Tom's teeth shone in the dim light of the 'tween decks.

'Reckon there was more to it than what you say, lad. Best keep out of his way and 'ope nowt comes of it. You keep your eyes sharp, Tom; Mister Vizzard would be a might upset if anything were to 'appen to you.'

'Um, well it were more about Mister Vizzard, Sergeant. He said that Mister Vizzard was a dirty, scruffy scoundrel and a Newgate attorney and what not. It got out of hand.' Tom Clutterbuck picked up the bayonet as it slid across the deck. 'And I won't have scum like that talking ill of Lieutenant Vizzard,' he said, spitting the words through his teeth. 'But, Sarge, please do not be telling Mister Vizzard about this.'

'Oh and why should I not, my lad? Think he might put you on punishment? And you think I'll not do the same?' Packer grinned. He would not discipline one of his best men for something he would have done himself. 'No more fighting, Tom. You save your energy for the French, whatever the provocation, or it's a floggin' for you, lad. Mister Vizzard would not be able to prevent you meeting the ship's cat. We ain't wanting to embarrass the lieutenant now, are we?'

Thus admonished, the only acceptable reply Tom could offer was a meek, 'No, Sergeant.'

* * *

A little before four bells in the afternoon watch, it appeared to those observing the French fleet, which included every man with the opportunity to do so, that the French were taking avoiding action, unwilling to take up the challenge of battle offered. Earl Howe threw out another signal for a general chase. Less than an hour later, they were no more than a mile apart; shots were exchanged, but the mêlée Howe desired to bring about failed to materialise. Not until the falling sand in the glass signified the end of the first dogwatch did full broadsides roar out across the rolling swell of the Atlantic.

'Damn this, Cracraft,' Harvey groaned to his first, as darkness crawled across the water, 'we'll not have a night action. Howe will want a full day to pound 'em,' he sighed. 'Why can we not get amongst 'em?'

'Sir, why not take some rest? You have walked the deck all day and look exhausted, if I may be so bold. It is plain we will not be in action this day, sir.'

Cracraft was a considerate man, fond of his captain who had given him his step and who, if he survived the coming battle, would again sponsor his advancement and perhaps even support his own command. Cracraft's mind drifted momentarily. He stretched his arms and rocked slowly on his heels. Four years since his commission as lieutenant. If he survived the coming battle, he could hope for a step to master and commander.

'I believe I will do so, William. It has been a long and largely thankless day. Call me immediately should the situation alter in any way.'

* * *

The pre-dawn found Harvey back on his deck wrapped in a boat cloak, sitting behind the helmsman, drinking hot tea from a pewter mug, as the routine of the ship continued around him. The ship's carpenter was growling at two of his mates, repairing a damaged companionway; a bosun's mate was teaching a pair of young boys some of the intricacies of tying knots, chuckling at their kack-handedness. The officer on watch, mindful of the captain's presence, ensured *Brunswick's* station keeping attracted no adverse criticism.

The wind was south by west and the stiff breeze and cloudy skies found the two fleets still on the larboard tack, about seven miles distant. A heavy swell from the westward caused *Brunswick* and the other line of battle ships to roll and pitch. Howe had been watching and waiting for the light. By seven of the clock, the British fleet was bearing down on their enemy; they hauled wind together and lay abreast the French. Captain Harvey could see the position of each fleet. As the fleet's van came abreast of the enemy's centre, Howe signalled his fleet to tack in succession once more, and shortly, signal thirty four broke out from his masthead; he meant to cut the French line in echelon and gain the wind.

Harvey watched the developing panorama from the elevated position on his poop deck. He saw the leading British ships tack and then lay up a little to windward of the enemy's rear. The French, evidently fearing their rear squadron might be cut off, began to wear ship in succession from the van and run down their line, hauling onto the wind on the larboard tack in a line parallel to the British line. 'Oh prettily done,' said Harvey to a passing gull screeching overhead, making his deposit on the side-rail a mere foot from where Harvey stood, glass extended. 'Very prettily done. They are not as lubberly as all we might believe.' He muttered in appreciation.

Another signal from Howe on *Queen Charlotte;* Harvey could decipher it without aid. Number thirty six: all captains were to steer for their opposing enemy and engage independently. Upward of fifty line of battle ships eyed each other warily.

Some sporadic fire startled Harvey as the van passed the enemy's rear. Lieutenant Cracraft ran up the companionway, paused in front of the captain and reported, 'The enemy have opened fire, sir.'

'I have ears of my own, Mister Cracraft,' Harvey snapped,

instantly regretting his unaccustomed terseness. 'My apologies, William. My remark was uncalled for and quite unforgivable in me.' He smiled at his premier, who waved away the apology.

'Think no more of it, sir. We all become tense in circumstances such as these.' Cracraft stood to his captain's left and pulled his telescope from under his left arm and opened it fully, watching the great ships pitch and roll toward their enemy. ''Tis akin to waiting in line for one's executioner, is it not, sir?'

'An apt but unfortunately accurate commentary on our situation, William.' Harvey shuddered as a premonition caught his mind and refused to leave. 'I find the waiting intolerable, I don't mind saying, William. The last few days of playing hide and seek have been wearing to us all. However, once action is joined and shot is flying, it seems easier to bear, if it ain't perverse in me.'

'Not perverse in any respect, sir,' said Cracraft. One is far too busy then to indulge one's fear, I imagine.' William Cracraft was facing his first action. He was fearful, naturally enough, but more concerned that he should perform his duty efficiently and with courage. He knew, should he survive the imminent battle, he might receive promotion. And promotion to master and commander meant a ship and command of his own.

'We shall face the battle as faithful servants of our king, William. The people will look to us for example and leadership. We must not fail them.'

Harvey coughed as a layer of smoke drifted across the deck and shrouded the quarterdeck, turning the crew into spectral apparitions. The crack of small arms fire grew louder, contrasting with the deeper cannonade of heavier guns delivering death and destruction with their thunder.

* * *

Brunswick's guns remained silent; the men however, did not.

'When are we getting to grips with the bastards, Sarge? Michael O'Farrell asked. This pussy-footing is doin' moi nerves no good. Got any grog?

'Just shut your bone box, Paddy. You'll have all the fightin' you want just as soon as M'lord Howe can arrange things. Then you'll end up sick of it, man.' Sergeant Packer passed a dark bottle across the bench to the wiry Irishman. 'Don't you guzzle it all at once, you bugger. When the time comes I want you sober enough to fire at the bastards an' not our lot.'

'What will it be like? I mean, have you been in a sea fight before, Sarge?' Tom Clutterbuck asked.

Sergeant Packer drank from the bottle and looked at the men gathering around in the gloom of the lower deck. He wondered how many would be there after the imminent battle. Then, in an unbidden moment, he became the frightened sixteen-year old recruit who had run away from a brutal father, his mother worn out from producing another child each year, worried beyond reason at the lack of food to sustain the expanding family.

In months, he had been sent to the fleet and aboard Howe's flagship, *Victory*, with a convoy of supplies and reinforcements for the garrison at Gibraltar. He had been sick with fear and sick from the storm off Cape Trafalgar and sick during the subsequent indecisive battle with the Spanish fleet.

'If you survive, young Tom, you'll never be the same again,' he grunted, haunted by the unwelcome images of carnage that slipped unbidden into his head. 'It ain't a pretty thing to witness.'

Joe Packer remembered the lieutenant who was commanding

the detachment that day nearly a dozen years past, as he cowered behind one of the giant guns, moments before it was blown aside, transforming the officer into a pile of oozing blood and shattered bones and tissue. He remembered too, the horror of splintering timber skewering the marine standing next in line to him, pinning the man to the deck like a child's rag doll with the stuffing spilling out. He remembered the blood slapping around the deck as the great ship rolled and pitched, flowing over his boots like a crimson tide. He remembered the noise and the smoke and being near deaf for days, while his eyes stung with tears, not all of them from the spent powder. He remembered emptying the contents of his belly on the deck, mixing with the blood and entrails of men he had spoken to only minutes before. He remembered his lungs choking with smoke, coughing until he felt he would die from the poisonous fumes. He remembered pissing his breeches at the horror. He remembered the screams of men, as limbs were torn from bodies. He remembered the crying of the ship's boys as they ran from the magazine to the great guns. He remembered the expressions of shock and disbelief on the men as they died. He remembered his own sergeant, on his knees crying, as blood poured from his mouth. He remembered one of the great guns exploding, scattering its crew in dismembered parts about the crowded deck. Joe Packer remembered it all; then drank hard and long from the bottle.

'Now don't worry lads,' he grinned, 'we're here to do our duty to king and country, and think on it boys; think of the fortunes to be made when we capture the French fleet and haul 'em all into Pompey!'

'Here's to that, Sergeant!' said Tom, emulating his mentor.

* * *

'We have the honour of escorting the flagship, William,' announced Captain Harvey. 'Look, he begins his turn. Be ready with your orders now.'

Queen Charlotte was carrying all the sail she could, but even so, it appeared to Harvey the French were slipping slowly ahead.

'Hah,' shouted Harvey, 'now is the time, William.'

The first lieutenant shouted three rapid orders and the men on deck responded, bringing the great yards around, as *Brunswick* turned sweetly towards the French line, which stretched before them like a line of cornered beasts spitting fire, directed at *Queen Charlotte* and *Brunswick* alone.

Chain shot and ball whistled into Captain Harvey's beautiful ship, tearing and ripping sails and making men duck down from the invisible, but audible, shrieking hail of death.

'For God's sake, sir, let us fire before we all are slaughtered.' A gun captain called out.

'Lie flat, you men,' shouted Cracraft. 'I'll tell you when to fire!'

'Well said, William. We must endure for some minutes, I fear, and I'll not waste powder and ball until we are in close to our enemy. There, see how handsomely Black Dick takes *Queen Charlotte* in amongst 'em! Ain't it a noble sight! Hah, look, William, her main and mizzen shrouds have taken the French flagship's flagstaff. My word, what a carronade she is giving them,' he shouted above the noise. 'We'll be there in a minute or two.'

'Sir, there is a gap in their line! Mister Stewart!' Cracraft shouted across to the *Brunswick's* master, 'there's a gap for us.' He pointed with his speaking trumpet needlessly as the master, Mister Stewart, his big hands on the ship's wheel, was intent on reaching the space first, willing his ship to sail faster into the French line.

The great ship pulled forward, but simultaneously, a French seventy-four, seeing Harvey's intention, trimmed sails to capture more wind and surged forward to deny him the space.

'We'll ram him, the rascal,' shouted Cracraft. 'Steady men,' Cracraft shouted through his trumpet. Musket fire from the French warship sang overhead and pulled splinters from the rail in front of him. Above him on the poop, the ship's band of fifes and drums, with men from the 29th Regiment, struck up a ragged rendition of 'Hearts of Oak.' The men below heard the strains of the march and loud and lusty cheers rose up through the decks, adding to the clamour swirling about the decks.

With a violent and crashing impact the two ships came together to begin a dance with death. The three starboard anchors of the *Brunswick* caught the larboard fore-channels and fore-shrouds of the French vessel, now identified by Midshipman Lucas as *Venguer du Peuple*. 'Avenger of the People, is she?' said Harvey when informed of the name of his enemy, 'well let us see what my *Brunswick* can do with her!'

'Sir,' shouted the master, Mister Stewart, 'I can have some men cut us free. We can cut the anchor cables.' He stood calmly as musket fire peppered the main deck, causing the guns' crews to cower.

'No, we have got her, and we will keep her!' Harvey replied with defiance.

At the same moment, *Venguer* released a full broadside with her main lower battery of thirty six -pounders and upper battery of eighteen -pounder cannons. *Brunswick,* her starboard side badly wounded, reeled under the punch; bleeding like a tortured bull, she roared out her pain into the French ship, a section of the lower gun deck firing through the closed gun-ports, her enemy too close to permit them to open fully, emitting a shower of lethal splinters into the French.

'Pass the word quickly to the main gun-deck, William, to expect another broadside.' Captain Harvey paced nervously across the deck.

It never came.

* * *

The men on the lower deck screamed defiance, abuse and profanity at their enemies, across a divide of only a few feet, then laughed as they realised the difficulty faced by the French, who could not reload quickly enough; moreover, their ramrods could not be used because of the proximity of the *Brunswick.*

'Look at 'em, Caldy. They can't work their guns; see mate,' said Jim Shadbolt, gun captain to his loader. 'French tools are too long for this work, the dozy Frogs!'

The ten-man crew of number four gun, starboard side on the upper gun deck, were working hard, sweat running down bare chests and backs, muscles bulging with tension, kerchiefs tied around heads and ears. They were a typical mix of trained men. Sailors all, with the gun's loader, Caldwell, a young Gloucestershire lad who had been at sea for five years. He happened to glance through the open port and spied a Frenchman sitting astride an open port, working with a rammer. With a poacher's instinct, he grabbed a round shot and, with the strength of a man fighting for his life, hurled it across the short gap and struck the Frenchman's head. The man fell from his perch to certain death as the swell pushed the two ships together, the great wooden hulls grinding him to pulp.

'Hey,' he yelled. 'Did ya see that, Jim?' he shouted to his mate. 'I got me a bulls-eye then!'

'Never mind that, Caldy, we need to keep pounding the bastards,' said Jim, pressing down on the quoin. 'Now load, you bugger, and be fast about it.'

The British now realised they had an immediate advantage, which they used to full effect. The Royal Navy had introduced flexible handles to their guns' tools; rammers, worms and sponges no longer had rigid handles, so a gun's crew did not have to expose themselves at the port, nor have to climb out in order to service the gun.

'Run out!' yelled the gun captains, almost in unison, sweat now glistening on backs and running down faces. 'Stand clear and... fire!' The noise became deafening and unbearable. Smoke, stinking and thick, rolled back from the muzzles, spreading along the low deck space, filling the deck and men's lungs and choking them. The *Venguer du Peuple* was being murderously attacked and badly wounded; blood already weeping from the seams. Screams came from within the hull as brave men and cowards died together.

Again and again the crews worked through the familiar routine: washing out, sponging, ladling the cartridge down the barrel, twisting the ladle over to drop the cartridge into position and ramming the shot and wad down the bore, before the gun captain aimed and fired the weapon. Little was called for to aim the gun at point-blank range, but today Captain Harvey had given orders for the guns to be alternately depressed and elevated, so as to inflict maximum damage to the hull and to the French crew within, and upwards into the rigging and sails to disable the enemy vessel.

Lieutenant Cracraft toured the gun-decks, instructing the junior officers, who were often young midshipmen, arranging replacements as casualties slowly mounted. He was horrified at the carnage developing; body parts on the deck and stuck to beams, a head rolling in the scuppers, wide-eyed boys struggling along the slippery deck with the weight of baskets about their necks, laden with eight-pound cartridges, relieved as they delivered their loads to the crews.

'Take men from the larboard side as you need 'em,' he shouted into the ear of another middie, struggling to make his voice heard above the cacophony of noise that made one's mortal body shake and tremble from the feet upwards. 'Keep 'em at it, youngster,' he shouted, slapping the boy on the back. 'You know what to do.' The boy nodded, his eyes mere slits against the heat and the burning, choking smoke,

Cracraft noted the damage to the ship, increasing every minute, memorizing the detail. The starboard gun ports from the first to the tenth were shot and blown away by their own gunners, the sooner to attack the French. Two half beams carried away as splinters, to wound and maim and kill.

He noted a similar scene on the upper gun deck as he made his way back to his station. Shot holes and spirketting holed and splintered; slings, beams and knees badly wounded. Skids and gang-boards cut to pieces, iron stations shot away. Cracraft noted the damage for his report to Captain Harvey. He watched and stood aside as two seamen appeared, coughing through the smoke, carrying a shipmate along the deck to the companionway leading to the hell of the orlop, the blood pumping from a gaping wound in the man's side. 'Thankee, sir,' one of them said as the trio crept along the deck. Cracraft nodded, thinking the man would be dead before he reached the surgeon.

* * *

'Vizzard, I need some more of your men in the foretop,' shouted Captain Saunders. 'I have lost half a dozen good men already and fear more will follow. This is hot work for certain.'

They were on the main deck just below the quarterdeck where Captain Harvey was still pacing across the quarterdeck. Small arms fire from the French had lessened during the last hour, but men were still being wounded. Jack Vizzard felt the wind of a ball as it passed by his right ear and struck a bucket hanging from the rail, punching a neat hole in the leather, between the letters G and R.

'I would rather take the entire complement across the gap and take the damned Frenchman, Saunders,' growled Jack. 'However, I agree we need to kill their sharpshooters; they are a greater danger to our company than their damned gunners are.'

Jack took but ten seconds to quickly reload his sea-pattern musket and aimed at a prominent target in the *Vengeur's* mizzen top. Drifting smoke obscured his aim and he paused, holding his breath, then fired. He noted, with great satisfaction, a spray of crimson against the grey smoke as a body fell from the top. 'One less to trouble us, Saunders.'

'To the foremast quickly, Vizzard. It is where we are most needed now.'

Saunders ran forward, pushing past sailors, jumping over the remains of one of his corporals and shouting for his men to follow. With a shout, he had two dozen of his detachment lined up on the fo'c'sle, in two ranks. Sergeant Packer followed with a dozen marines and Vizzard, who ordered them aloft.

'The fore-top, Joe, quick as you can, and direct fire onto those devils massing over there.' With practiced speed, he again loaded his weapon and noted a large, bearded Frenchman on the larboard bulwark of *Venguer,* shouting abuse at the British officers. Taking aim, Jack was unbalanced as a wave rolled beneath the two ships and his shot went wide. 'Blood and thunder,' he yelled, reaching for another cartridge and ball. As he did so, a gang of Frenchmen reached the *Vengeur's* larboard cathead, intent on boarding the *Brunswick.*

'With me, marines,' he yelled, throwing aside the musket, reaching for his sword and running towards them. Three Frenchmen, with more courage than their shipmates, made the short jump onto the *Brunswick's* starboard bulwark. Jack bellowed as his sword scythed across their faces, catching one and opening the man's left cheek with a vivid scarlet line from ear to chin. He was aware of a sea of fearsome faces behind the leaders and the sound of volley fire in his ears.

Smoke from a musket filled his vision, making him choke, and he dropped to one knee as a pike reached for his chest. With his left arm, he parried it, thrusting upward with the sword and feeling it strike bone. A French sailor collapsed in front of him, more blood pouring onto the deck.

Rising to his feet, he turned and saw with alarm, Captain Saunders on his knees, head slumped forward, a trickle of blood staining his shirt and coat.

'Ensign Vernon! Where are you?' he shouted through the smoke. 'Captain Saunders is wounded. Get him taken below, will you. And I need more of your men up here now, or we will be boarded again.'

The young officer appeared, eyes wide with fear, cheeks smeared with uniform blackened, his eyes wide. 'Here I am, sir. I'll look after him.'

Jack looked around as a breeze took the smoke along the length of the ship and saw at least half a dozen of the 29th Regiment's men heaped together in death. 'Stand firm, 29th and strike hard,' Jack shouted. The French had retreated in the face of determined resistance from the infantrymen—and a row of vicious bayonets. Their repulse had come at a price: the detachment's senior officer would play no further part in the battle.

Looking up at the foretop, Jack was relieved to see the grinning face of his sergeant looking down on the scene of death. He grinned in return, in spite of the carnage about him.

'I was hoping your section would keep them at bay, Sergeant Packer!' He laughed. 'You're not up there to admire the view, you know!'

'Thought you were doing fine without my 'elp, sir.' Packer called down, 'Best be quick, sir, they may have enough guts to try again. The Vein Openers are doin' good, though ain't they, sir?' Packer grinned, giving the regiment grudging respect by referring to the nickname by which it became known after the Boston affair ,some twenty-five years previously. A sergeant of the 29th in the rear rank, hat missing and a bloody rag around his head, looked up at Packer and raised two fingers in salute.

'Mister Vizzard, sir,' said a blackened, dirty sailor, 'they shot off The Duke's hat, sir. 'Tain't right for His Lordship to face the enemy bare-headed, sir.' The man grinned, the marines' humour infecting the sailors around them.

'Well then man, I suggest you go report to Captain Harvey and tell me what he wishes to do about it.' Vizzard's bemused smile sent the sailor scurrying along the shattered deck to report to his captain the news of the figurehead's damage. 'I think we have enough to worry about without the loss of Duke's headgear. You men, get your wounded comrades down to the surgeon. The dead will have to go over the other side,' he shouted at men immobilised by a mix of fear and exhaustion.

The sergeant reacted and moved forward. 'You 'eard wot the officer of marines said. C'mon, lads let's get to it.' He stepped forward, bent over, grasping the arm of a wounded man, as a musket barked and shattered his left leg, sending him tumbling to the deck.

The sound of cannon fire intruded again, but this time it was from the other side of the ship. Looking over to larboard, Jack saw, through wisps of smoke, another French seventy-four line of battle ship, already damaged from a previous encounter, bearing down on *Brunswick*. Jack absently noted the missing main and mizzenmasts.

'Dear Christ in Heaven,' said Jack to the sky. 'Another of the bastards comes to add to the slaughter. 'Sergeant Packer,' he called up to the foretop, 'Joe Packer! Wake up you bugger. Get your men ready; here's another on the larboard quarter! I'm going aft to speak to the captain.'

Shaken by the damage on the upper deck, Jack strode aft, pushing aside trailing lines and strips of canvas, stumbling on a wet rolling deck. The ship's boats were shattered, strips of planking strewn across the deck. Shreds of sails littered the deck, acting as shrouds for the dead. Severed ropes lay amongst severed limbs and blood pools and trails were everywhere. The same bloodstained sailor passed him, returning to the bowsprit. ''Tis the captain's own hat, sir. He says he will not see *Brunswick* without 'is hat, sir.' The man grinned, grim determination in his eyes.

'Sir,' Jack shouted, as he climbed the companionway to the quarterdeck above the continuing noise of gunfire, lessening now from the Frenchman alongside. 'Captain Saunders is wounded and I have taken command of his men forrard. Do you have any orders, for me?' He pointed to the second seventy-four, now closer on the larboard quarter as he paced alongside Captain Harvey, before he realised the captain, too, was injured. 'Sir; you are wounded - your hand!'

'Captain Saunders was dead before he reached the orlop, Mister Vizzard. Please take command of his detachment. As for my wound, 'tis nothing for you to be concerned with.' The handkerchief wrapped around his hand concealed the loss of two fingers. 'I am losing too many good men today, Mister Vizzard. I would encourage you to keep walking, sir,' said Harvey seeing Jack halt, 'they still have many sharpshooters, which you would oblige me by removing as soon as convenient, please. They are a damned nuisance!'

'At once, sir,' Jack replied.

'And have more men in the tops to deal with the new threat, if you would be so kind,' added Harvey, his eyes failing to conceal the pain.

Jack nodded and turned away and saw a youngster at number two gun fall wounded in the ankle as he passed cartridges to the gunners.. He watched as smoke wrapped around the boy, shrouding him, as if taken by angels, insulating him from further harm. He stood there, unconscious of time passing, his mind thinking of Mary and the rolling fields of home. Jack's left ear sang as a musket was discharged behind him, bringing him back to the carnage all around. The youngster was stumbling, trying to stand, dropping to his knees, pulling himself up again, crying with pain. Jack saw the glistening white bone protruding from the shattered ankle.

But there was something wrong with the voice. He stepped forward to help. The boy dropped again, blood appearing from a second wound in the right thigh. He looked around and saw one of his men, jacket covered in stains and grime and hair burnt. 'You, over here to me and help this lad,' he shouted. 'Get him below to the surgeon, now.'

The man turned and he saw Tom Clutterbuck, face bleeding from a small splinter in his left cheek. 'Tom, for pity's sake get this lad below and have the surgeon stitch your own wound.'

Together they picked up the youngster. 'What's your name, lad? Jack asked kindly, and almost dropped him in surprise at the answer. 'Mary, sir. Mary Talbot. But I'm on the books as John Taylor,' she whimpered in pain.

'Blood and sand, boy,' exclaimed Jack. 'Can you carry him... her, Tom? Get her below at once. This is no place for a girl. Here, I'll help you down.' Together they carried the girl to the main deck and Jack left Tom to manage the tortuous descent to the orlop deck far below.

'Mister Willis,' Jack shouted at the tall midshipman supervising some of the surviving guns on the main deck. 'Lieutenant Bevan tells me you are a decent shot—good enough, he says, to join my marines. What say you, Willis? Can you leave the guns for a time and help us deal with their sharpshooters?'

'I am a fair shot, sir; so much is true. Better with a fowling piece on my father's estate than a soldier's Brown Bess though, I fancy.' In spite of his fear the youngster smiled.

'We are losing too many from yonder French marksmen. Get aloft, would you, and keep them busy, please.' He handed him a musket, quickly removed the cross-belt and pouches from a dead infantryman of the 29th and slid down the companionway to the upper deck; running forrard to his station, he all but collided with Lieutenant Bevan giving orders to the reduced crewmembers there.

'The captain is wounded, Bevan. He should go below, but it is not for me to suggest so,' Jack said.

'Jack, he has been hit before but has concealed it. I will speak to him when I have finished here.' Lieutenant Bevan shouted above a sudden sporadic broadside from the *Venguer*. 'Have you noted we are to be attacked on our larboard side? I believe we have only a few minutes.'

'Where is the first lieutenant?' Jack asked.

'Cracraft is on the main gun-deck, Jack. We have lost some good fellows down there. He is preparing the larboard guns to give the new arrival a warm welcome!' Bevan showed a row of teeth from the grime and powder covering his face. More musket balls peppered the deck around their feet, forcing the two officers to move.

The *Brunswick's* larboard battery released its broadside, an orderly, concentrated fire someone had controlled with skill and determination until the second French ship was close alongside. The devastating fire visibly shook both ships and deafened men, throwing some to the deck. Jack shook his head to clear the confusion and saw sails on the second French ship's foremast start to shiver as the surviving mast fell to starboard. He heard the cheering and grinned.

'I need more men aloft, Rowland. Those French sharpshooters are becoming better at this game! Rowland, you, too, are wounded; look at your leg, man.' Jack indicated the blood staining the lieutenant's breeches.

'So it would appear, Jack. It is a minor matter, I shall see to it when time allows.'

'Rowland, may I suggest you have the surgeon or one of his mates take a look at it sooner. Now, I must organise some men.'

Jack ran toward the fo'c'sle, yelling at two sailors to extinguish a small fire amongst the remains of one of the ship's boats, gathering isolated soldiers of the 29th and ordering them into ranks, directing their fire into the mass of Frenchmen opposite. The soldiers of the 29th Foot were methodical and well trained. The young, enthusiastic ensign, Harcourt Vernon, shrilled various orders to reach the point of firing. Laborious and too slow. Jack's expression darkened. The volley roared out in an irregular, ragged crackle of fire.

'Mister Vernon, they must work faster than they are, for their own preservation. Crack the pace along, man!' Jack shouted, his voice rising, 'like this, men!' he shouted, loading his own weapon, raised it to present well before the first of the soldiers were replacing their ramrods. Harcourt shouted the final order, 'Present and... fire!'

A more consistent volley and the smoke became a curtain before them, as the sequence was repeated, the high-pitched, anxious voice of Ensign Vernon barely audible above the thunder of the guns and the shouts and screams. Then Jack realised the orders had stopped coming. Looking about him he saw the young officer on the deck, blood pouring from his head, unseeing eyes staring at the grey clouds, crying above the rolling consuming battlefield.

* * *

'Sir, let me take a boarding party across, please.' Jack looked hard at Captain Harvey. 'Your officers have work enough fighting the guns. Give me your top-men and let me try and take the *Venguer.*'

He paced alongside Harvey as the captain considered the suggestion. Then, as the captain turned to answer the impatient officer of marines, he collapsed, struck by a large splinter blown from the bulwark, ripping his elbow to shreds. He stopped walking, watching the blood flow from his shattered arm.

'Sir, said Jack, 'you are wounded again.'

As he spoke, Captain Harvey was again hit on the head and he staggered about the deck as Vizzard jumped to catch him, calling to a pair of seamen to help.

'Belay that,' said Harvey, 'I will have no man leave his quarters. I have two legs left yet to go down to the doctor.'

As he walked coolly to the horrors of the orlop deck, deep in the darkest area of the ship, he called out to the watching sailors, 'Persevere, my brave lads, in your duty. Continue the action with spirit, for the honour of our king and country; and remember my last words, the colours of the *Brunswick* shall never be struck.'

Jack watched in wonder at the courage and example of the ship's captain, then deciding to take the fight to the enemy, ran forward and called the squads of marines away from the larboard guns, urging them to follow. 'Sergeant Packer,' Vizzard bellowed from the foot of the foremast, 'Joe Packer, on deck now with everyone—as many of the *Brunswickers* and the 29th as you can muster.'

Sulphur pots started landing on the deck, spilling onto wounded men, who screamed in agony as their wounded bodies burned, men were blinded as raw ore was discharged into their midst and heated shot drilled into *Brunswick's* timbers. 'The bastards, the fucking bastards,' Vizzard swore as another fire was started amongst the pile of fallen canvas and tarred fallen rigging. He shouted at a dazed sailor. 'Get some water on that fire, man, on the double, now.' The startled sailor ran to a fire bucket, galvanised into reality as flames kissed and embraced the base of the mainmast.

Moments later, Sergeant Packer, having managed the forestay without injury, joined Vizzard on deck. 'What's afoot, sir?' he said, ramrod straight as a pair of musket balls thudded into the mast behind him. 'Bloody Frogs, they couldn't 'it a barn door at twenty paces.' He sneered at the enemy, a mere pistol shot distant, as a sailor fell dead at his feet, his belly ripped open by chain-shot, which nearly cut him in half.

'We're going to have a go at taking her, Joe,' shouted Vizzard. 'I'm damned if I'll strut around this deck being shot at by a bunch of piss-poor French bastards. Grab some pikes and cutlasses and let's cut the buggers apart!'

With a growl of agreement, the marines gathered up weapons— anything that came to hand, pikes, dirks, cutlasses, even a weighted monkey's fist or slungshot, as sailors called them. Vizzard saw Tom Clutterbuck attempting to hide behind the big Irishman. 'Tom, I need you and another three good marksmen at the maintop to keep their heads down. No arguments with me, corporal.' He grunted as Tom's mouth opened in protest. 'If I should signal thus, I need very quick and accurate support. Move it, now!'

He gave Tom and his chosen men half a minute to scramble up the larboard ratlines and then he made for the *Brunswick's* bow with a roar, with two dozen marines and as many of the 29th at his back, all shouting, screaming and swearing. They reached the bow to see a group of Frenchmen waiting. 'Shit,' said Joe Packer, 'a reception committee.' He roared defiance and ran past Jack, as both vied to be first aboard the *Vengeur*. The boarders rushed across as the swell rolled under the hulls, pulling the vessels apart. Steel struck steel as Packer and Vizzard leapt across the void of a yard and a half between the two vessels, slashing and stabbing with the fury of wild men. A bearded face appeared from the smoke and Jack slashed at it with the cutlass, bringing the blade back to slice into the midriff of another, spilling glistening innards onto the deck already slippery and red.

A wild but controlled surge of energy brought him up against two hesitant French sailors being pressed forward by an officer. He swung his blade in a wide flat arc, sending the pair to the deck in a scarlet spray, which spattered those next to them.

A slow marine screamed as a French pike spitted him to the bulwark, Joe Packer instantly bringing a cutlass down hard on the neck of the French sailor wielding it—dead before his head rolled across the deck like a spent cannon ball.

Another face appeared through the mist and smoke, wildly waving a useless musket. Vizzard side-stepped, kicked at the man's legs, slashing his bloody blade across the startled face as it disappeared from his sight.

The resistance was fierce, and although Jack caught glimpses of the French captain bellowing from his quarterdeck, he and his marines were not making progress. The attack was faltering. Another of his marines fell to a dagger thrust by a short, wiry man, who also died when Michael O'Farrell, with a roaring Gaelic curse, skewered the man through the throat with his bayonet.

'Joe, this will not do,' Jack shouted, 'it's time for us to leave. Get them back—now.' He slashed again at a young French petty officer who displayed more courage than many, and who was exhorting his men to attack harder. The man was able to leap sideways and avoid the blade as Jack held him at bay. Through the din and smoke he heard Joe Packer shouting, and realised that he was in danger of being left behind. A step backwards and he raised his free arm. Instantly a volley of fire sprayed the French fo'c'sle, spinning the petty officer around in a final dance of death. Jack seized the moment to run, slipping on blood, which probably saved him as the wind of a ball brushed his neck. He made the larboard cathead of *Venguer,* leaping the crevasse between the two protagonists and land in a tumble at the feet of Joe Packer.

'Is that what you call an orderly withdrawal, sir?' He grinned as Jack rose to his feet.

'Is that what you call providing your commanding officer with support, Sergeant Packer?' He returned the grin and grasped the NCO's arm. 'Let's get the men organised and provide the bastards with some disciplined fire.'

'Mister Vizzard, sir,' said a corporal of the 29th, 'Mister Cracraft has been wounded and Mister Bevan has taken command, sir. He wants a word, sir.'

The fire from *Vengeur* was light and sporadic, with only occasional musket shots now cracking across the deck. Jack ran the length of *Brunswick's* larboard side, seeing the wounded men waiting to be taken below, the shattered timbers of a once proud ship of war, the streaks of blood running into the scuppers, the tears of a severely wounded vessel. He ran up the companionway to the quarterdeck where his new friend, Rowland Bevan, was standing, daring the French.

'Vizzard, you bloody fool. If I thought we could have taken the *Venguer,* I would have ordered it; no—I would have led a boarding party myself.' His anger was patently contrived and unsustainable, his face breaking into a smile. 'But damn me, it was a glorious sight. I even thought you might make it, for a moment.'

'Bevan, if I thought you could have taken the *Venguer,* I would have let you take my place. Boarding is for marines, not sailor boys.' He chuckled aloud, clapping his hand on Bevan's shoulder. 'It was worth the try, but damn my eyes, the Frogs over there have some spirit. I lost some good men.' His face darkened at the thought. He never could accept the loss of good men.

'They cannot sustain this pounding, surely. We've been pouring iron into her for an age, but her captain shows no sign of surrendering. Can you see the bugger, Jack? He looks a calm one.'

The smoke parted and allowed Jack a glimpse of the officer in question. Who was he? Why had he not struck? His ship was fast becoming a wreck. The hull was peppered with holes and studded with shot that had not penetrated; masts were severely mauled, her sails mere shreds of dirty canvas. Her larboard side was streaming crimson and the sounds of the dying carried above the din of *Brunswick's* guns.

'Whoever he is, Rowland, he has courage, and is to be respected for his determination. Why will he not strike? Call on him, Rowland. We have surely spilled enough blood, and his ship cannot survive.'

Bevan picked up a battered speaking trumpet and hailed the French officer, whose shadowy form could just be discerned through the swirling smoke. The man was striding his rolling deck and shouting at his crew. Bellowing across the divide, Bevan saw the Frenchman turn and look directly at him.

'*Monsieur Le Capitaine, au nom du Roi George, je vous exhorte à vous rendre. De rechange vos hommes courageux.*'

The Frenchman might have smiled; Bevan could not be sure. What he did see was the two-finger salute Henry V's archers gave to the French at Agincourt. The man's intention was clear. There would be no surrender.

A ripping screeching of timber and the twang of tangled lines snapping from the weight of hundreds of tons of force drew Bevan's attention to the bows once more. The two ships, bound together for over three hours in a dual for survival, now slowly parted. As they drifted apart, Jack noted the approach of another ship. 'Rowland, there is another of the bastards approaching. We will be hard pressed to fight two of them!'

Bevan raised his glass and focused on the new arrival creeping as a ghostly apparition through the smoke. His anxious face broke into a grin. 'You may relax, Jack. That is no enemy but our captain's brother; that's *Ramillies*, Jack. Another of our seventy-fours; Henry Harvey commands her.'

A slow tearing noise from the bows diverted Bevan from his observation of *Ramillies.* 'What the devil? We're losing her, Jack.'

'Quickly now, Rowland. Her stern. She will be exposed and we can rake her.'

'Damn me, Jack. I'm failing in my duty—Mister Kemble,' he bellowed at the third lieutenant, who was directing fire on the main deck, 'get the larboard quarter guns busy. We can rake her as she tries to slip away.'

'Right away, sir,' said the young officer, calling away a surviving gun captain from an exhausted crew.

Vizzard and Bevan watched as the *Vengeur* pulled away with the sounds of lines parting and grinding timbers and smoke drifting apart, allowing the observers to witness a French officer attacking his own men.

Within moments, more fire exploded from *Brunswick's* larboard quarter with a thunderous roar, cannon shot whipping across the growing void between the two exhausted protagonists.

'Hah, look Jack; we've struck her rudder pintle. She'll not steer. By God, I believe she is sinking. Yes, she's settling low in the water. My goodness, *Ramillies* is going to finish her. We must keep before the wind, else we lose our masts; look how the foremast shivers.'

A murderous broadside poured in a rolling thunder of iron, tearing the innards of the French ship to shreds. Men died or were maimed by the score. *Venguer* settled lower, the surging ocean willing her to give up the fight.

'Rowland, look to windward,' he shouted. 'Do you see the French van? I think we are cut off and at risk of being taken.'

Lieutenant Bevan seized the situation and bellowed an order to the helm. 'Bear away. I believe we can do no more, Jack. We are too badly wounded and this battle is over.' As he spoke, a defiant shot tore a section of the mizzen and sent it spinning into Bevan's legs. He collapsed with a scream of pain, the deck beneath his crumpled body stained red.

A disciplined broadside from *Ramillies* shattered the enemy's stern, sweeping the interior with death and opening the ship to the consuming ocean.

'We have her, Rowland. She's finished for sure,' croaked Jack, his throat dry and tongue thick in his mouth. 'Look there, he's raised the Union flag over her Republican colours. She's finally surrendered, Rowland. She's your prize.' He watched as the once proud ship rolled slowly on to her beam ends, men scrambling to hold on, many of them sliding into the icy water.

'I'll lower a boat and try to save some of the wretches,' Bevan muttered, voicing a sailor's sympathy for other men of the sea. Then he realised he had no boats left, they had all been turned to matchwood. 'God help the poor devils,' he said, as *Brunswick* drifted slowly north and away from the ship's graveyard, and the graveyard of so many men.

'God help you, Rowland!' he said, kneeling by his friend. 'You're wounded again.' Vizzard shouted at a dazed sailor, 'Go and fetch the surgeon or one of his mates for Mister Bevan. He can't leave the deck.' He sat on a coil of rope and reached for his water canteen, swigging the warm water, as he surveyed the scenes of devastation about him. The blood-stained deck timbers, pockmarked with musket balls, the smouldering shreds of canvas and tarred rope, body parts still visible; there a boot with a stump of bone protruding, a thumb and finger next to an overturned nine pounder.

'Was it worth it, Rowland? Was it worth the loss of so many men? I have yet to take a roll of my killed and wounded, but *Brunswick* has lost many.'

'How are such things measured, Jack? In truth, I do not know. We have yet to find the convoy, but we have surely defeated the French battle fleet and that must be worthwhile, do you not think?'

'It remains to be seen, Rowland. I would we had found the convoy first and destroyed it. It is the Prime Minister's wish to see it taken, so much I know. But a victorious sea battle will delight the country.'

'For now we must be content with our achievement, Jack,' Bevan answered. 'We have done well. Now I must see to *Brunswick's* return to England.' Lieutenant Bevan summoned the carpenter, seeking a report, and mentally prepared a series of orders to ensure the ship's return to Portsmouth.

'If nothing else, Jack, we will be the glorious first with the news.'

EPILOGUE

Jack Vizzard sat in his father's armchair as the summer evening spilled warmth and dappled sunshine into Sir Henry's study. He read again the order from the first secretary:

> *On conclusion of your leave of absence, you will report to the Port Admiral at Portsmouth and acquaint him with your orders as detailed above, and, at the earliest opportunity will take transport with the men under your command to place yourself under the orders of Vice Admiral Lord Jervis, Commander in Chief of the Mediterranean Fleet...*

He looked up at the portrait of his father. Sir Henry had not survived the winter of 1794 and had been buried in the frozen earth of Woodchester, the village he had loved and served all his life. In accordance with his last will, drafted in his own hand and witnessed by his two servants, Madeline and Edmund Neave, he was buried in the same plot as his beloved Caroline. Vizzard sighed and rose from the leather, staring out at the hills above the house. Lampern was now his, but at times it felt empty, until his wife and children returned and laughter filled the old house. He missed his father; missed his humour, missed his wisdom and his counsel.

William Pitt had been fulsome in his praise. Vizzard had even been presented to King George and Queen Charlotte on the occasion of Their Majesties' visit to Portsmouth, following the return of Howe's glorious fleet. His sister, also Charlotte, had been green with envy when informed of the news. Mary had simply glowed with pride. Honours and awards had been generous and controversial. Several of the senior officers had received hereditary honours, others knighted and all first lieutenants promoted to commander, including his friend Rowland Bevan, who was now impatiently awaiting his first command. Some officers, omitted from Lord Howe's despatches, were furious and let it be widely known. Funds had been raised for a monument to be installed in Westminster Abbey, to honour the memory of Captain Harvey, who died of his wounds shortly after *Brunswick* returned to Portsmouth; the courage he displayed on that bloody day more than a year past now. Jack had declined a captaincy, much to the irritation of Colonel Souter, not wishing to lose the camaraderie of his Vandals, he had insisted on remaining in his rank.

'There you are, Jack,' said Mary, entering the study and intruding on his thoughts. 'Our Freddie is here to say good-night to his papa.' The little boy ran unsteadily until Jack swept him up and held him tight.

'My darling boy,' Jack whispered into his ear. 'I fear I will have to leave you and will not see you again for a long, long time.'

'Oh,' said Mary, her face crestfallen. 'You have new orders?

'The Mediterranean fleet, my dear. Lord Jervis commands, and where Jervis leads there will surely be action!'

M Howard Morgan is a *nom de plume* of Malcolm Mendey.

Born in Carmarthen in South Wales, he spent his childhood years living in France, Belgium, Gibraltar and Germany. Following an initial career in civil law, he moved into loss adjusting, acting for and advising underwriters at Lloyd's of London and multi-national insurers. With his family he spent nearly twenty years in New Zealand, has traveled extensively on assignments within the UK and Europe, the Far East, Oceania, and North America.

An interest in genealogy resulted in the surprising discovery of an ancestor who was a marine with the First Fleet of convicts sent by Britain to Australia in 1788. Always a student of history, the discovery triggered an ever more consuming investigation into the Royal Marines and the history of the Golden Age of Sail and tangentially, the conflicts with Revolutionary and Napoleonic France.

First Fleet is a debut novel. The sequel, *The Glorious First* set in 1794, describes the first major naval engagement between Britain and France in what was the first world war, known in Britain as The Glorious First of June. The third novel finds the two principal characters, Jack Vizzard and Joe Packer, back at sea in 1797. They join the Mediterranean Fleet commanded by Sir John Jervis. The story concludes with the major fleet engagement known as the Battle of Cape St Vincent, in which a young captain Horatio Nelson distinguished himself and won his knighthood.

A qualified boat master, a failed golfer, enthusiast of aviation, consumer of fine wines, real ales, and spirits, the author has absolutely no interest in celery.

He lives in the beautiful Cotswolds in Southwest England with his beautiful wife, affectionately known as SWMBO (credit H Rider Haggard: *She Who Must Be Obeyed*) and a wonderful Sprollie dog called Molly.

First Fleet

By

M Howard Morgan

Love, murder, betrayal, and adventure with the transportation of convicts from Britain in 1787 and the founding of the penal colony that became Australia.

With the American colonies closed to Britain the gaols overflowed and the criminal under-class posed a growing threat to the property-owning classes. A solution was required to deal with the overcrowded prisons. The answer lay in colonising the continent on the far side of the world – *Terra Australis Incognita*; the unknown continent.

Claimed for Britain by James Cook during his first voyage of discovery in April 1770, the government of the day launched an ambitious project; to make use of the criminal class to develop a new colony. Its aim to find a new source of trade and a establish a new base for Britain's Royal Navy to support the burgeoning empire. The First Fleet of eleven ships left Portsmouth in May 1787 tasked with those objectives. The First Fleet of convicts. The great experiment so nearly failed.

Jack Vizzard, a young and raw marine officer of affluent background, becomes a member of the expedition. Lawyer, newly commissioned subaltern and a murderer, Vizzard finds his acts of betrayal follow him to New Holland. But what awaits him there? Retribution and reconciliation? Or ignominy and death?

PENMORE PRESS
www.penmorepress.com

The Chosen Man

by

J. G Harlond

From the bulb of a rare flower bloom ambition and scandal

Rome, 1635: As Flanders braces for another long year of war, a Spanish count presents the Vatican with a means of disrupting the Dutch rebels' booming economy. His plan is brilliant. They just need the right man to implement it.

They choose Ludovico da Portovenere, a charismatic spice and silk merchant. Intrigued by the Vatican's proposal—and hungry for profit—Ludo sets off for Amsterdam to sow greed and venture capitalism for a disastrous harvest, hampered by a timid English priest sent from Rome, accompanied by a quick-witted young admirer he will use as a spy, and bothered by the memory of the beautiful young lady he refused to take with him.

Set in a world of international politics and domestic intrigue, *The Chosen Man* spins an engrossing tale about the Dutch financial scandal known as tulip mania—and how decisions made in high places can have terrible repercussions on innocent lives.

PENMORE PRESS
www.penmorepress.com

GREEK FIRE
BY
JAMES BOSCHERT

In the fourth book of Talon, James Boschert delivers fast-paced adventure, packed with violent confrontations and intrepid heroes up against hard odds.

Imprisoned for brawling in Acre, a coastal city in the Kingdom of Jerusalem, Talon and his longtime friend Max are freed by an old mentor from the Order of the Templars and offered a new mission in the fabled city of Constantinople. There Talon makes new friendships, but winning the Emperor's favor obligates him to follow Manuel to war in a willful expedition to free Byzantine lands from the Seljuk Turks. And beneath the pageantry of the great city, seditious plans are being fomented by disaffected aristocrats who have made a reckless deal to sell the one weapon the Byzantine Empire has to defend itself, *Greek fire*, to an implacable enemy bent upon the Empire's destruction.

Talon and Max find themselves sailing into perilous battles, and in the labyrinthine back streets of Constantinople Talon must outwit his own kind—assassins—in the pay of a treacherous alliance.

PENMORE PRESS
www.penmorepress.com

On the Lee Shore

by

Philip K.Allan

Newly promoted to Post Captain, Alexander Clay returns home from the Caribbean to recover from wounds sustained at the Battle of San Felipe. However, he is soon called upon by the Admiralty to take command of the frigate HMS Titan and join the blockade of the French coast. But the HMS Titan will be no easy command with its troubled crew that had launched a successful mutiny against its previous sadistic captain. Once aboard, Clay realizes he must confront the dangers of a fractious crew, rife with corrupt officers and disgruntled mutineers, if he is to have a united force capable of navigating the treacherous reefs of Brittany's notorious lee shore and successfully combating the French determined to break out of the blockade.

PENMORE PRESS
www.penmorepress.com

Penmore Press

Challenging, Intriguing, Adventurous, Historical and Imaginative

www.penmorepress.com